THE UNLIKELY JOURNEY
OF LELAND AND DIANE

Also by Edward M. George

Poetry:

Midnight Coffee

Espresso Evenings

Cosmic Latte

Dark Roast

Short Fiction:

Starlight and Other Stories

The Unlikely Journey of Leland and Diane

A Novel

EDWARD M. GEORGE

TNSB

Montgomery

TNSB
105 S. Court Street
Montgomery, AL 36104

The painting on the cover is *Libertytown Depot,*
by Donna Pate of Deatsville, Alabama.

Cataloging-in-Publication Data

ISBN 978-1-961938-05-2

Design by Randall Williams

Printed in the United States of America

To Sherry

Good fortune is light as a feather, and few are strong enough to carry it.

—Chuang Tzu

Introduction

LIBERTYTOWN IS A SMALL CITY IN SOUTH ALABAMA. AS IS THE CASE with many small cities in Alabama, Libertytown is controlled by a handful of prominent families who have embraced that control for generations. Melanie and Beth, known in the community as the "Moore sisters," are members of one of those prominent families, and they have each married into another of those prominent families.

As part of their effort to keep up with everything that happens in Libertytown, the Moore sisters become curious about the lives of Leland and Diane Johnson, an unassuming young working-class couple who live in a rented trailer on the outskirts of town. This story describes how during the period of 1990 through 1996, the Moore sisters slowly come to realize that there may be much more to Leland and Diane than they ever imagined.

Chapter One

Libertytown is a city of about sixteen thousand located in Creek County in southeast Alabama. It lies seventeen miles south of Carleton, the county seat, and a half mile west of the ironically named Creek River.

It is a few minutes after eight on a warm Monday morning in May of 1990. On a brown leather sofa in the comfortable living room of a stately two-story colonial house at 232 Main Street sits Melanie Pebworth, a petite dark-haired woman of twenty-seven years, tying the laces of the K-Swiss walking shoe on her left foot.

Standing across the room, in an identical pair of white walking shoes, and looking out one of the tall front windows, is Melanie's twenty-nine-year-old sister, Beth Lancaster. Beth is slightly taller than Melanie, with a more athletic build. With her creamy complexion and light brown hair, Beth favors their father, Dr. Horace Moore, who's a sandy-haired former Auburn linebacker. Melanie favors their mother Sarah, a slender lady of Italian ancestry.

Dr. Horace Moore and his father Dr. Andrew Moore own the Moore Clinic at the north end of Main Street. The education of both Doctors Moore was financed by Horace's grandfather, Randolph Moore, who made his fortune in cotton farming, as had his father before him. The Moore Clinic, which started out as a solo practice, now employs five physicians in addition to Horace and Andrew, as well as a full crew of nurses and physician assistants. Because of its reputation for excellent service and its location on the Carleton side of Libertytown, the clinic almost always operates at near-full capacity, and Horace sometimes calls on Beth, a registered nurse, to assist when demand is high or the clinic is short of staff.

Still looking out the window, Beth says to Melanie, "This is a gorgeous day."

Melanie replies, "I know. I'm so glad that the rain moved out over the weekend." She rises from the sofa and stretches a bit. "Okay. I'm ready now. Do you think that we need to wear a jacket?"

Beth looks at Melanie in her red Alabama sweatshirt and blue jeans. "No, you're fine." As they walk toward the front door, Beth smiles and shakes her head. "I swear, you look good in anything."

Melanie takes a slight bow as she opens the door. She motions for Beth to walk out and says, "Thank you very much, but I'm not the sister who was Miss Libertytown Prep."

"That was a long time and twelve pounds ago."

"Well, I think you look better now. You were too skinny in high school."

"Well, be sure to tell John how good I look the next time you see him. Tell him how lucky he is to have me."

Melanie grins as she locks the front door behind them. "I'm sure he knows, but we can stop by the bank if you want to walk that far, and I'll go in and remind him."

The sisters walk down the stone pathway toward the gate.

Beth opens the gate. She says, "It would probably just annoy John if we dropped in on him at work with something that silly. How about we just walk as far as Danny's, as usual, and have a cup of coffee there?"

As they exit the gate and turn right, Melanie says, "Sounds good to me. By the way, where'd you get that shirt? I really like it."

Beth rubs her right hand down the left sleeve of the red plaid flannel shirt that she's wearing with her jeans. "One of John's. He says it's the tartan of his mother's Scottish ancestors, the MacDougalls, but I have no idea if that's true."

"I don't see how that shirt would fit John."

"It doesn't, but he's had it since high school when he was a lot smaller. He's probably only worn it maybe three times. He hates plaid. Says it's too busy. He won't even wear a striped shirt."

"Well, anyway, it looks good on you."

The sisters walk another block down Main Street without saying anything before Beth asks, "How are things going with the art gallery plans?"

"Frank and I finished the final version of our draft plan and gave it to the architect a few days ago. He's drawing up the blueprint based on our final draft, so we're close to starting the renovation. We'd like to open this fall, sometime in late September or early October."

"Was it your idea to convert that old furniture store building into a gallery?"

"No, Frank came up with the idea. But he knew that I had an interest in running a gallery, because I had talked with him about that when he was one of my art instructors at Sewanee. It was he who suggested that I get a master's in art history after I graduated there. So, when he retired from teaching and moved here, he came to me with the idea of our running a gallery together. He had seen the empty furniture store and thought that it was the perfect site for a gallery. And Mister Henderson agreed to make the necessary renovations and rent us the building."

"I didn't even know Frank was from Libertytown."

"He's not. He's from Mobile. But he decided to retire here because he wanted to live out what he calls his 'twilight years' in a small town."

"That makes sense. Is he married?"

"No. He's what in polite society is referred to as a 'confirmed bachelor.'"

Beth nods and says, "I see."

Melanie continues, "When I was a student of Frank's, he had what he called his 'life partner,' a guy named Jim. I liked Jim. He was a very nice man, and very cultured. He was also a talented artist. As a matter of fact, we're going to have a few of Jim's paintings on permanent display once we open the gallery."

"Really. Be sure to show them to me sometime."

When they get to the corner of Main and Union, Melanie says, "Let's go see if the Holman house has sold yet."

They turn right and walk another block and a half to a one-story Spanish style house with a Madison Realty sign in the front yard. They stop in front of the house and study it for a few minutes.

Beth says, "Seems it's still for sale. I hope somebody buys it soon. It's beginning to show signs of needing some repairs. We certainly don't need any rundown houses this close to ours."

Melanie nods in agreement. "Yeah, but I've always liked this house. I was in it many times when Emma lived there. Do you remember her?"

"Vaguely. Kind of a chubby girl, always giggling. Terrible dresser. What happened to her?"

"She married an Air Force pilot."

"That so. Where's she now?"

"I don't know. Last I heard they were in Texas. I'd sure like to hear from her sometime. She was a sweet girl."

"Probably weighs about two fifty by now."

"Oh, you be quiet. You have no idea what she looks like now. But I do hope that she started taking better care of herself than she did when she was a teenager. She was the world's worst junk food addict."

"You know, it's pathetic how some women just let themselves go. I've never understood that. . . Ready to get some coffee?"

The sisters start walking back toward Main Street. Melanie says, "I could sure use a cup or two of coffee. I stayed up late last night reading a book about Sylvia Beach."

"Sylvia Beach? Was she the one who opened that bookstore in Paris back in the twenties?"

"Yeah. The bookstore was called Shakespeare and Company. Sylvia was American, but she wanted to be in Paris at that time because it was *the* center for the arts. And it was amazing how many famous people came into her bookstore. I mean people like James Joyce, Hemingway, Fitzgerald, Thornton Wilder, Henry Miller, Aaron Copland, T. S. Eliot, Gertrude Stein, Picasso, and I don't know how many more."

Beth thinks for a moment. "You know, a couple of cool sophisticated gals like us would have fit right into that scene, wouldn't we?"

"Yeah, it would have been fun. Too bad there'll never be another place like that with all those artists, writers, dancers, composers, and musicians hanging out together and inspiring one another."

"Maybe your gallery will be like that, with all the famous artists, writers, and musicians in Libertytown hanging out there."

Melanie snickers. "That would be a small crowd indeed."

Danny's Diner is a little café across the street from Libertytown City Hall, on the first floor of a two-story red brick office building. The diner has a wide front door of thick tinted glass with stainless steel trim, and it has a large picture window that faces the sidewalk. On the second floor of the building are four law offices that provide some of Danny's most loyal customers, including retired circuit judge Hollis Bailey, who is the owner of the building.

Ever since Greek immigrant Nicholas Bellos opened the diner in 1948, Danny's has been a meeting place for lawyers, politicians, and businessmen, as well as a rest stop for women out shopping. The café is now operated by Nick's nephew, Theo.

The sisters reach Danny's at around 8:40. Beth holds open the front door for Melanie, then follows her inside. They look around and see that about half the tables are occupied, mostly by people having breakfast. They see Mayor Steadman in a corner booth and wave to him. The mayor is a tall, thin gray-haired man who almost always seems to be in a good mood. He smiles and throws them a kiss.

The sisters also wave to Mrs. Edna Sinclair, who owns a ladies' dress shop, then they nod toward a table where three local lawyers are eating.

Melanie says, "Let's sit at the counter since all we're having is coffee."

Behind the long white Formica-topped counter is an attractive young blonde woman in a white apron. She's folding napkins. She smiles and says, "Miz Pebworth, Miz Lancaster, how are y'all doing this morning?"

Beth says, "Well, Diane, we're doing fine. Been out for our usual morning walk . . . You know, you look different today. What have you done to yourself?"

Diane strikes a modeling pose. "Well, I've got this new hairdo, and

I'm wearing new makeup. Gloria down at the beauty salon did my hair and gave me some lessons on makeup. What do you think?"

Melanie says, "I think you look just gorgeous."

Beth smiles and says, "So do I. You look a lot like a young Grace Kelly with that new hairstyle."

"I wish. But, coming from y'all, that's quite a compliment, y'all being probably the two prettiest women in town."

Beth looks at Melanie. "I think she's fishing for a big tip."

Diane blushes. "Oh no, I'm not doing that. I just think that y'all are both so pretty."

Melanie reaches over and pats Diane's hand. "Don't take what Beth said seriously. That's just her trying to be funny."

Diane nods then smiles again. "Well, anyway, what can I get for y'all?"

Beth says, "Just coffee."

Melanie adds, "I think I'll have a chocolate donut with mine."

Beth looks at Melanie as though she just ordered a hand grenade.

In a few moments Diane brings the coffee and donut. She asks, "Anything else?"

The sisters shake their heads as they begin to drink their coffee.

Once they leave the diner and start back home, Beth asks, "Chocolate donut? What's that about?"

"I don't know. I just saw the donuts sitting there in the glass case and got the urge to eat one. I thought it might give me a little energy. By the way, it was delicious. That's the first donut I've eaten in years. I'd forgotten how good they are. But don't let me do that again, okay?"

At the window of the diner watching the sisters walk away is a Black woman who looks to be about twenty years old. She is wearing the same type of white apron as Diane. She is about the same height as Diane and has short, naturally curly black hair. When Diane walks over to see what Earline is looking at, Earline turns to her and says, "Those Moore sisters are two snooty white ladies. They just think they're better than the rest of us."

Diane pats Earline on her shoulder and softly says, "Aw, they're not so bad. They were just raised that way. Have you ever seen their mother?"

Earline nods and laughs. "Oh, yeah. Me and my sister Katherine were hired by their mother one time for one of her fancy dinner parties. We got so tickled at her flouncing around and putting on such a big show that we had to go back in the kitchen and laugh about it. We started calling her 'Queen Sarah' to ourselves."

The sisters are about half a block away from Danny's when Melanie asks, "Didn't Diane look beautiful today? I had no idea she could look that good. She's always worn so little makeup."

"I'm sure that was because of her mother. You've heard about her. She's one of those religious nuts who don't wear any makeup at all. Strange woman. That's probably why her husband left her when Diane was a child. But, you know, even if she is a little different, I have to give Missus Randall credit, she's pretty self-sufficient. You know she started working over at that glass plant out on Highway 74 right after her husband left her, and she's managed to provide for Diane and herself ever since. But, still, she is a bit anti-social. Doesn't talk to anybody much."

"Yeah, but even if her mother's that way, Diane's not like that. And now that she's married to Leland, it appears that she feels free to spruce herself up a bit. But tell me about Leland and her. They got married when I was off at Bama working on my master's. Why'd they get married so young?"

"Well, here's the deal. Even though Diane's a year younger than Leland, they wound up in the same English class their senior year. She was a semester ahead of her graduating class because she took advantage of that experimental summer school program that the high school had one year when they let a handful of students take a full load during the summer. And Leland was a semester behind his class because he had to take a semester off to work and support his family after his father got drunk and ran his car into that huge oak tree in front of the nursing home and broke his leg and tore up his shoulder. You may remember that Red Johnson was known for driving drunk back then, and everybody knew that it was just a matter of time before something like that would happen."

Melanie asks, "But how did they wind up getting married?"

"Well, it just so happened that the teacher asked Diane to help Leland catch up on his English studies so that they could both graduate mid-year as scheduled, and evidently the time they spent together somehow led to sweet, innocent Miss Diane Randall getting impregnated by roughneck Leland Johnson about two months or so before they graduated. As things turned out, Diane's mother and Leland's parents got together and agreed to take Leland and Diane over to Baldwin County where they were secretly married not too long after Diane found out that she was pregnant. No one else knew that she was pregnant until after they graduated, and she started showing."

"But they don't have any children, do they? What happened to the baby?"

"Miscarriage."

"Oh, no. To such a nice girl. I'll bet it broke her heart."

"From what I heard, it did. Myrtis, Grandfather's nurse, told me that Diane is still on birth control pills because she's not yet psychologically ready to try to have another baby."

"I can understand that, but evidently they decided to stay married and make the best of it."

"Oh, yeah. You should see the two of them together. You've never seen two people more in love. It's sweet."

"Where do they live?"

"They live in a little single-wide trailer that they rent from the bank. It's on Highway 74 about two miles south of town, about a half mile before you get to the glass plant. The bank got the trailer they're living in and the land it sits on in a foreclosure, and John okayed the bank's renting the land and trailer to them as a favor to Leland's father who had done a lot of work on our house over the years, as well as some at the bank and at John's dad's house."

After a moment Melanie asks, "Is Leland's father still a drunk?"

"Oh, no. Evidently that wreck straightened him out. As far as I know, he's been sober ever since. He's still working for Mister Henderson's sawmill, but he also does carpentry work on the side. Matter of fact, Leland and he have a carpentry business together, and they're really good at what they do. And they do custom cabinetmaking as well as general carpentry. They're never at a loss for work. And I believe that Leland also works at the lumber mill."

"Hmm . . . How old are Leland and Diane now?"

"Let's see. They graduated a year and a half ago, so Leland would have just turned twenty and Diane is nineteen."

"So, we've got two poor, relatively uneducated, uncultured, almost teenagers with no apparent prospects who live in a rented trailer on a country road. What chance do you give them?"

"Not much. The only thing that they've got going for them is that they're both so good-looking and, of course, they're both very well-mannered."

"Well, you know how fast that good-looking part can change. Remember what you told me about your high school reunion last year?"

"Yeah. That was pretty much a freak show. I almost didn't recognize some of my fellow prep school beauties. And it was the same with most of the men. You know, I just don't understand why some people don't take more pride in their appearance, especially when they know better. I'm glad Mother drilled into us how important appearances are."

Melanie smiles. "I remember that Mother used to tell us that when you look good, you feel good."

"She still does that. And remember she also used to tell us that when you look special, you are special . . . Yeah, even now, every time I'm tempted to go out in public without putting myself together first, I think of what she might say if she saw me. I was that way even when I was off at nursing school at Auburn."

"Melanie laughs. "I'm the same way. Crazy, isn't it?"

"Yeah, a little."

When they get back to Melanie's house, Beth says, "By the way, I didn't see Baby George while ago. Is he at Mother's?"

"Of course. She asked me to have Mattie take him over there. I believe she'd adopt him if we let her. But Mattie's going to bring him home around five. Big George always wants to see him first thing when he gets home from work. He'll probably be in around seven tonight. He's meeting with the manager of his Carleton Shopping Center pharmacy about an expansion they're considering. But whatever time he gets home, I want Little George to have had his nap first."

"I don't see how in the world George keeps up with those three pharmacies that he owns. That would drive me crazy."

"He loves it. Says it keeps his brain sharp. But sometimes I can tell that he's aggravated with something. That's when he likes to go out on the porch and sit in the swing with Little George and wind down."

Beth says, "You know, I probably shouldn't say anything about working too hard. John's the same way. Sometimes he's at the bank till midnight. I guess banker's hours don't apply when you own the bank. And the girls really hate it when they don't get to see him at night."

"How are the girls? It's been a couple of weeks since I've seen them."

"They're fine. You know Charlotte's just about to finish the fourth grade, and Daphne is finishing the first grade. Can you believe that?"

Melanie shakes her head. "Nope. It seems like just yesterday they were babies."

"And Mother's the same way about them as she is Little George, as far as wanting to monitor everything they're doing. Sometimes I think that she doesn't understand that we're grown up, college-educated women and perfectly capable of raising our own children. Why do you think she's that way?"

"She's probably worried to death that we might not raise our kids the way she raised us, you know, to be proper little southern ladies."

Beth snickers. "With a sense of propriety."

"Of course. Our kids must be imbued with a sense of propriety above all else."

"Again, why do you think Mother's the way she is?"

Melanie thinks for a moment. "It could be because she grew up poor on a tenant farm in Georgia with a dysfunctional family, and she remembers how difficult and demeaning it was to have to live that way. So, I'm thinking that she doesn't want you or me or any of our children to ever know what that feels like."

Beth says, "Yeah, you're probably right. Father told me that when he first met Mother over in Atlanta, when he was at Emory Medical School, he could tell that she had some rough edges and probably came from a not too well-off family. But he said that she was so pretty and tried so hard to come across as refined and sophisticated that he found her absolutely fascinating.

"Father said that when he brought her home one weekend, Grandfather could also tell that Mother must have come from a disadvantaged background, because a lot of Grandfather's patients are poor country folks. But Grandfather, when he got a chance, took Father aside and said, 'Son, you need to marry that girl. I like her a whole lot. I can tell she's got a lot of potential, and I'd like to see her get a rich husband so that she can be the Cinderella that she wants to be.' Father said that Mother was the first girlfriend of his that Grandfather had ever liked, and that was the reason he married her. Of course, I don't believe that, but it makes for a good story, doesn't it?"

Melanie nods. "Well, whatever the reason, I think that Father made the right decision for himself, don't you? And even now he still gets a kick from how fervently Mother plays the genteel Southern lady. I heard him tell George the other night when they were in the library having drinks that sometimes he feels like he's living with Scarlett O'Hara. George almost doubled over laughing."

Beth has a pensive look on her face. After a moment, she says, "But think about it. With Mother's background, she could have easily wound up pregnant at sixteen or seventeen and living in a single-wide trailer on the side of a county road with some dumb redneck husband."

Melanie looks upward, as if picturing the scenario that Beth just conjectured. Still looking up, she says, "And you and I would have grown up sharing a tiny bedroom in that little trailer, with no private schools, and no colleges in our future, looking for our own dumb redneck husbands."

Beth makes a face. "Good lord, sister. Don't even joke about that sort of thing."

Chapter Two

It's a mild day in early September 1993. Fall is in the air. Beth and Melanie are about twenty minutes into their morning walk when Beth says, "It seems that I owe you ten dollars, sis."

"How's that?"

"Do you remember back in 1990 I bet you ten dollars that five years from then Leland and Diane would still be living in that rented single-wide trailer?"

"I remember. What happened? Have they moved?"

"No, but they're no longer living in a rented trailer. They bought the trailer and the ten acres that it sits on. So, technically I think I lost the bet."

Melanie ponders that for a bit. "Well, I don't know about that, but how about you buy us breakfast with that ten dollars, and we'll call it even?"

"That sounds good."

"So, how'd you find out that they bought that property?"

"John told me. He said that back when the bank first rented the trailer and land to Leland and Diane, Leland asked for a five-year lease-purchase agreement with one of the provisions being that if they bought the property within five years, a designated portion of the rent that had been paid would count toward the purchase price. John said that he really didn't want to keep the property tied up that long, but when Leland agreed to pay a higher rent in exchange for the purchase option, he went along with it, never thinking that they'd exercise the option. Well then, last month Leland came to John and said that he was ready to buy the property. John said he checked out their rent payment record and their financial situation, and then he and Leland worked out the terms for a mortgage, and he had the bank's attorney draw up a deed."

"Interesting. What *is* their financial situation?"

"John wouldn't tell me that, but he did say that Leland had gotten a promotion at the sawmill and was now Mark Henderson's assistant."

"What does that mean?"

"Beats me. But it must mean more money. It sounds impressive, anyway."

After a few minutes of walking without further conversation, Melanie asks, "Do you mind if we go by the gallery before we eat? There's something that I have to check on before we open this afternoon for that youth exhibit."

They pass by Danny's Diner on their way to the gallery, which is two blocks past the diner on the opposite side of the street. They see Diane through the window taking the mayor his breakfast.

Melanie says, "She looks very good for somebody who had a baby just three months ago."

"She does, and that baby boy is just beautiful. I saw him at the clinic when she brought him in for a checkup."

"Of course he is, with those two for parents. But how did the pregnancy go? Was Diane anxious about it?"

"Oh, yeah. She was a nervous wreck. I was helping out at the clinic one day when she came in for one of her prenatal checkups. When Doctor Chambers, our ob-gyn, was examining her, he did more counselling than he did doctoring. But Father said that after the first trimester, she got more relaxed about it and was a good patient. She did everything that Chambers told her to do, and the baby turned out great. Seven pounds, nine ounces. I was at the clinic when Chambers got back from the maternity ward over at Saint Michael's."

"I'm so glad for her. You know, today's the first time I've seen her since the baby was born."

"Me, too. We'll have to congratulate her. And I am so glad to have her back. I mean, Theo's little sister is a nice girl and all, but she's a lousy waitress."

Melanie says, "You got that right. But I know that, being an elementary school teacher, she was glad to have a summer job, especially being that she just got rid of her sorry husband. I heard that they almost lost their house because of his compulsive gambling."

"Yeah, I heard the same thing. Polly at the bank told me that he spent way too much time in Biloxi."

While Melanie is unlocking the front door of the gallery, Beth stands in front of the building, which is now painted ivory with pastel green trim. The dark walnut front door is tall and wide with brass fittings. Beth comments, "I still can't believe the way that y'all have transformed this old furniture store. What did Mister Henderson say when he first saw the completed transition?"

"He said that his former tenant, Mister Simmons, would have been proud of how good his old furniture shop looks. By the way, did you know that Mister Henderson has an art collection in his house? He showed it to me the other day went I went by to give him a rent check. It's not a huge collection, but it's high quality. He had the paintings hanging in his living room, his big family room, and in the hallway to his library. They were mostly Hudson Valley style paintings, landscapes and river scenes, but there were also a couple of Southwest landscapes mixed in. He said that his parents gave him a few of the pieces, but that he had bought most of them himself."

The sisters enter the gallery, and Melanie turns on the lights. Beth says, "You know, I never would have taken Mister Henderson for an art lover, as big and coarse, and boisterous, as he is. What did the inside of the house look like? I've always been curious about that. Father says that it's the biggest house in town, over six thousand square feet. It looks beautiful on the outside, now that Mister Henderson has spent years refurbishing it. It looks like an antebellum plantation home that you'd see in a movie. But, for some reason, I can't imagine that the inside would be very stylish. What did you think of the interior?"

"Well, I didn't see many of the rooms, but those that I saw were pretty old-fashioned, and I don't mean that in a good way. I mean they looked worn down and years out of style, except for the library and the kitchen. He told me that those two rooms were redone a couple of years ago. The kitchen has this gorgeous custom hickory cabinetry, and the library has floor to ceiling mahogany bookshelves on each side. And I don't mean mahogany stained. I mean actual mahogany wood. Those two rooms look great, but everything else that I saw left a lot to be desired."

"Who do you think did the cabinet work? I'm sure that Mister Henderson would know who the best craftsmen are."

"He told me that Red and Leland Johnson did it all. And, I mean, it was some of the best cabinetry that I've ever seen. Just beautiful."

"Well, John says that Red and Leland do very good work. But, you know, I still can't picture Mark Henderson as an art lover. That surprises me."

"It caught me off guard, too, particularly when he said that he had many happy memories of when he and his wife Stella used to go to New York and visit the museums."

"That's interesting. Missus Henderson seemed like just a good ole country gal to me. Can you envision her standing there studying a Van Gogh in a New York art museum? By the way, do you know if they had any children?"

"They had a son, Virgil, who was killed in Kuwait. He was an Army helicopter pilot. I saw some photos of him in the library. He was a good-looking young man. He had dark brown hair like his mother, but otherwise favored his dad, just not as stocky. Father says that Mister Henderson has never forgiven himself for not talking his son out of volunteering for Kuwait, and somebody, I can't remember who, told me that Missus Henderson was never the same after her son died."

"I can certainly understand that. Lord knows what my reaction would be if I lost one of the girls. But as for Mister Henderson, other than his lack of social graces and his godawful taste in clothes, he seems to be a good man. Is he a good landlord?"

"The best. He's done way more than anyone else would have done for us. But I agree with you about his taste in clothes. Sometimes when I see him in town, he'll be wearing dress pants but have on one of those dark green work shirts with the sawmill logo on it."

Melanie checks the thermostat in the gallery to make sure that it's working properly, and then she looks through the mail that came in today. She puts the mail down, and she and Beth walk toward the front where Melanie turns out the lights. The sisters walk out the gallery door, and Melanie locks the door behind them. Then they start walking back toward the diner.

They walk into Danny's at about half past ten and see that it's more crowded than usual. Beth points out to Melanie all the shopping bags sitting beside the tables and speculates that many of the large crowd are people doing last-minute shopping for school clothes.

Diane confirms Beth's speculation when she comes over to wait on them. "We've been snowed under this morning. The Target over in Carleton is having a big back-to-school sale, and it looks like every mother in Libertytown went over there early this morning to get in on it."

Melanie gently lays her hand on Diane's left forearm. "Speaking of mothers, how's our new mother doing. And how's the baby?"

"We're both fine. Thanks for asking. Except that I'm worn out from not getting enough sleep for the past three months. Bret's a night owl like his daddy."

Beth says, "Well, you look great. And John told me that y'all bought the mobile home y'all had been renting from the bank."

"We did. Both of us love where we are, so we plan on building a house on that same spot one day. Leland says we can stay in the trailer while we build the house."

Beth says, "Sounds like a good plan. I'm sure John will help all that he can when y'all get ready to do that."

"Mister Lancaster's been really good to us. Tell him we really appreciate it."

"I will."

As they leave the diner after having a light breakfast, and start back home, Beth asks Melanie, "Can you imagine Mother shopping at Target for *our* school clothes?"

"Good lord, no. Remember that time when she got all over Father for buying a suit at Sears?"

"I do. She took it back the next day while he was at work."

They both giggle at the memory of their father finding out the next day that his new suit was gone.

After a few more minutes of walking Beth says, "Don't you just love the way Diane and Leland are making big plans for their future? They're going to move out of that little ole trailer and live in a *real* house."

"Well, let them have their dreams. They're young."

"Speaking of plans, do you have any plans for this afternoon?"

"No. Why?"

"Let's go look at that trailer we've been talking about so much. I've never seen it."

"Neither have I. Let me change clothes and freshen up when I get back to the house, and then we can go look at it."

Not too long after they get home, the sisters get into Beth's silver BMW 7 and head for Highway 74. About a mile down the highway, "Allegheny Lumber Mill and Millworks, Libertytown Division" comes into view. Melanie says, "My Lord, that place is *gigantic*. I never knew it was anything like that."

"John says that it was modeled after one that Mister Henderson's family has in Pennsylvania. He says that sawmill is a few miles outside of McKeesport, which is where Mr. Henderson grew up and where his family still lives. Evidently, his family has been in the lumber business up there for generations and has made a fortune."

"How in the world did he wind up in Libertytown?"

"From what Mister Henderson told Father, he met his wife and married her when he was stationed at Fort Benning, and they used to sometimes come through here on their way to Panama City. For whatever reason, they took a liking to the town. I'm not sure about this, but I think that Libertytown is about the same size as McKeesport. And

Mister Henderson, of course, couldn't help noticing the potential for a lumber business in this area. So, after he was discharged, they moved here, bought that big old rundown house, and opened a sawmill and lumber company, and here they stayed. But, of course, the lumber company was nowhere near as big when it first opened as it is now."

"Interesting. I had no idea he was a Yankee."

"Well, he seems to have done a good job of shedding whatever Yankee he had in him. He's just a good ole boy now."

"A very wealthy good ole boy. He may not look or act the part, but Mattie heard from Mister Henderson's former housekeeper that he's from a very well-off Pennsylvania family that's been there since before the Revolutionary War."

"Now that's what I call *old* money. But we sure can't begrudge him for that. Particularly since he's been so good to you and Frank with the gallery."

Melanie nods. "Yeah, you're right about that. He lowered our rent a while back, and he's one of the biggest donors to our non-profit. He doesn't come by the gallery very often because he's so busy with his sawmill and his other business dealings. But when he does come by, it's surprising to Frank and me how much he knows about art and art history, particularly for someone who has never formally studied art. He told us that he grew up in the lumber business and was a business major at the University of Pittsburgh, but that he's always been fascinated by artists. Says his favorite is Edward Hopper."

Beth is surveying the countryside along the highway. "Do you know how much farther it is to their trailer and which side of the road it's on."

"Judging by the address it should be just ahead. And I think I remember Diane saying that it was on the same side of the highway as the glass plant. So, it should be on your side."

Beth says, "I think I see it now." She looks in the rearview mirror as she begins to slow her car down. She pulls off the highway onto the shoulder on Melanie's side and looks toward the mobile home across the road. "Not exactly what I expected. It's actually pretty cute. It's teeny, but it appears to be in very good shape."

Melanie peers around Beth at the light beige single-wide mobile home sitting at the end of a long concrete driveway.

Beth says, "John told me that before they moved in, Leland repainted the trailer and put up new shutters. And Leland must have also added that front porch. They've done a good job of landscaping, too. I like those rose bushes next to the trailer . . . Of course, I wouldn't live there for anything, but it doesn't look bad at all."

Melanie asks, "Can you pull up into the driveway. I think something's being built in the back yard."

Beth drives her car onto the concrete driveway and turns off the engine. The sisters get out and walk to the left side of the trailer. Behind the house they see a wooden building that's well under construction. It looks as though, when completed, it will be around fifty feet wide and twenty feet deep.

Melanie says, "Whatever that is, it's going to be about as big as the trailer. We'll have to tell Diane that we were driving by and noticed that something was being built back there and ask her what it is."

Beth looks at her watch. "We need to start back. I've got to pick up the girls at school. I told them that I'd take them shopping for shoes today."

Chapter Three

THE NEXT MORNING, AS THE SISTERS ARE DRINKING COFFEE AT DANny's, Beth says to Diane, "We passed by your home yesterday, and I love your rose bushes. And we couldn't help but notice that something was going up in the back yard."

"Why, thank you. Leland and his daddy are putting up a building back behind our trailer. They've almost finished it. They've been working on it almost every day after work and on weekends when they weren't doing jobs for somebody else. Anyway, most of the building is going to be a workshop for Leland, but on the right side there's going to be an art studio for me.

"They've done a lot of work on the workshop part, and they've almost finished the studio part. I pestered Leland so much about when the studio was going to be finished that they stopped working on the workshop and are going to finish the studio before they get back to the workshop."

Beth looks at Melanie, who says, "Leland sounds like a good husband, but I didn't know you were an artist."

"Oh, I'm not really an *artist*, but I like to paint pictures. I used to do it all the time, but since we moved into the trailer, I haven't had room. That's why Leland's building me a studio."

"What type of paintings do you do?" asks Melanie.

"I don't know yet. Back when I was painting a lot, Mama wouldn't let me paint anything but religious pictures. She said that painting secular paintings was a waste of time and a sin. Now, I never believed that, but all the same, that's what I painted, pictures of Jesus, and John, and Mary, and Moses, and Samson and Delilah, and so forth."

Beth asks, "Could you show us some of your paintings?"

"Afraid not. As soon as I finished one, Mama would give it to our church or to some other church or religious organization. And she gave two to Kirkwood Academy. I think one was a nativity scene and the other was a portrait of Jesus."

Beth says, "Kirkwood. That's where my girls go to school. Do you know if your pictures are still hanging there?"

"I really don't. I think that the portrait was in the lobby, and the other one was in the headmaster's office. But I really don't know if they're still there."

Melanie looks at Beth. "We're going to have to check that out. I'd love to see them."

Kirkwood Academy is on the northern edge of Libertytown on the way to Carleton. It is a small but prestigious K-12 preparatory school whose students are children of well-to-do families from all over Creek County as well as from surrounding counties.

Beth and Melanie are friends with Kirkwood Headmaster Jeffery Bolden. So, right after Diane walks away to serve another customer, Melanie calls Dr. Bolden on his cell phone with her cell phone.

"Jeffery, this is Melanie Pebworth . . . Why, thank you . . . Beth and I just found out that our waitress here at Danny's Diner once had some paintings hanging at your school. Her name is Diane Johnson, but at the time that her mother donated the paintings, her last name was Randall. Does any of this ring a bell?"

Melanie waits for an answer, then says, "Would you mind terribly if Beth and I came by to take a look at them . . . That's wonderful. I'll let you know when we can come by."

As soon as Melanie ends her call, Beth asks, "What did he say?"

"He says the two paintings are still there and that they're very good. Are you picking up your girls this afternoon?"

"I could. John was going to, but I can call and tell him that I will."

"Great. I'll call Jeffery back and tell him we'll be coming by this afternoon."

The sisters arrive at Kirkwood Academy about thirty minutes before Beth's girls are scheduled to get out of class. The school, except for a separate gymnasium and physical education center, is in a long, classically styled two-story speckled gray brick building. There is a covered walkway leading from the front entrance to a concrete driveway that encircles a well-manicured lawn in the middle of which stands a tall flagpole with the U.S. flag flying above the Alabama flag. Beth enters the driveway and parks her car in front of the school in one of the "Visitor" parking spaces.

As they're walking to the front door, Beth asks Melanie, "Remember when we were going to school here, back when it was Libertytown Prep?"

"Yeah, but it didn't look anywhere near this nice, and it was only about half this size."

They enter the front door, and Melanie notices that the lobby now has an arched doorway and a terra cotta tile floor.

"This really looks good," says Melanie, "and I see that the hallways have been redone, too. That high tuition y'all are paying is being well spent."

"It does look good, doesn't it. We're proud of it." Beth points down the hall to their right. "They moved the headmaster's suite down this hall to where the library was when we were going here."

Melanie looks at where Beth is pointing. "Where's the library now?"

"Second floor. Right above us."

When they get to a partially opened door marked "Headmaster's Office," Beth raps lightly on the door before she walks in and Melanie follows. As she walks through the door, Beth waves to a well-dressed, middle-aged Black woman sitting behind a large walnut desk at the front of which is a walnut nameplate stating, "Louise Kilmer, Administrative Assistant."

Beth says, "It's just us, Missus Kilmer, my sister Melanie and me. Is Doctor Bolden available to see us?"

"He will be in just a moment. He's finishing up a phone call right now. Would y'all like some coffee?"

"No, thanks. We've had our quota of coffee for the day. But we appreciate the offer."

Mrs. Kilmer points to a burgundy loveseat on the wall facing her desk and says, "You can have a seat right back there if you like, while you wait."

Melanie says, "Thank you."

When they get situated in the loveseat, Beth and Melanie look at each other, and Beth mouths "Wow." Beth asks, "Missus Kilmer. Where did y'all get this loveseat? I'd love to have one of these for my parlor."

Mrs. Kilmer looks at the loveseat and says, "It's one that Doctor Bolden brought with him from Pennsylvania. He said that it was in his grandfather's law office before he retired."

"What company made it, do you know?"

"Doctor Bolden said that it was a Pennsylvania company that makes expensive office furniture. I don't remember the name of the company, but I believe he said that it was 'Durham' or something like that."

Melanie says to Mrs. Kilmer, "We need to ask him about this loveseat. I'd also like to have one like this. I love this color, and this leather is fantastic."

Beth leans back in the loveseat. "And it's unbelievably comfortable."

Mrs. Kilmer says, "Yes, ma'am," and goes back to her filing.

In a few minutes the office door is opened by a tall, well-built middle-aged man dressed in gray slacks and a starched blue dress shirt with a red regimental striped tie. He smiles and says, "I thought that I heard voices out here. Why don't you two come on in. Can we get some coffee for you?"

Beth answers, "No, thank you. Missus Kilmer's already been kind enough to have offered us some, but we're fine, thanks."

"Well, come on in. I'll show you one of those paintings that Melanie asked about."

The sisters enter the classically decorated office. Jeffery follows them and points to a painting that's hanging above a credenza that's situated against the wall to the right of his large walnut desk.

Melanie walks over and stands in front of the painting, which looks to be about fourteen by twenty inches. It's a nativity scene in the style of a Dutch master. Melanie studies it for quite a while before she turns to Dr. Bolden and asks in a low voice, "Are you sure that this was painted by Diane Johnson?"

"Yeah. Her name and address are on the back of the canvas."

"May I look?"

"Sure."

Melanie carefully removes the painting from the wall. On the back of the canvas in black ink, in block letters, is written: "Diane Randall, 704 Jefferson St., Libertytown, Alabama, 1987."

Melanie thinks for a moment. "That date means that she would only been about sixteen when she painted this. I can't believe it. This is really well done."

After Melanie rehangs the painting, Beth looks at for a while. "This looks familiar. Is it a copy of a famous painting?"

"It's a copy of a painting called 'Adoration of the Shepherds' by Jacob van Oost, a Flemish painter from the sixteen hundreds. This copy is done on a cheap canvas with low quality paints, but it's very faithful to the original, except that Diane has made the faces of Joseph and Mary look a little more Semitic than in the original. That's a very clever change if she did it intentionally because it makes the portrayal probably truer to what they really looked like."

Melanie studies the painting a little longer before she says, "Jeffery, Diane said that the other painting is a portrait of Jesus that was hanging in the lobby, but we didn't see it out there."

"It used to be in the lobby, but now it's hanging in the library conference room. I'll call Miss Gleason, our librarian, and she can show you where it is. Why don't you two just head on up there, and I'll ring Miss Gleason while you're on the way."

Beth says, "Can we ask you about something else before we go?"

"Sure, what's that?"

"That loveseat out front. Missus Kilmer said that you brought it with you from Pennsylvania."

"I did. It was in my grandfather's law office. When he retired, he doled out his office furniture among the family members. I got that loveseat and an end table that's in my den at home. The loveseat had been in storage until I decided to take it out last week and use it in out there. I'm glad you like it.

"All of my grandfather's office furniture was made by an old company in Lebanon County, Pennsylvania called Dunham Fine Furnishings. It's a company that's known worldwide for its high end office furniture, so I was happy to get those two pieces."

"Do you know where their furniture is sold in this area?"

"It's not. It's only sold in Pennsylvania, New York, and Connecticut."

Beth looks surprised. "Why is that?"

"Dunham has always been a family owned and run company, and they monitor the quality of everything from the milling of the lumber to the selling of the furniture. That means that they handpick the stores that they want to handle their merchandise and then keep a close eye on them. Of course, most of their business is not done out of furniture stores, it's from direct sales by their representatives to corporate customers."

Beth says, "Interesting. But how do you know so much about the company?"

Jeffery smiles. "I worked there for two years when I was in college. That was a long time ago, but not much has changed."

Melanie asks, "Is there any way you could help us get some loveseats? We'll be glad to pay full retail and pay for shipping. And we'd owe you a huge favor."

"I'd love to help you, but I really don't know if I can. As I said, it's been a long time since I've worked there. But I can ask around and let you know."

"Oh, thank you. If you'd do that for us, we'd really appreciate it."

"I'll see what I can do, but you two had better head upstairs before Miss Gleason leaves for the day. She doesn't like to stay late on Fridays."

As they're walking up the stairs to the second floor, Beth asks Melanie, "Don't you think that we should have asked how much those love-seats cost?"

Melanie laughs. "Yeah, probably. I'd hate to have to get a divorce over a chair."

Miss Gleason, a thin, pale woman in her late thirties, is waiting for the sisters when they reach the open library door. She greets them and motions them in, then leads them to a conference room where a portrait of Jesus is hanging on the back wall. She stands near the door watching the sisters, now and then checking her wristwatch.

"Wow," says Beth, as she walks nearer to the painting, which is approximately the same size as the nativity painting in Dr. Bolden's office and in the same type of simple brown wooden frame. "This is so pretty." The painting is of a standing Jesus in a pale robe with a white sash over his left shoulder. There's a soft faint golden glow behind Jesus's head. His left arm is situated in front of his left side, and his left hand shows two fingers outstretched and separated.

Melanie is standing next to Beth and is also admiring the portrait. Melanie quietly says, "That's a copy of 'Christ the Savior' by Heinrich Hoffman, a German painter from the late eighteen hundreds. I can't believe how good it is. It's even better than the painting downstairs. We must find out where Diane learned to paint like this. This is professional level."

"What does that two-finger sign mean? Is it some sort of religious symbol?

"Yes. It's called the 'benediction sign' or 'benediction symbol.' It represents Christ's duality, human and divine."

Chapter Four

On the following Monday morning, Melanie is standing at Beth's wrought iron gate when Beth comes out from her front door, which she closes and locks behind her. Halfway down the walkway to the gate, Beth says, "What's this? You're never early. I almost always have to wait for you."

"I can't wait to get to Danny's and ask Diane about those paintings. I've been thinking about them all weekend."

When Beth gets to the sidewalk and starts walking along side Melanie, she says, "I'm kind of curious about that myself. Do you want to get breakfast or just coffee when we get there?"

"Just coffee. I already ate."

Melanie has a small transistor radio with her. She tunes the radio to a local station to hear the news. Then, just as the newscaster begins to speak, she turns off the radio and says, "I can't help thinking that her mother is the key. What do you think?"

Beth shakes her head. "I have no idea. But then I haven't been obsessing about it all weekend."

"Yeah, that was kind of crazy. Anyway, I'm sure that we'll find out today from Diane."

"Turn your radio back on. I want to hear the weather for tomorrow."

The sisters listen to what's left of the weather report before Melanie turns off the radio again.

When they reach Danny's Diner several minutes later, Melanie quickly opens the door and walks in. Beth follows. Melanie looks around to see where Diane is. She doesn't see her. Earline sees the sisters. She walks up to Melanie and asks, "Looking for Diane?"

"Yes. Is she here?"

"No, ma'am. She had a dentist appointment over in Carleton."

Beth snickers. Melanie gives her a dirty look, then chuckles to herself. Beth turns to Earline and says, "Oh, well. Where would you like us to sit, Earline?"

As they're drinking their coffee at a two-person table near the front window, Beth grins and points at Melanie. Melanie glowers at Beth over the edge of her mug as she takes another sip of coffee. Then both Beth and Melanie start chuckling softly. Mrs. Joan Bailey, wife of Judge Bailey, is sitting at the next table. She hears the chuckling and turns and looks at them. Beth smiles and nods to Mrs. Bailey, who nods in return and goes back to eating her waffles.

On their way home, Melanie says, "I'm going to call Diane tonight at their trailer. I'm not going to wait another day for the answer."

"She'll probably think you're a nut."

"No. I'll finesse it. I'll tell her that we saw her paintings and thought they were really well done and ask her where she took art lessons."

"She'll still think you're a nut. Have you ever had anyone call you at home out of the blue and ask you where you took art lessons?"

"Not that I can remember. But I'm still going to do it."

"Suit yourself. Just be sure to call me right afterward and let me know what she says."

It's six-thirty that evening when the phone rings in Diane's trailer. Leland is walking through the front door on the second ring. He picks up the handset. "Hello . . . Oh, hello, Miz Pebworth . . . Yes, ma'am, she's here, but she's cooking supper right now. Can she call you back?"

Leland picks up the black pen that's laying on top of a small writing pad next to the phone. He writes down a phone number. "I'll give it to her right now, Miz Pebworth . . . Yes, ma'am. Goodbye."

Leland walks into the small kitchen where Diane is stirring a pan of spaghetti sauce. He places the page with the phone number that Melanie gave him into Diane's apron pocket. As he is washing his hands in the sink, he says, "That was Miz Pebworth. She wants you to give her a call when you get a chance. She said something about seeing your paintings at Kirkwood Academy."

"Okay, thanks. Wonder what she thought about the paintings?"

"I'm sure she liked them."

Diane smiles at Leland's comment. "You don't even know what they look like."

Leland sits down at the counter that separates the living room from the kitchen. "Just trying to be a supportive husband, babe."

"Well, thank you. Speaking of art, how close are y'all to finishing the studio? I am so anxious to get in there I can't stand it. I've never had a studio before."

As he's picking up his dinner fork, Leland says, "We got a lot done last night and this evening. All that's left is installing the light fixtures in the ceiling, and installing the track lights once they come in, and then finishing the painting and clear coating. Sam finished the wiring today, so I can go ahead and hook up the fixtures that we have. I could do that tonight if you want. Shouldn't take but about an hour, maybe an hour and a half. And then you can come check it out."

"Would you do that for me? That would be great. As soon as you get the lights working, come get me. I want to see how everything looks."

Diane is relaxing in Leland's recliner in her pink flannel pajamas watching an old black and white movie on television when Leland comes to the door at eight-twenty. "Want to come look?"

"Let me get my shoes on."

Diane hurriedly puts on a pair of old pink house slippers and almost stumbles on her way to the door.

Leland catches her and lightly kisses her on the right cheek. "Whoa, babe, be careful. It'll still be there when we get there. Did you call Miz Pebworth?"

Diane says, "I did, but I didn't get any answer, so I left her a message. I said that I was sorry I missed her call tonight but would be at Danny's tomorrow. And if I didn't see her there, I'd call her again tomorrow at around seven."

When they get to the studio, which is about thirty feet behind the mobile home, Leland opens the door. Diane walks in. All the overhead lights are on. Diane can see that Leland has completed the cabinets along the back wall. On either side of the room is a worktable in front of a tall window. To the sides of each window are shelves on the wall. The front wall is paneled with plywood and will serve as the display wall.

Leland says, "Like I said, all that's left is to clearcoat the concrete floor with waterproofing and to paint the cabinets and the walls. The walls will be antique white, and the cabinets are gonna be a real light peachy color. And we'll put up the track lights as soon as they come in. You can see that we made the two sides symmetrical except that the overhead lights on that side—he points to the right—are a little brighter. Those bulbs are similar to natural light. And the lights on the left are softer, like house lights."

"I would have never thought of that. How'd you come up with that? Did you see it in a book somewhere."

"No. It just seemed like a good idea to be able to look at a painting under different lighting, because I know from painting walls and cabinets that colors look different in different light."

Leland looks at Diane. "Did I overthink it?"

"No. I like the idea of seeing a painting under different lights. And I'll also have natural sunlight coming through the windows on each end. This is just great."

Diane wraps her arms around Leland and kisses his neck. "Y'all are so smart, you and your daddy."

"It was actually kind of fun. This is the first studio we ever built."

"I'm sure it won't be the last once everybody sees it."

The next morning at around 9:30, Diane is taking an order from a retired couple visiting from out of town when she sees the Moore sisters come into the diner and take seats at the counter. After she gets the order from the older couple and gives it to Theo through the kitchen window, she walks over to the Moore sisters and asks, "Just coffee today?"

Beth says, "Just coffee, no donuts."

Melanie lightly punches her sister on right arm and says, "Smarty."

As soon as Diane returns with the coffee, Melanie asks if Leland told her that Beth and she had seen her paintings at Kirkwood Academy the previous Friday.

"He did, and that made me nervous, because that was all he told me. He didn't say whether y'all liked them or not."

Melanie says, "We thought they were great. I couldn't believe that you painted that well at just sixteen."

"Well, thank you. I can barely remember them, but I'm glad y'all thought they were good."

"The reason that I called the other night was because I couldn't wait to ask you where you learned to paint."

"My mother."

Beth and Melanie look at each other, obviously picturing the nondescript, solemn Mrs. Randall in their minds.

Beth asks, "Is your mother a painter? We had no idea."

"Well, she was when she was young. She told me she took lessons when she was growing up in Dothan, then, when she was seventeen, she ran off and joined an art commune somewhere in California. That would have been back in the hippie days. Mama's never told me the full story on that, but I do know that she was there for several months before she came back home and married my daddy and moved to Niceville, Florida, where he was from. Then, shortly after she got back, Daddy got a job delivering furniture for Simmons Furniture Company that was in that same building where the gallery is now. He'd been a truck driver in the army. That's when they moved here."

Beth says, "We never knew your father. Please forgive me for bringing it up, but we had heard that he divorced your mother when you were a small child."

Melanie notices Diane's eyes tearing up as she takes a deep breath. "That's true, but that's not the whole story. He left us because when he got so awfully sick with cancer that he didn't want to be a burden on Mama. He spent his last six months in a V.A. hospital in Mobile. We used to go visit him there. Mama didn't know it when they got married, but he had first been diagnosed with lung issues not too long before they got married. He didn't tell her about it until years later. I mean, we knew that he was going to the doctor for what he called his 'lung problem,' but we had no idea it was cancer. And even after he told Mama that he had cancer, she didn't tell me until he got so sick that he had to go to the hospital."

Beth reaches out and takes Diane's left hand. "Good lord, I'm so sorry. We had no idea. I'm sorry now that we brought it up. It was really none of our business."

"Oh, that's okay. Y'all are friends."

Melanie quietly asks, "Why did your mother give up painting?"

"Well, she hasn't completely given it up. Every once in a while, I can get her to do a painting. But it's always a religious painting, and she always gives it away as soon as she finishes it. I wish she would keep some of her paintings because they are really good. I'd love to have one in our trailer, or maybe hanging in my studio."

Beth asks, "Is your studio finished? Can we see it?"

Melanie says, "Beth, don't be so pushy. I'm sure that Diane will invite us to see at the proper time."

Diane says, "Excuse me. I'll be right back," and she goes to wait on Mayor Steadman who has sat down in his usual corner booth after glad-handing all the customers, including the visitors from out of town.

In a low voice, Beth says to Melanie, "How about that story? Pretty sad, huh?"

"Extremely so. But I'm glad you got her to talk. We were completely wrong about how her father left her mother."

"Yeah, I always assumed it was because of how hard she must have been to get along with, being such a religious nut. Now, I'm kind of ashamed of myself."

"You've got nothing to be ashamed of. It just seemed logical, husband leaves crazy wife . . . Now, how can we get Diane to let us see the studio?"

"Beats me."

Diane returns and says, "Sorry about that, but Theo insists that the mayor gets served as soon as he sits down. If y'all are really interested in seeing the studio, Saturday would be a good time. Leland tells me that all the paint and the floor coating should be dry by Friday night, so I can move my easels and paint supplies from my mother's house on Saturday morning."

Melanie immediately perks up. "Would four o'clock Saturday afternoon be all right?"

"That would be great. I can't wait to show you what Leland and his daddy have done."

Melanie turns to Beth. "Is that okay with you, Beth?"

"No, we'll be down at our beach house on Saturday, but you go ahead and then give me a report when we get back home on Sunday night."

Melanie stands up and hands Diane the money for their coffee and her tip. "Beth and I won't be by here for the rest of the week. We're going to be helping my mother redecorate her living room. But I'll see you at four on Saturday, Diane. I can't wait."

"Yes, ma'am. Me, too."

Chapter Five

MELANIE'S SIX-YEAR-OLD LEXUS SEDAN APPROACHES THE JOHNSONS' trailer at 3:56 on Saturday afternoon. She sees that there are four vehicles already there. Two are identical green Ford pickup trucks parked in the back yard, one is an old red Toyota Camry that she recognizes as Diane's, and parked in the driveway behind Diane's car is a newer white Toyota Corolla that Melanie doesn't recognize.

Melanie pulls her car into the driveway and parks behind the white Corolla.

As she's exiting her car, Melanie sees a smiling Diane in faded blue jeans and an oversized white t-shirt, trotting out to greet her. Diane meets her in front of the car and, to Melanie's surprise, gives her an affectionate hug. Melanie, being uncertain of how to react to being greeted this way, gives Diane an awkward squeeze in return.

Diane says, "I'm so glad you came. I can't wait to show you the studio. Would you like a Coke or a cup of coffee?"

Melanie smiles. "No, thanks, I'm good. Maybe later."

Diane takes Melanie's right hand in her left hand and leads her around the right side of the mobile home toward the entrance to the studio. Melanie notices that the building that she and Beth saw under construction not long ago is now almost complete and is in the process of being painted the same shade of light beige as the trailer. She hears a clanging sound from above and looks up to see Leland and his father installing a metal roof. Leland sees Melanie and waves. She smiles and waves back. She asks Diane, "Do those two ever rest?"

Diane laughs. "Not that I've seen."

Diane opens the studio's hunter green door and motions Melanie in. Melanie walks in and immediately sees Beverly Randall, Diane's mother, standing at an easel situated in front of the left-side window. "Good afternoon, Missus Randall, are you looking at a painting that Diane's working on?"

"Afternoon, Missus Pebworth. Actually, this is a painting that I started about a month ago at home."

Melanie then notices that Mrs. Randall is holding a round bristle brush in her right hand, and the tip of the brush has on it red paint.

Melanie and Diane walk closer to the painting, and Melanie sees that it is of a field of poppies with the sun going down behind the flowers and lighting up a sky of gray and pink and purple clouds. Melanie is unsure of what to say, in view of what she's heard from Diane about her mother never painting secular pictures. She says, "This is just beautiful."

Seeing that Melanie is at a loss for anything else to say, Diane says. "I finally got Mama to paint something besides sacred pictures. I told her that I had to have one of her paintings for Bret's bedroom, and I wanted it to be flowers. This is going to be so pretty that Bret will keep it for the rest of his life."

Melanie steps closer to the painting. She says, "Missus Randall . . ."

"Please call me Beverly."

"Okay, if you'll call me Melanie."

"Deal."

"Well, Beverly, what I was going to ask is where did you see this poppy field?"

"In my head."

When she sees the surprised look on Melanie's face, Beverly explains, "Oh, I'm sure that I saw it somewhere, sometime in my life, so I'm painting it basically from memory and feeling."

Melanie continues to study the details in the painting. She says, "I'm sure you've heard that I'm a painter. I studied at Suwanee and Bama, as well as taking private lessons when I was growing up, but I don't believe that I could do what you're doing here, especially from memory."

"You're too kind. I probably couldn't do what you do."

"You'll have to come by our gallery sometime. I'll show you some of my work, as well as pieces by some other artists from around here. By the way, where did *you* learn to paint?"

"Oh, here and there. I was just lucky enough to have met several really good painters when I was young, and I tried to learn something from each one of them. I'm sure I must have been a pain asking all the questions that I did. Anyway, I don't want to talk about me. You two visit with each other."

Diane takes Melanie by the hand and leads her to a small, canary yellow crib next to the easel that's standing on the other side of the studio. "This sleeping beauty is Bret."

Melanie says, "He's a handsome boy. Who takes care of him when you're at work?"

"Miz Spencer from across the road. She's retired now, so she told us that she could watch Bret for the next several months before she goes to visit relatives in Detroit. Do you know her?"

"Very well. She was our neighbor's housekeeper for several years. Seems like a nice person."

"Oh, she is, and she gave us a great deal on the babysitting. I wanted to pay her more, but she wouldn't accept it. She said that she knows how hard it is for young couples to get by. And she said that she loves watching our satellite TV. Anyway, she comes over every morning just before I go to work, and we have a cup of coffee and watch the morning news on television and gossip a little while, then I kiss Bret goodbye and leave him with her."

Melanie turns to look at the canvas on the easel next to the crib and sees that Diane has been sketching a picture of a cocker spaniel.

Diane says, "This is also going to be for Bret's room. He loves dogs. This is Otto, our brown cocker spaniel."

"I saw him running around in the back yard when I was driving up." Melanie studies Diane's sketch for a moment. She says, "Yeah, that should be a nice picture."

Melanie walks over to look at one of the cabinets on the back wall. She notices the attention to detail. She says to Diane, "You know, I love the color of these cabinets. Where'd you find this paint? It looks like a cross between peach and light salmon."

"Leland came up with it for me. Mixed it up from some paints that he had left over from other jobs. Pretty, isn't it?"

"It is. Maybe Leland should be an artist, if he's that good with colors."

"No way. I tried to teach him to paint one time, and you should have seen the mess that he made. He painted a cow that looked more like a hippopotamus and got paint all over his jeans."

Melanie smiles at that. "Well, I can see that you and your mother are busy, so I won't take any more of your time. But please let me know when y'all finish your paintings for Bret's room. I'd love to see them. And thanks so much for showing me your studio and introducing me to Bret. I'll see you at the diner on Monday. And when y'all get a chance to come by the gallery, I'll show you my studio there. After seeing this one, I kind of wish that we had hired Leland and Red to build ours."

"Oh, I'm sure that yours is perfectly beautiful."

Melanie walks over to take another look at Beverly's poppy field painting and say goodbye to her. "It was good to finally meet you, Beverly, after seeing you around town so many times. And, as I said, I absolutely love this painting."

Beverly looks up from her painting. "Thank you, Melanie. It was good to meet you, too. Maybe we'll drop by your gallery sometime soon. I really appreciate what you and Frank have done with that old store. It went from being a rundown eyesore to being a credit to downtown Libertytown."

As Melanie is walking back to her car, she's thinking: *That wasn't anything at all like what I expected. I've got to tell Beth as soon as she gets home.*

That night at around nine o'clock, Melanie calls Beth at her house. Beth tells her that the family has just gotten in from their beach weekend and that right before they left, they had a "marvelous" seafood dinner at a local beachfront café.

Melanie anxiously waits for Beth to finish her detailed description of their dinner. Just as Melanie is about to run out of patience, Beth says, "Now, tell me all about your visit to Diane's studio. Was it worth driving out there?"

Melanie relays the story of her visit, and Beth is very intrigued by what she's hearing, especially by what Melanie is telling her about Mrs. Randall. Right before they end their conversation, the sisters conspire to do everything they can to unravel the mystery of Beverly's time in California.

Melanie says, "We just have to find out what happened out there. I just can't visualize Beverly Randall as a hippie girl."

"Neither can I. Except that hippie girls didn't wear makeup either. At least, that's what I've always heard."

"Yeah, but they certainly weren't religious fanatics. From what I've heard and read, and seen in the movies, they lived for sex, drugs, and rock and roll. That's what makes it so hard to envision Beverly as part of that scene."

"Well, maybe it'll all make sense once we hear the whole story, and if I know you and me, we will somehow manage to get that whole story."

Chapter Six

IT'S THREE O'CLOCK ON A SUNDAY AFTERNOON, ABOUT A MONTH after Melanie's visit to Diane's studio. Beverly has come by today to visit Bret and to see if the poppy field painting that she completed has fully dried. When no one answers the doorbell at the front door of the trailer, Beverly walks into the backyard to see if Diane is in her studio. She sees that the lights are on, so she goes to the studio door and lets herself in.

Beverly finds Diane at her easel putting the finishing touches on her painting of Otto. She compliments Diane on how good the painting looks. Diane smiles and turns to thank her mother for the compliment. She takes a long look at Beverly and says, "Why, Mama, you look so pretty today. Is that a new hairdo? And you've got on some makeup, too. Do you have a boyfriend you haven't told us about?"

Beverly tilts her head and smiles seductively. Then she strokes her strawberry blonde hair, which is loosely flowing to her shoulders. She says, "Of course not. You have to give Gloria credit for the new look. She talked me into it. I have to say that I do kind of like it, now that I've gotten used to it. But as for a boyfriend, that would be the last thing in the world that I would need right now."

Beverly turns to say hello to Leland whom she sees on the other side of the studio sitting in a folding chair and reading a story to Bret, who's listening attentively from his yellow crib.

Leland rises from his chair and walks over to Beverly. He gives her a quick hug and says, "Diane's right. You look very pretty. How was church this morning?"

"Oh, it was nice. I saw three new members. Are y'all still satisfied with First Baptist?"

Diane looks up from her painting and laughs. "Mama, quit trying to recruit us. We're just fine where we are. I'm sure that God has no trouble locating us there."

Beverly looks at Bret who's now playing with a red ball in his crib. "Bret, did you hear that blasphemy coming from your mama's mouth? I'll bet you'll come to my church when you get old enough."

Leland looks at Bret, then back at Beverly. He says, "Tell you what, Miz Beverly, if that's where Bret wants to go when he gets older, he'll surely have our blessing. But we don't need to talk any more about churches right now. I bet that you came by to check on your painting and see how Diane's doing on hers."

Beverly walks to Bret's crib and reaches in. She carefully lifts Bret and holds him to her bosom. She says, "And to see my precious grandson." Beverly carries Bret over to her painting, which she lightly touches. She finds that it's now dry enough to handle. She turns Bret around so that he can see the picture. "Bret, this painting is just for you. Don't let your mama hang it anywhere but in your bedroom, okay."

Leland walks over to look at the painting again. "Miz Beverly, that has to be one of the prettiest paintings I've ever seen."

"Why, thank you, Leland. Maybe I'll do one for you sometime. What type of picture would you like? Maybe a landscape?"

Leland closes his eyes, then opens them and says, "I've always wanted a painting of the Creek River where the old wooden pier is, maybe at sundown on a cloudy evening with the fog kinda hanging in the air and the sun shining through the fog from behind the trees on the other side of the river."

"Wow, for a carpenter, that was pretty creative. Why don't you wait for a day like you described and take a photo for me. I could paint a picture from the photo."

Leland feigns being offended. "Excuse me, what was that about a carpenter and creativity? Did you forget that Jesus was a carpenter? But thanks anyway for the offer. I'll take that picture and bring it to you."

Diane, still applying final touches to her painting, says, "He will absolutely not forget that you made him that offer, Mama, even if it means going down to the river every day until he gets the exact picture he wants."

Beverly smiles at Leland. "That's one of my favorite things about Leland. He always follows through."

Beverly gently places Bret back into the crib and hands him the red ball. Then she again lightly touches her painting with her fingertip and satisfies herself that it's fully dry.

Diane turns on her stool and says to Beverly, "Mama, I've been meaning to tell you that every time the Moore sisters have come into the diner for the past month, they've asked me about your painting."

"That so. What do they ask?"

"Mainly they want to know when they can see it. Since it's dry now, how about we go by the art gallery one day this week and take the painting with us."

Beverly ponders that for a moment. "Sure, why not, if it'll stop them from bothering you. As a matter of fact, tomorrow would be a good day for me. The glass plant's going to be closed tomorrow afternoon for some equipment replacement. Would that work for you?"

"I get off at four, but I can ask Miz Spencer if she'll stay with Bret for a little longer than usual, and if that's okay with her, we can go by the gallery right after I get off. Of course, I'll have to call Miz Pebworth tonight and make sure it's okay with her."

"Why don't you call her right now?"

Diane gets up, wipes a splotch of black paint off her right hand and says, "Good idea. I'll do that."

While Diane is standing just outside the studio door making the call on her cell phone, Beverly picks up her poppy field painting from its easel. As she walks toward the door with the painting, she says, "Leland, I'm going to take this out to my car, so that I don't drive off without it. I've got a frame at home that I bought for it on sale over at the art store in Carleton Plaza, and I'll frame it tonight."

"Yes, ma'am. By the way, I'm going to be making some frames for Diane. I'd be glad to make some for you, too."

Beverly nods. "I'll take you up on that. You can make a frame for your river painting once we know what size it'll be."

Just then Diane comes back through the door smiling. "I talked with Miz Pebworth. She said that anytime between four and five tomorrow would be fine with her. Turns out, her sister, Miz Lancaster, was there in the room with her, so she's also coming by the gallery tomorrow. Her sister said she has to pick up her girls at Kirkwood at three-fifteen, so she can stop by the gallery on the way home."

Leland says, "I'd kinda like to be there myself, but there's no way I could go. I'll be meeting with Mister Henderson about our trip to Pennsylvania."

Diane says, "You never did tell me what that trip was about."

"That's cause I still don't know. All I know is that it's about some business deal that Mister Henderson is trying to work out with somebody in Pennsylvania. I don't even know who we're going to be meeting with. He told me that he'll fill me in once the details are closer to being worked out."

"Well, then, why does he even need you there, if you don't know anything?"

"Beats me. But one thing that I've learned working with Mister Henderson is that he always has a reason for everything he does. I do know that we'll be meeting with Mister Henderson's brother Sean while we're up there. He runs the sawmill in Pennsylvania that our mill was modeled after."

Beverly asks, "When are y'all leaving for Pennsylvania?"

"I think it'll be in about two weeks. Mister Henderson says that he has some more research to do before we go."

"How long will y'all be gone?"

Leland is walking toward the studio door. He stops and turns around. "Probably two or three days. Could y'all please excuse me. I've got to go over to my shop and finish a screen door that Daddy needs."

Still standing next to the door with her painting in her hand, Beverly says, "Well, thank you, Leland, for letting me know about your trip that's coming up. That'll give me an excuse to come by and spend more time with Diane."

Diane laughs. "You mean Bret."

"You know what they say, grandkids are a blessing."

"What about daughters?"

"Oh, I guess they're a blessing, too, especially you. Do you know how long Leland's going to be in his shop? There's something that I've been wanting to talk to you about."

"Oh, he'll probably be in there until I call him for supper. You know how he is. Once he finishes the screen door, he'll find something else to work on. Also, there's a Packers game about to start, and he's got a TV in there."

"That reminds me. One of the girls at work asked me the other day if my grandson was named after Bret Favre. I had no clue who that was, so they told me that he's the quarterback for the Green Bay Packers. I told them I'd ask you if Bret was named after him."

"Yes, he was named after Bret Favre, but it wasn't because of the Packers. It was because Leland's daddy is a Southern Miss fan. He went there for two years before he had to drop out to take over his daddy's carpentry business after his daddy's arthritis got so bad."

"I didn't know that Red's father went through that. That's sad to hear, but what was that about Southern Miss?"

"That's where Bret Favre played college football. Red said that he always liked the name Bret, and when he found out that I was going to have a son, he asked us if we would name him Bret. I already liked the name Bret from watching reruns of old Maverick shows on television. You may remember the main character was Bret Maverick, played by James Garner. But I let Red think that we were doing him a favor by agreeing to that name, until one night at supper at their house, I finally told him that I was already considering naming our son Bret before he asked us. Leland's mother got a kick out of that. By the way, have you ever noticed that Leland looks like a young James Garner?

That's probably why I'm such a fan of the show."

Beverly answers, "I have noticed that, and I think that Bret is going to look just like Leland when he grows up, and he's going to be tall like Leland. But to get back to my question, can I just tell the girls at work that Bret was named after Bret Favre without getting into your convoluted story about Southern Miss and James Garner."

"Sure. Is that what you were so anxious to talk to me about?"

"No, it's something else. When I said while ago that grandkids are a blessing, it reminded me of something that I've been meaning to talk to you about for some time now, something really important that I probably should have already told you."

Diane leans toward her mother. "Now, you've got me worried, Mama. What in the world are you talking about? You're not sick, are you?"

"No, I'm fine. But I think that it's past time that I told you about my life in California and all the things that part of my life led up to."

Diane studies her mother's face. "Did something bad happen out there, something that you didn't want to tell me? Is that why you've been putting it off?"

"Just sit down and relax, and let me tell you what I should have already told you."

Diane sits down in the chair that Leland had been sitting in. She leans back and says, "Okay, I'm listening."

Beverly lays her painting on the nearest worktable and slides a folding chair to a spot close to where Diane is sitting. Beverly sits down in the chair and takes a deep breath. "You know that I went to California to join an art colony when I was seventeen, right after I finished high school. Remember, I finished early because I was in an advanced study program."

"Yes, ma'am. I know that you graduated early and left for California as soon as you graduated. But that's about all I know, except that one time Daddy told me that he had to drive cross country to rescue you from what he called 'all that,' whatever 'all that' was."

"Your daddy coming to get me is an important part of the story, but it's not the most important part.

"Remember, I told you that I never knew who my birth parents were, because I was adopted as a baby by your grandpa and grandma when they were in their late fifties. They treated me wonderfully when I was growing up, but even so, when I started taking art lessons at around thirteen, I hung around with a lot of older kids who taught me some bad habits, like drinking and experimenting with drugs, and everything that comes with that."

Diane raises her eyebrows. "Wow. Knowing you now, I can't imagine that. Is that why you went to California, to live that lifestyle?"

"That's exactly why. And my parents didn't know that I was leaving. I just packed a suitcase, got together all the money I had saved up, and left in the middle of the night. I walked down to the bus station and bought a ticket to Fresno, because I'd heard from some of my art friends that there was a new art commune not far from there.

"I didn't call my folks until I'd been in that little art colony for about two weeks. Needless to say, they were worried out of their minds by then, and my dad was not in good health at the time, so it was just an awful thing that I did by running off to California without telling them. And that was just the first of my transgressions."

Beverly pauses for a moment. "This art commune was just south of Fresno on what was once a cattle farm, and it was run by a guy named Will Stanton, who was a well-known and very successful artist from San Francisco. Will had said that he was fed up with the big city rat race and that it was a good time for him to invest in something that he had always wanted to do. So, he bought the farm and fixed up several of the main buildings. He turned one of the buildings into a dining hall, and he built separate living quarters for men and women. He also converted what had been the bunkhouse for the farm hands into what he called the art center where he and anyone else who wanted to would paint and share ideas with each other, and also give lessons to younger artists like me.

"Now the commune went great until about six months after I got there. That was when Will and some of his close friends started getting deeper and deeper into the drug scene. I was lucky in one sense, at least from an art point of view. Because during the first three or four months

I was there, I was able to learn almost everything that I know now about painting. I mean, the art center was going literally twenty-four hours a day, and you could walk in anytime and ask as many questions as you wanted, and somebody there could answer your questions. And you could try out new techniques and styles with somebody right there to help you. It was great. And the commune provided all of the art supplies, and books, and space, and whatever else that you needed."

"What exactly went wrong?"

"Well, first of all, bear in mind that I've just turned eighteen at that time, and I'm very impressionable, and dumb as a rock. And I'm also very pretty, with a sexy young body."

Diane blushes and turns her head. She cannot believe what she's hearing from her pious mother.

Beverly grins. "See why I've been putting this off."

Diane takes a long look at her mother. Then she takes a deep breath and lets it out. She says, "Sort of, but don't hold anything back. I'll understand."

"Well, anyway, I'm this cute, gullible eighteen-year-old who's suffering from hero worship of all these older guys but having no idea of where that could lead. In particular, I was madly in love with this really cute guy named Burton Webber, who was twenty-two years old and a really talented artist who had studied under Will Stanton. Burton was also, as I realize now, completely void of morals or scruples. Well, as I mentioned earlier, I'd been around people in Dothan who were experimenting with drugs, mainly marijuana and uppers, so that made it easy for me to get convinced to expand the scope of my drug use and try LSD and mushrooms, and eventually heroin."

Diane blinks. "Wow, I didn't see that coming. I can sort of understand LSD and mushrooms, because those might have been considered party drugs in that situation. But heroin's another matter."

"Not to me it wasn't. I was convinced by Burton that heroin was just another step along the path of expanding my mind for creative purposes. And I was a huge fan of the Doors, and I had heard from some of the musicians in the area that Jim Morrison did a lot of heroin. So, in my immature mind, if a drug was good enough for Jim Morrison, it was certainly good enough for little old me. And, besides that, I didn't want to be a square, because in that community being square was the ultimate sin."

Beverly pauses and takes a quick breath. "I'm getting close to the most important parts of the story now. This is still hard for me to say, even though I've rehearsed this conversation a thousand times in my mind. But here is it: Burton finally got me to try heroin not too long after I became what he called his 'lady.' I didn't like the way that heroin made me feel, but I liked the idea that Burton and I were getting high together. Well, one Saturday night after he and I had been doing drugs together for a couple of months, we did some heroin that Burton had gotten from a dealer who he didn't really know, and of course I didn't know, and the heroin that we got that night turned out to be probably three times stronger than any we'd done before.

"I woke up the next afternoon in a bed in a hospital feeling absolutely horrible. The first thing that crossed my mind was that I must have over-dosed, so I asked a nurse if Burton was okay. Instead of answering my question, the nurse called for the doctor. When the doctor got there, he told me how lucky I was to be alive and how lucky I was that the heroin didn't kill my baby. I screamed out, 'What baby? And where's Burton? Is he all right?' The doctor asked the nurse how long it had been since I'd been given some shot that he named, and when she told him, he said that he'd be back in a little while to talk to me.

"I don't know what they gave me, but by the time the doctor got back, I felt much more relaxed and not so sick. The doctor asked me, 'Is Burton the young man who was with you when you were taking the heroin?' I said, 'Yes, sir, is he okay? Can I see him?' He said, 'I'm afraid that you won't be seeing Burton. He wasn't as lucky as you. He didn't make it.' I felt myself starting to get hysterical again. I said, 'Are you saying that Burton's dead?' The doctor came over and sat on the bed next to me and kind of whispered, 'I'm afraid so.'

"That's when, as tranquilized as I was, I lost it and started crying uncontrollably. Then, for some reason, I remembered the comment about a baby. So, I calmed down as best I could and asked, 'What was that about me being lucky that the heroin didn't kill my baby? What baby?' The doctor and the nurse looked at each other. The doctor took my hand and he said, 'As you can imagine, when you got here, we had to do all sorts of tests on you because we didn't know for sure what had happened to you. Well, one of the tests showed that you were pregnant, but not very far along, so I can understand if you didn't know.'

"By then I was sobbing again. I said, 'No. I didn't know. But are you sure that the baby's going to be all right?' He said, 'We didn't see anything that would indicate that there is any problem with the baby, as long as you stay completely away from all illicit drugs during the pregnancy, and alcohol, too, for that matter.'"

At this point of her mother's story Diane is holding both of her mother's hands, and tears are streaming down the cheeks of both Diane and Beverly. Knowing the pain of losing a baby, Diane is almost afraid to ask, "What about the baby, Mama? Did the baby survive?"

Beverly squeezes Diane's hands. "Yes, the baby was born a beautiful and healthy girl, and she's right here with me now."

Diane leans toward her mother and whispers, "You mean me . . . but what about Daddy? I thought he was my father. I don't understand."

"Diane, Burton Webber was your father. It couldn't have been anyone else."

"Did Daddy know?"

"Yes, he did, and now you're the only other person I've ever told. Not even the doctor who delivered you, Melanie and Beth's grandfather, suspected that Charlie wasn't your father. It was probably because he thought we'd been married longer than we had."

"I still don't understand. When and how did you and Daddy get married?"

Beverly takes a deep breath and slowly releases it. "This is what happened. As soon as I was well enough to leave the hospital in Fresno, I called your father in Niceville, Florida, which, as you know, is where he's from. And you'll remember that I told you that your daddy and I had met in Dothan when he was stationed at Fort Rucker and was in Dothan with some of his army buddies. Not long after we met, we became very close friends, even though I was sixteen and he was twenty. And after that, we stayed pen pals when he was stationed in Missouri. Well, when I called him from California, I asked him to please come out there and get me, that I was ready to come home. I told him about the overdose, but not about the baby.

"At the time that he got my call, he had just gotten discharged, and he was waiting to start a job at Simmons Furniture Company here in Libertytown a few weeks later. Well, anyway, when I asked him to come get me, he said that he'd be leaving right then. I gave him the address and phone number for the commune, and around midnight about four days later, I got a call from an exhausted Charlie asking me for directions. He was only about ten miles away, so I was still packing when he got to the commune. We loaded my stuff in his Chevelle, and I went by Will's apartment to leave him a note thanking him for everything and telling him that I was needed back in Alabama.

"I was crying so much as we were leaving the commune that Charlie thought I had changed my mind. So, he pulled into the parking lot of an all-night gas station, and we had a long talk. That was when I told him about Burton and the baby. Then I started crying some more and bawling, 'What am I going to do with a baby?' As I said, he was four years older than me and an Army veteran, so he didn't freak out. He just waited for me to calm down some and then he said, 'This is what you're going to do. When we get to Nevada, you and I are going to get married. Once we do that, everything else will take care of itself. How about that?'

"I said, 'I can't let you marry me just because you feel sorry for me.' He said, 'But you can let me marry you because I love you and want to take care of you and your baby.' I didn't say yes or no about marrying him right then, but he started driving toward Nevada and said that the city he had in mind wasn't too far out of our way in case I decided against marrying him.

"As I'm sure you've figured out by now, we got married in Nevada. After we got married, we spent the next day and that night in Las Vegas and then left for Florida early the following morning. And we actually had a good time traveling to Florida. We took turns driving and sleeping, and when we were both awake, we sang along with the radio. And we stopped a couple of times to get some sleep in a motel and take a shower.

"Then, when we got to Niceville, I called my parents and begged their forgiveness for running off like I did, and I told them about Charlie and me getting married. I didn't tell them that I was pregnant until a couple of months later, so that they would think that the baby was Charlie's. Well, they had met Charlie several times before and liked him a lot, and they were so relieved that I was okay that they had no problem accepting our marriage.

"We went to visit them right after Charlie and I moved into our house here in Libertytown, and, as you know, everything turned out just fine with them from then on. You remember how crazy they were about you."

Diane says, "Yes, I do. I miss them so much. I wish that they were here to see Bret."

Diane gets up from her chair and walks over to Bret's crib where she pulls his blanket up onto his neck. She strokes his pink cheek then comes back to sit in her chair. After thinking for a moment, she looks at her mother and asks, "Mama, why in the world did you take so long to tell me this?"

"Mainly because I didn't want you to think any less of Charlie because he wasn't your natural father, and, of course, because I didn`t want any of the snoops in Libertytown to ever know about it. So, I just never told anybody until now."

Diane looks into her mother's eyes and touches her cheek. "You know that I could never, ever think anything bad about Daddy. But, believe me, I completely understand what you mean about not letting the town gossips find out, because I hear how they talk about folks every day at the diner." She shakes her head and smiles. "They are just so *nasty*."

Beverly takes a handkerchief from her pocket and wipes the tears from her cheeks, and then she wipes away those on Diane's cheeks. The two of them embrace and smile as more tears flow. Beverly looks over

Diane's shoulder at a sleeping Bret and softly says, "I am so blessed."

After a few moments, Dianes softly says, "Mama."

"Yes, honey."

"Where is Burton Webber buried?"

"I'm not really sure, baby. Right after Charlie and I got settled here in Libertytown, I called Will Stanton and asked him where Burton was buried. He said that Burton was buried in a cemetery in Salem, Oregon, where he was from. Will told me that some of the people from the art colony went to the funeral. But to this day, I don't know why I wanted to know where Burton was buried. It wasn't like I was planning on visiting his grave."

"Well, I'm glad you did ask where he was buried. Do you think we could go there sometime?"

"Sure, honey. I don't remember if Will told me the name of the cemetery, and, unfortunately Will's gone now, but I'll see if I can get a copy of Burton's obituary from his local paper. That should give us the name."

Diane is dabbing her eyes with the little white handkerchief that she keeps in her purse. She says, "Mama, once we're out there, do you think that we could find one of Burton Webber's paintings for me to see?"

"Tell you what. Once we decide on when we're going to Oregon, I'll start calling every art museum in Salem or in that vicinity and see if I can find one for us to look at while we're there. I would especially love for you to see one from his Monterey series if I can find one. That series is just unbelievable."

"Thanks, Mama."

Chapter Seven

It's around 3:55 on the following Monday afternoon. Diane is looking out the front window of Danny's Diner, waiting for her mother to arrive. In a few moments, she sees Beverly's Toyota pull into a parking spot across Main Street from the diner. She sees Beverly exit the Corolla and look both ways before crossing the street. Diane takes off her apron and folds it before she places it in a drawer behind the counter. She motions to Theo that she's on her way out, and Theo waves goodbye to her.

A smiling Beverly is waiting for Diane on the sidewalk in front of Danny's. She takes Diane's left hand and walks her across the street to the white Toyota. After they're both seated and belted in, Beverly says, "You know, I've been looking forward to this all day. I can't remember the last time we went anywhere together."

"I know. It seems that the only times we're together are at your house or ours."

"Just regular homebodies, aren't we?"

"Afraid so, Mama."

"Well, that ends as of today. Is that a deal?"

"Yes, ma'am." Diane drops her head down and inhales deeply. "Do I smell like grease? I never can tell until I get home and take off my clothes and take a whiff of them."

"I can't tell, baby, my head's stopped up today."

"I know what I'll do." Diane reaches into her purse and pulls out a travel-size spray cologne bottle. She shows it to Beverly, then sprays a little on her neck and on the inside of each wrist. "There, I feel better now."

"Okay, baby."

They arrive at the Main Street Gallery just after four. Beth, Melanie, and Frank are all standing in the lobby of the gallery talking. Melanie sees Beverly and Diane approaching the gallery and walks over to open the door for them. She takes a slight bow and says, "Afternoon, ladies." Once Beverly and Diane are inside, Melanie leads Beverly over to Beth and Frank. "Beverly, let me introduce you to my sister Beth and my partner Frank Dupre. Diane already knows them both."

Beth and Frank each shake Beverly's hand, and Frank welcomes her to the gallery. "Is this your first time in our gallery, Beverly? I know that Diane has been in here once before."

"It is. I've admired your building from the street, but this is the first time I've been inside this building since years ago when it was a furniture store."

Beverly shifts her painting, which is wrapped in brown packing paper, from her left hand to her right. Then she looks around the gallery. She notices that the tile floor is light gray, and the walls are painted a lighter shade of gray. She sees that the ceiling is the same shade of gray as the floor, and the doors and wooden trim are charcoal gray. Beverly says, "This is very nice, Frank. Would it be a bother to give Diane and me a quick tour?"

"No bother at all. I'd love to. Do you want to put your package down? You can leave it right here on this desk."

Beverly places the painting on the reception desk and says, "Thank you. That's the painting that Beth and Melanie wanted to see."

"As do I. They told me that it is a perfectly marvelous painting of a poppy field."

Diane says, "Mama did it for my son Bret's room. I just love it. I know you'll like it too."

Frank looks at the wrapped painting lying on the desk. "I'm sure I will. I can hardly wait to see it. If it's all right with you, Beverly, we'd love for you to unveil it as soon as we get back from our walk through the gallery."

"Sure, why not."

For the next ten minutes or so, Frank takes Diane and Beverly on an intimate tour of the gallery. Beverly can hear the pride in Frank's voice as he points out and gives details about each separate area of exhibits, and each of the gallery's two conference rooms, as well as his and Melanie's studio and the three rooms that are set aside for classes and other special activities.

As they're walking toward a high school art exhibit near the front of the gallery, Beverly tells Frank that she particularly liked the abstract art exhibit they just looked at. She says, "That's the one type of art that I simply can't do, no matter how hard I try. I guess that I'm just too much of a realist. But to me, abstract art is probably the most creative form of painting."

Frank says, "Personally, I've never cared that much for abstract art, but that exhibit does seem to be very popular. My favorite style is impressionism, particularly paintings of young women."

Diane says, "Oh, I love that style. I've always been a fan of Degas's dancer paintings."

Frank nods. "Oh, yes. Those are lovely, aren't they?"

When they get back to the lobby, Frank says, "Well, that's the gallery, ladies, except for the second floor where we have our offices and storage rooms and mail room and copy room, and such as that."

"Thank you so much for taking the time to show us around," Diane says. "Now, Mama, why don't you unwrap your painting and show it to everybody."

Beth and Melanie, who have been entertaining Beth's girls while waiting for the gallery tour to end, look to other as if to say, "Finally." Out loud, Melanie says, "Yes, Beverly, show Frank and Beth your painting now, so they can see that I've haven't been exaggerating about how beautiful it is."

Beverly starts unwrapping the painting, being careful not to tear the packing paper that she intends to put back over the painting once everyone has seen it. As the painting comes into view, one area at a time, Diane sees Frank's face evolving from that of a cheery tour guide to one of an earnest art professor. Once the painting is fully unveiled, Frank stands over it for a while then slowly backs away, never taking his eyes from it. Finally, he turns to Beverly and says in a soft voice, "This is stunning, Beverly. I simply love the way that you give each flower a life of its own, and the way you use light and shadow. It's just perfectly done."

Beverly is amused by Frank's dramatic reaction to her painting, but with a straight face she says, "Thank you, Frank. That's quite a compliment coming from someone of your expertise. I'm glad you like it."

"Oh, no. Thank you so very much for showing it to us."

Melanie laughs and says, "I'm pretty sure that we never would have seen it if it had gotten to Bret's bedroom first."

Beth says, "Thank you, Beverly. I was skeptical, but that painting is just as beautiful as Melanie said that it was. I really appreciate your going to the trouble to bring it by here."

"You're welcome, Beth. It was no trouble, and I was glad to get to see the gallery. It's even nicer that I thought it would be."

Beth says, "Well, you have to give all the credit to Melanie and Frank for how good the gallery looks. This is all their doing."

Beverly bows toward Melanie and Franks and says, "Thank you, Melanie and Frank for bringing such a lovely gallery to our little town." Then she turns to Diane and says, "Baby girl, it's time for me to get you on your way home. The babysitter's waiting."

Diane says to Frank and the Moore sisters, "Thank y'all so much for your courtesy and for how much you appreciate Mama's painting. Now I've got to get her interested in doing more paintings because I'm her biggest fan."

Frank looks at Melanie and then at Beverly. "Beverly, please let us know if there is anything that Melanie or I can ever do for you as far as your art career. We definitely want to see more of your work, and we'd love for you to have an exhibit here sometime if you're ever interested in doing that. And, believe me, your art will sell once people get a chance to see it."

Beverly smiles. "Well, I've never really had an art career, but thank you, anyway."

After Diane and Beverly leave, Frank says to Melanie, "Thank you so much for bringing her to me. I am astounded at how good that painting is. Even if she never paints another piece, that one picture makes her a star in my mind. But I think that, based on what I can see from that painting, there could be a huge demand for her work."

Melanie puts her arm around Frank's shoulders. "And you'd love to be the first one to exhibit her, wouldn't you?"

"Heavens, yes."

As Beverly and Diane are walking back to Beverly's car, Beverly turns and takes a long look at the gallery. She says, "That's a really nice place. I'm glad we came. But it was sad how it reminded me so much of Charlie. I could almost feel his presence in there."

Chapter Eight

A FEW MINUTES AFTER THEY START RIDING BACK TOWARD DANNY'S, Diane says, "They really liked your painting, but I knew they would."

"Yes. I believe they did. But one of the things that I learned from my time in California, as brief as it was, is that there is a dichotomy between those who look at a work of art as a gift from God and those who look at it as a commodity or a status symbol."

"I'm not sure what you mean."

"I mean that I see the ability to create art as a gift that God has given us to help bring more beauty into the world, and I always have a hard time thinking of a work of art as a commercial product, something to be bought and sold. And I got the impression, maybe I'm wrong, that Melanie and Frank are quite a bit more of the commercial orientation than I am."

"Well, of course they are. They sell art for people who want to sell their art, and they sell to people who are looking to buy art. I don't see anything wrong with that. I'd love to be able to sell some of my art. And I don't see how a sales transaction would make a work of art any less a thing of beauty."

"That's because you have two gifts from God, my dear, the gift of creativity and the gift of common sense. As for me, I guess that I'm still an old hippie at heart, too idealistic for my own good."

"So true, Mama. But that's one of the things I love the most about you. You're not like the rest of us, you're a romantic soul."

Beverly laughs. "Yeah, that's why I'm a forty-year-old single woman working in a factory."

Diane reaches over and gently lays her hand on Beverly's right shoulder. "But a romantic forty-year-old single woman working in a factory."

When they get back to Danny's, Beverly drives down a narrow alley to the rear of the building where the employees park. Instead of getting out of the car right away, Diane turns to her mother and says, "Mama, before you go, there's something else that I have to know."

"What's that, baby?"

"When and how did your strong religious feelings come about? You know without me telling you that some people think that you're a little bit on the overly religious side."

"It was because of you."

"I don't understand. What did *I* do?"

"It's not anything that you did. It's that before you were born, I was constantly feeling sad and stressed out because I was afraid my past drug habits might somehow increase the chances that you would be born with some kind of serious problem, and there were many nights that I cried myself to sleep about it."

"Did Daddy know how you felt?"

"No. I kept my feelings from him. I didn't want to make him worry, too. He had enough on his mind at that time."

"How'd you cope with that stress?"

"Not all that well. But late one night when Charlie was out on the road delivering some furniture to a house in Florida, I was feeling even more miserable and worried about you than usual, and that's when I decided that I needed to talk to Jesus. That was totally out of character for me, because I was far from a religious person at the time. But on that night, sometime after midnight, I went out on the front porch and bared my soul to the Lord. I asked for forgiveness for my sins and begged that you wouldn't have to pay for what I had done. I promised Jesus that if he would protect you, I would be his servant for the rest of my life. It's that simple. And when you were born so healthy and beautiful, I knew that Jesus had watched over you, and I felt so much joy and gratitude on the day you were born that I recommitted to the promise that I had made."

Diane takes her mother's hand in hers. With a tear in her voice, she says, "So, all of the sacrifices that you've made over all these years were because of a promise that you made so that I would be protected. I wish I had known that before now. Maybe I would have been a better person, and maybe not gotten pregnant at seventeen."

"Baby, don't think like that. Think about how great everything has turned out. You're healthy, you're beautiful. You have a great husband and the best son in the world, and . . ."

"The best mother in the world."

Beverly laughs. "Of course, that too, the best mother in the world."

Diane squeezes Beverly's hand. "I've got to think for a while about all that you've told me lately, Mama. There's a lot to take in."

"Above all, remember that Jesus came through for us when it counted."

Diane takes a deep breath and exhales it. "Mama, since you've been so open with me, there's something that I've got to tell you."

"What's that?"

"When I had my miscarriage, I felt as guilty as you did when you thought that maybe you had done something to harm me before I was born. You don't know how many nights I couldn't sleep because I thought that I had done something to cause my precious baby to die."

"But, honey, the doctor told us that the miscarriage was not due to anything like that. It was because of a chromosomal problem that was purely random, a matter of chance. He said that there was nothing that anyone could have done to prevent a miscarriage. The fetus just couldn't develop."

"But I didn't know that when it first happened. Remember, they had to do some tests to find that out."

Beverly takes Diane's hand in hers. "I'm so sorry you felt that guilty. But do you remember what I told you when it happened? Always know that the soul of your unborn baby went back to the Lord."

"I remember."

Mother and daughter tearfully embrace in the front seat of that white Corolla until Beverly lifts her head from Diane's shoulder and says, "Okay, enough crying. Let's go home."

Chapter Nine

IT'S A PLEASANT SATURDAY AFTERNOON IN MARCH OF 1994. SINCE their heart-to-heart conversations in October of the prior year, Beverly and Diane have been spending every available moment together in Diane's studio, where they have been drawing, painting, talking about life, and watching Bret flourish.

On this day, Diane is working on a painting of a fishing pond that she photographed a few weeks ago. Beverly is painting a picture of flowers wilting in a small concrete vase at the head of a gravestone that is chipped and stained almost black and into which is etched:

PVT. OSCAR O'CONNOR

1843–1864

1ST ALABAMA CAVALRY, CSA

While the women are painting, Bret is sleeping peacefully in his yellow crib. He's clutching the toy brown cocker spaniel that Leland gave him the night before.

Diane hears a vehicle coming up the driveway. She knows that Leland is working in his shop, so she puts her paint brush into an old coffee cup on her worktable and walks out into the yard and looks toward the driveway. She sees a familiar dark blue 1992 Mustang fastback come to a stop. Diane walks toward the car and sees Leland's mother exiting the driver-side door and waving to her.

"Hey, Diane. You must be working in the studio."

"Yes, ma'am, Mama and I are in there today. Come on back."

Diane waits for Leland's mother to reach her and gives her a warm embrace. "I was hoping you'd come by today. I want to show you the painting that I'm working on for y'all."

As they're walking to the studio, Leland's mother says, "You're doing a painting for us. Does Red know?"

"I don't think so, unless Leland told him. I haven't seen Daddy Johnson lately."

"Yeah, he's been building some cabinets for Pauline Livingston's dining room, and it seems to be taking forever. She keeps changing her mind about different little details. Red says he doesn't care because he's being paid by the hour."

"That may be what he says, but I bet that he winds up not charging her for all his time."

"Of course he won't."

Once they get inside the studio, Beverly rises from her stool and comes over and hugs Leland's mother carefully, trying not to get any paint on her. "How are you, Jeanette. It's been a while. Good to see you."

"You, too, Beverly. I'm glad you're here. I want to run something by y'all. But first, let me look at this painting that Diane is doing for us."

Jeanette walks over to Diane's easel and studies the painting. She turns to Beverly and asks, "Isn't that just beautiful?"

Beverly says, "It sure is."

Diane says to Jeanette, "Thank you, ma'am, but what is it you want to tell us, Mama Johnson?"

"Don't look so worried. I just wanted to let you and Leland know that I just recently got in my twenty-five years with the Creek County Board of Education, and I'm about ninety-nine percent sure that I'm going to file my retirement papers on Monday morning. I've been talking to Red about it for several months now, and I think that he wants me to go ahead and retire so he won't have to hear about it anymore."

Beverly says, "Well, if you and Red are agreeable to it, then what's to discuss?"

"It's just such a big step for me."

"Believe me, if I could retire on a pension right now, I'd do it in a minute."

Jeanette thinks for a moment, then nods. "You know, you're right, Beverly. It's not like I'm indispensable. They can find another payroll clerk in no time."

Diane says, "Then it's settled. Now, where are we going to have your retirement party?"

"I haven't even thought about a retirement party. But it would be nice to see some of my co-workers one last time, because almost all of them live in Carleton, and I rarely see them except at work."

Beverly says, "Sounds like the retirement party needs to be in Carleton."

Jeanette says, "Let me talk to Red about it. I'm sure that he can come up with an idea of a good place to hold the party because his band used to play a lot of events in Carleton."

Beverly asks, "When did he have a band?"

"Oh, he played in a band for years until that wreck convinced him that he needed to stay away from anywhere he might be tempted to drink again. The only time he plays music now is when Leland and him are writing songs together, or sometimes at our church or at a social function. I believe that the last time they played in public was for some kind of party at the country club. You know, I hadn't thought about it, but Red's been sober for about seven years now."

Diane says, "I've never seen him any other way."

"You're lucky. He was a terrible drunk. He didn't get into fights or anything. He just wanted to party all night when he was drinking, and he'd get louder and louder as the night went on, and it was almost impossible to get him home. And then he'd have a terrible hangover the next day and just be miserable the whole day. No sir, I don't miss that mess even a little bit."

Beverly asks, "So, what are you going to do when you retire? Do you want to start painting with us?"

"Lord no. I've always been terrible at art, but I know I'll read a lot more than I do now. And maybe join a bridge club, and, of course, spend more time with my grandson, if Diane will let me."

Jeanette walks over to Bret's crib and touches his cheek. Diane comes over and stands next to her. Diane smiles at how attached Bret is to the new toy dog that he is cradling and says, "Of course, I will. I'm sure that he'd like to have more time with both of his grandmas."

Beverly looks at Bret and smiles. "He is going to be *so* spoiled when we get through with him."

Diane reaches down and strokes Bret's hair. "Not once he gets old enough to hang around with his daddy and granddaddy. He'll be out hunting and fishing, and building stuff, and playing Hank Williams on his guitar. Nope, Leland will unspoil him in a hurry."

Jeanette says to Beverly, "She's right. My husband and my son don't have one ounce of refinement between them. They'll probably have him chewing tobacco and driving a truck in the first grade."

Beverly says, "Well then, we better get to work on getting some gentility instilled into Bret before those two get a hold of him."

Diane walks back to her easel and surveys her fishing pond painting. She starts cleaning her brushes and says, "I've done about all I can do on this painting today. What do y'all say we grill some hamburgers?"

Beverly picks up one of her paint brushes and points it at her painting. "I need about fifteen more minutes on this one. Why don't y'all go fire up the grill and also tell Leland that it's about to be hamburger time."

Chapter Ten

The next Monday morning, Mrs. Spencer and Diane are sitting at the small dinette table in the trailer's kitchen drinking their morning coffee when Mrs. Spencer stops buttering her toast and says, "You remember when I told you that I was going to have to take some time away from Bret this summer to visit my folks in Detroit?"

"Yes, ma'am. Have you scheduled your trip yet?"

"Not quite, but we decided that I'll go up there sometime in late May or early June. But there's been a change of plans. Instead of me just spending the summer with my sister, she wants me to come live with her permanently."

"Gracious, Miz Spencer, I don't know what I'd do without you being across the road from us. You're like part of the family."

"I know. This was a hard decision for me, too. But all my family is going to be in the Detroit area now. Even my sons have decided to stay up there instead of moving back here like they had planned on doing. And I'm not getting any younger. I want to spend what time I have left with my people."

Diane nods. "That's the right thing to do. You need to be with your family. You don't have to be concerned about us. We'll miss you, but we'll be glad for you."

"What about babysitting Bret? Can you find somebody?"

"Oh, don't worry about that. Leland's mother will be retiring at the end of April, and she's been strongly hinting at wanting Bret to stay with her during the day. I think she'd love to keep him for us."

"Oh, I'm so glad you told me that. I wouldn't want just anybody tending to my Bret."

Diane gets up and stands behind Mrs. Spencer. She puts her hands on Mrs. Spencer's shoulders and kisses the top of her head. "Now, I can't promise that Bret won't be heartbroken. You're the only babysitter he's ever had, and he's going to wonder where you went. You know how he lights up every time he sees you."

When Diane sits back down, she notices that Mrs. Spencer's eyes are glistening. "I'm going to miss him, too. Will you send me pictures and keep me up on how he's doing?"

"Of course. Just be sure to give us your new mailing address and phone number. Oh, and leave us a photo of you that I can put in Bret's room."

"I'd be proud to, Miss Diane."

Diane kisses Bret goodbye and leaves for work.

When Diane gets to the diner, she tells Earline about Mrs. Spencer's plans. Earline says, "Gosh, I hate to hear that. Mama and Miss Ethel have been good friends forever. I don't know how many times we've been to her house, and she's been to ours."

"I know. I've seen y'all over there."

"No, Mama's not going to be happy about this at all. She's lost so many friends already, moving away or passing away."

"Well, you need to console her as best you can. It's hard to lose a good friend like that. But they can still call each other."

Earline and Diane hear voices and turn to see Judge Bailey coming through the door, followed by Mr. Henderson and a short, well-tanned middle-aged man.

"Earline asks Diane, "Who's that with Judge Bailey and Mister Henderson?"

"That's Mister Bernstein. He owns all that farmland across from us. He also owns that little house that Miz Spencer lives in. His grandson manages the farm now. Mister Bernstein moved to somewhere down on the Gulf Coast years ago."

The three men who just came in join John Lancaster, Earline's first customer this morning, at a corner table. Earline says, "You know there was a time black folks would worry if they saw four of the richest white men in town meeting together."

Diane shakes her head and smiles. "Well, that's your table, Earline. Why don't you go over there and ask them what they're up to."

Earline gives Diane the evil eye, then she walks over to the table with a smile. Each of the men orders scrambled eggs, pancakes and coffee.

Diane waves at Mr. Henderson on her way to see to the needs of two of the city's society matrons who have dropped by for coffee on their way to a book club meeting at the Libertytown Library.

When she and Earline meet at the counter later, Diane asks, "Well, did they tell you what they're up to?"

"Well, right now, they're talking about football, but Mister Henderson had a stack of papers in front of him."

"I'm going to ask Leland if he knows what they might be up to. He has a way of knowing these things."

Earline says, "Let me know what you find out." Then she points toward the front door. "Speak of the Devil."

Diane turns to see Leland coming through the door. He walks over and winks at Earline, then gives Diane a quick hug and says "Morning, babe." He waves to Theo as he heads for the table where the four power brokers are sitting. When he gets there, he hands Mr. Henderson a folder containing more documents. Then he pulls up a chair and takes a seat between Mr. Henderson and John Lancaster.

Diane says, "Now I really am curious."

"Like I said, let me know when you find out what's going on."

The Moore sisters enter the diner, and Beth waves to her husband John. The sisters take seats at the counter. Diane walks behind the counter and says, "Good morning. How are y'all doing?"

Beth asks, "What's going on over there in the corner with John and that bunch?"

Melanie looks over at the men and says, "Whatever it is, there's got to be a lot of money involved."

Beth says, "Or a deer hunting trip . . . Isn't that your husband, Diane?"

"Yes, ma'am, but don't ask me what they're up to."

"I'll have to ask John when he gets home tonight."

Melanie says, "Well, I guess we'll find out soon enough. How's your painting going, Diane?"

"Oh, fine, especially because I've been spending so much time with Mama. I'm learning a lot from her. I guess I never knew just how talented and how smart she is."

Melanie asks, "Did you know that your mother was offered an art scholarship out of high school?"

"I think I heard her, or maybe her mother, mention that one time. How'd you find out?"

"A friend of mine who's an art teacher at Dothan High School was a classmate of your mother in high school. She said your mother won several art awards when she was a teenager and was offered an art scholarship to South Alabama."

"I'm not really surprised at that, but I guess she had other plans. She wanted to go to California instead. I don't know that much about the art world, but I think that Mama could have been something special if she had concentrated on her art."

Melanie tilts her head and says, "Well, personally, I don't think it's too late. As a matter of fact, I think that both of you could be something special."

"Oh, I don't know about that. I'm still learning, and she doesn't seem to be that crazy about being part of the art scene. She's happy just doing paintings for her family and for fun."

"Would it be an inconvenience if Beth and I came by your studio sometime to see what y'all are working on?"

Beth says, "Yeah, I'm still looking forward to seeing the studio."

"Sure, that'd be great. Saturday afternoons are our favorite painting times. Why don't y'all come by this coming Saturday if you don't have something else to do?"

Melanie says, "I'm good. George is taking Little George fishing, so I'll be free all day."

Beth adds, "Charlotte has a soccer game, but it'll be over by twelve. So, how about if we come by around two?"

Diane reflects for a moment. "That'll be fine. Just come on over, and don't worry if you run late. We'll be there all afternoon."

Chapter Eleven

BETH AND MELANIE ARRIVE AT DIANE'S TRAILER AT A FEW MINUTES after two on Saturday. They notice that there are three cars in the driveway. Melanie says, "The white car is Beverly Randall's. I don't know about the Mustang."

The sisters approach the studio and see Diane's head peering from the doorway. Diane smiles and comes out the door. "I thought I heard a car drive up. Come on in."

When they get inside, Melanie is pleasantly surprised at all the paintings that she sees in various stages of completion. She says, "My goodness, you two have certainly been busy."

Diane points toward Beverly, who's working at her easel. Diane says, "Y'all both know my mother." Then Diane puts her arm around Jeanette and says to Beth and Melanie, "This is Missus Johnson, Leland's mother. Mama Johnson, these are the famous Moore sisters, Beth Lancaster and Melanie Pebworth."

Jeanette smiles and extends her right hand. "Of course I know who you two are. I've been hearing about y'all since you were babies."

Beth shakes Jeanette's hand. "Nothing bad, I hope."

Jeanette laughs. "Nothing that you can't be forgiven for."

Melanie smiles as she shakes Jeanette's hand and says, "Missus Johnson, aren't you amazed at what these two are doing here. This is some high quality artwork."

"Well, I don't know much about art, but it sure looks good to me. And please call me Jeanette."

"Okay. Jeanette, do you think that you could help me convince these two to let our gallery put on an exhibit of their works."

Jeanette's face lights up. "Oh, I think that's a wonderful idea. And I'll be glad to loan you the painting Diane gave to us. It's a picture of the pond where Leland and Red fished when Leland was a boy."

Beth turns to Melanie. "Well, that's makes one painting for the show."

Diane says, "Actually, I had already been talking to Mama about us having an exhibit together at the gallery, and she said that if it's that important to me to have a show, she'll go along with it and exhibit some of her paintings, too, as long as none of hers are put up for sale. She knows that I want to sell some of my paintings to make some money to use toward building a house, so she understands why an exhibit would be a help to me. But I made it clear to Mama that I want the exhibit to be a mother and daughter exhibit. I don't want all the attention to be on me."

Melanie looks at Beth. "I love the idea of a mother and daughter exhibit. We've never done that before, and I know that Frank would also love that approach. We have a summer show coming up in June, Diane. It opens on June twentieth, and we'd need the paintings a few days before that. Would that be too soon for you two?"

Diane looks at her mother and says, "I don't know. How many paintings would you need?"

"Let's see, if we dedicate one section to your mother and you, it would mean between eight and ten paintings, depending on how we space them. So, the minimum number would be eight. And I see at least five or six in here right now that could be finished by that date."

"And all of them wouldn't have to be for sale?"

"No. This would be mainly a show, not a sale. Still, you can sell as many or as few as you want. The gallery would handle the sales and keep a reasonable commission."

Melanie turns to Beverly. "Missus Randall, you haven't said much, what do you think?"

"Well, as much disdain as I have for art dilettantes, it's still important to me for my baby girl to be happy, so I'm in."

Melanie says, "I can't deny that our galley does attract its share of dilettantes, especially some of the old money crowd from Carleton, but you'll see that at the summer show, there will also be a whole lot of just regular people who are true art lovers. And I promise you they're going to love your work and Diane's."

"Well, as I said, I'm doing this for Diane. So, I'll put in three paintings and Diane can put in five."

Melanie smiles at Diane. "Or six . . . or seven."

Diane runs over to hug her mother and then goes to hug Leland's mother. "You are the two best mothers in the world."

On the way home, Melanie asks Beth, "What do you think? Do you think the mother and daughter exhibit will be a success? Personally, I love that idea."

"Well, I'm no expert, but I think those two are phenomenal. I saw a couple of pieces in there that I'd like to have myself. I can see the exhibit being a big success, especially if y'all promote the mother-daughter angle as part of your publicity. And, you know, I don't think that Diane's life will ever be the same again after her work gets shown."

"Yeah, I feel the same way, and as much as Beverly was grousing this afternoon, I still can't help feeling that she wants her daughter's talent to be appreciated. You can see the pride in her eyes when we talk about Diane's work. By the way, is John still being mum about that get-together we saw at the diner on Monday morning?"

"All he's told me so far is that they went from there to the bank conference room to talk some more. He gave me absolutely no clue what they were talking about except to say that they were working on a complicated business deal."

"We've just got to find out what's going on. Anytime that many heavy hitters get together, something big has to be going on."

That night, after Leland comes in from a renovation project that he and Red have been working on, Diane tells him about the upcoming exhibit.

Leland hands Diane the pepperoni pizza that he brought home. "That's great, Diane. People are going to be surprised at how talented you and your mother are. I want to be there to see their reactions."

"You'll have to wear some dress pants and a sport coat."

"Well, you can tell me about it when you get home."

Diane did a pirouette. "But don't you want to share in my glory?"

Leland kissed her on the cheek. "Well, since you put it like that . . ."

"There's still one more thing we need to talk about. When are you going to tell me what you and Mister Henderson and those other men were talking about on Monday?"

"I told you before that everything is hush-hush right now because there are a lot of moving parts to the thing that we're working on, and everything has to be in place before we can make it public."

"What are you, the CIA?"

Leland smiles. "Might as well be. But it's just not my call, babe."

"I'm going to ask the Moore sisters on Monday when they come in the diner. They know everything that's going on in this town."

"Yeah, do that."

Chapter Twelve

IT'S JUNE 20, 1994. THE MAIN STREET GALLERY IS CROWDED WITH people attending the opening reception for the summer show.

When Leland arrives, he spots Mr. Henderson admiring the paintings in the Mother and Daughter Exhibit. Mr. Henderson notices that Leland has arrived and waves him over. "Leland, your wife and her mother are both gifted artists. Every single one of these paintings is first rate. Would it make you uncomfortable if I bought two of Diane's paintings?"

"Lord, no. I'd be proud for you to have two of her paintings, and I know Diane would. She thinks the world of you."

"She wouldn't think that I was doing it just because you're my most important employee?"

"Now you're just teasing me. But which two do you like?"

"Oh, I like all of them, but the two that I particularly like are the painting of the daisy field and the painting of the train depot. What do you think?"

"Well, you're the art expert, but I think those would be good choices."

"I'll get back with you later. Right now, let me go tell Frank Dupre that those two are sold."

Mr. Henderson spots Frank standing across the room. He motions to him as he walks in Frank's direction. A few minutes later, Diane walks up and tugs at the left sleeve of Leland's navy-blue sport coat as Leland is intently looking at a painting of a deer in a cornfield. When Leland turns to her, Diane says, "I see you made it. You look very handsome tonight. What does Mister Henderson think about the exhibit?"

"Oh, he left already. He didn't care for it."

"No, he didn't leave. I can see him over there talking to Mister Frank."

Leland puts his arm around Diane. "He loves your paintings. He's going to buy two of them."

"Really, which two?"

"The daisy field and the train depot."

"Great, that'll be some more money to put aside for our new house."

"About the house. I found out something from Mister Henderson this afternoon that will affect that. I'll tell you about it after the show."

"We're still going to build a new house, aren't we?"

"Yeah, but I'll tell you more later. It's all good, don't worry."

Diane looks puzzled. "Okay, but don't forget to tell me." Then she says, "Look at that. Mister Henderson's talking to Mama, and they're both laughing about something."

Leland looks. "I bet he's telling her how much he likes y'all's paintings." He takes Diane by the arm. "How about walking me through the gallery and telling me about the rest of the show."

As they're looking at the various exhibits, several people come up to Diane and tell her how much they think of her paintings.

With an amused look on his face, Leland says, "It looks like you're becoming quite a celebrity."

"I know you think that all this is a little phony, Leland, but it makes me feel good to have people like my work. Your daddy and your mother were in here while ago, but they had to leave early. Your mother was just great. She was telling everybody that she was my mother-in-law and telling them about the painting that I gave her at her retirement party."

"She's proud of you, babe, just like I am. And there's nothing wrong with you feeling good about the attention you're getting tonight. But you know that these are just not my kind of people. I mean, I'm sure they're great people and all, but I just think that all this fancy to-do is a little silly."

Diane smiles. "Except for me, you mean."

"Well, you're a little silly, too, but in a good way."

Diane sees Mr. Henderson coming their way with Beverly by his side. When Mr. Henderson gets near enough to be heard above the din of the crowd, he says, "Diane, I've been telling your mother how much I love your work and hers. Did Leland tell you that I'm buying two of your paintings?"

"Yes, sir. I really appreciate that, because I've heard how much you know about art. But I'm not really sure I deserve all this attention."

"Oh, you deserve the attention, all right. And, believe me, this is just the beginning."

Diane blushes. "Now you're embarrassing me."

"Just watch. By the way, did Leland tell you about the little real estate deal that we're working on?"

"No, sir, but he did say that there was something that he was going to tell me tonight after the show."

"That's fine. I'll let him tell you. Well, I must go now. My brother Sean's coming in tonight to spend a few days with me. I've got to pick him up at the Mobile airport. But, once again, I think that both you and your mother have a special gift, and I'm going to enjoy having your paintings in my house."

Mr. Henderson turns to Beverly and says, "Good evening, Beverly. I enjoyed our conversation."

"Thank you, Mark. And thank you so much for buying Diane's paintings."

Beverly looks down at her watch. "I think that I'll be going, too. I'm teaching a Sunday school class tomorrow morning, and I want to go over my notes before I go to bed tonight."

Leland says, "We'll walk you to your car. Where'd you park? When I got here, the parking lot was full, and I had to park a block away."

"Oh, I got here early. I'm right behind the gallery."

As Leland and Diane walk Beverly toward the front door, they are stopped twice by people who tell Diane and Beverly how much they like the Mother and Daughter Exhibit. When they get to Beverly's car, Diane gives her mother a goodbye hug. As he watches Beverly drive away down Main Street, Leland says to Diane, "I know you noticed how happy your mother looked tonight. Maybe this sort of thing is good for her."

"Yeah, no matter how much she plays it down, she's still an artist at heart, and she loves to be surrounded by other artists. It gets her creative juices flowing. And did you notice how good her hair and makeup looked tonight, and how nicely she was dressed? I think that she did that as much for my benefit as hers. Now, what in the world is this mysterious real estate deal that Mister Henderson mentioned?"

Leland points to a marble bench in front of the gallery. "Let's sit over there, and I'll go over it with you. But I don't want you to mention what I tell you to anybody, at least for a while."

"Okay."

Once they're both seated, Leland starts, "Because of the raise I told you about, and some other things that are in the works, it looks like we're going to be able to start on our house sooner than we expected. For one thing, Mister Henderson's property company owns the six-acre lot next to us, the one on the town side, and he's going to sell us that lot and buy our ten-acre lot."

"I like our lot."

"The other lot is exactly like ours, except smaller. And we don't need ten acres. We don't really need six acres. But the deal is that Mister Henderson's going to pay us the same amount per acre for our lot as what he's going to charge us per acre for the six-acre lot, and he's going to let us stay in the trailer just where it is until we move into our house once it's finished.

"Then, after we move out of the trailer, he's going to pay us a fair market value price for the trailer. So, if you take into account the money that we've saved up, the increase in pay that I'm getting, the money coming in from our carpentry business, along with what we'll make on the land sale and the trailer sale, and, of course, your art money, we'll be in a position to move up the starting date on building our house."

"How much sooner are you talking about?"

"Well, that depends. At the most, it'll be a year from now, but it could easily be sooner. We're working on a three-party contract with the bank and Henderson Properties that'll make it possible for us to get a construction loan as soon as some things that I can't talk about yet are worked out. But, if everything else that needs to be done gets done as soon as I think it'll be, the construction on the house could start in probably six months or so."

"Really? That would be a lot sooner than I thought. Did you and Ron already finish the design for the house?"

"Ron has everything done, and it's ready to file with the construction loan papers once all the other details are taken care of. And the design that he came up with is exactly what we wanted. The house will be three thousand square feet with a two-car garage, and the design allows for us to add another bedroom if we ever need to, without having to disturb the original construction."

"Will we have city water and sewer like you told me?"

"Yeah, all of that's in the process of being finalized, but you can't tell anyone because, like I said, there are some other related things taking place, and everything will have to fall into place at about the same time in order for all of the pieces to fit together the way we need for them to."

"Okay, that doesn't tell me anything, but what can I say as of right now?"

"It's better that you don't say anything to anybody right now, but I promise you that everything is headed in the right direction."

"What if some of these other mysterious things don't work out?"

"Then we'd just have to wait a little longer to start on the house, but still no longer than a year or so."

Leland reaches over and pulls Diane close. He kisses her on the cheek and says, "Don't worry, babe, we can't lose either way."

Diane returns Leland's kiss and says, "Well, while I've got your attention for a change, there's something else we need to talk about."

"What's that?"

"Remember that I told you that Miz Spencer is moving up north in a few weeks?"

"Yeah."

"Well, there's two things. First, are you okay with your mother keeping Bret while I'm at work, and second, what do you think about me giving Miz Spencer one of my paintings as a going away present?"

"I'll let you and my mom work out the babysitting arrangements. I'll support whatever y'all come up with. As for Miz Spencer, I think that she would love to have one of your paintings to take with her. Just let her pick one out. And I'd also like to give her some going away money, whatever amount you decide is appropriate."

Diane pulls back and looks at Leland, "Boy, you are really easy to get along with tonight."

"Hey, I'm in a good mood. I'm proud of how the mother and daughter thing went."

Chapter Thirteen

At noon on Labor Day, 1994, Mr. Henderson hears his front doorbell chime. He excuses himself from his conversation with Red and Jeanette Johnson and walks from his library to the front door. He opens the tall, stain glass-paneled oak door for Leland and Diane. Diane is holding a sleepy Bret in her arms. Mr. Henderson shakes Leland's hand and says, "Come on in. Red and Jeanette are already here." Mr. Henderson leans over to look at Bret, whose eyes are barely open. "Welcome to my home, Master Bret."

As Diane follows Mr. Henderson and Leland through the foyer and into the library, she surveys the rooms that she is seeing for the first time. She seems awed by the size of the rooms and the tall ceilings with their wide crown molding and antique crystal chandeliers.

Mr. Henderson points to a sofa where Leland and Diane can sit. As Diane sits down, Jeanette walks over and reaches for Bret. "Let me hold our little darling for a while and give you a break."

"Thanks, Mama Johnson. He's getting to be a load. I'm glad that he's walking now. He's almost too big for me to carry."

Bret cuddles up in his Grandma Johnson's arms and smiles. Then, after a few moments, he starts to squirm, indicating that he's ready to get down.

Diane asks, "Mister Henderson, is it okay if we let Bret walk around?"

Mr. Henderson looks at Bret and smiles. "Of course. Whatever he breaks, I'm sure Red and Leland can fix."

Jeanette gently lowers Bret to the floor and says, "Well, let's hope that he doesn't break anything. But he's never been in a house this big. You can tell that he's fascinated by your home."

Bret walks slowly from one chair to the next, holding on to each one as he reaches it. When he gets to where Leland is sitting, he reaches up and pulls on Leland's sleeve. Leland picks him up and places him in his lap. Bret looks content.

The doorbell chimes once more. Mr. Henderson excuses himself and goes to let Beverly in. As he opens the door, Mr. Henderson sees that Beverly is wearing a jade green silk blouse, gray woolen slacks, and a modest white pearl necklace.

Mr. Henderson leans back to get a better look at Beverly. He smiles and says, "Welcome, Beverly." Then he takes her arm in his and tells her, "Everyone's in the library except for my brother. He's upstairs making a phone call. By the way, you look striking today."

"Why, thank you, sir. You're not so bad yourself."

Beverly looks around as they're walking to the library. "I've always wondered what the inside of this house looked like."

"Well, what do you think?"

"Very impressive. I noticed your art collection in the hall. Would you mind if Diane and I take a better look at it afterwhile?"

"I'd love for you to. I'd like to know what you two think about it." Mr. Henderson points to a wall just behind where Beverly is standing and says, "The two paintings that I bought at the Mother and Daughter Exhibit are hanging back there."

Beverly turns to look at the paintings. "I'm so proud of Diane. Did you know that she sold two other paintings that night?"

Mr. Henderson smiles. "I didn't, but I'm not surprised. Maybe I should have bought all of them. I think that Diane's light is just beginning to shine."

"I believe you're right. I just hope it doesn't change her."

"Oh, I wouldn't worry about that. She has a good mother who'll keep her grounded."

Diane, who's been watching her mother and Mr. Henderson, sees

Earline standing in the hall behind them in a fancy white apron, waiting for the right time to come in and tell Mr. Henderson that lunch is almost ready. Diane rushes over and hugs Earline. She asks, "Are you and your sister catering our lunch?"

Earline curtsies and says, "Yes, ma'am, Miss Diane. We have been out back barbequing ribs and chicken breasts on Mister Henderson's fancy grill." Diane smiles and says, "Wow. I'm looking forward to that. Can I do anything to help y'all?"

With feigned indignity, Earline asks, "Why weren't you here earlier when we could have used some help?" They both laugh, and Diane hugs Earline again.

Diane turns to Mr. Henderson and asks if it would be okay with him if Earline and Katherine ate lunch with them.

"Sure. But right now, my brother and I are going to be discussing some business plans in here with Leland and Red, so why don't you ladies, including Earline and Katherine, go on into the dining room and start without us. We'll join you in a little while."

Not long after the women leave the library, Sean Henderson walks through the door of the library and apologizes for his tardiness. He appears to be about five years younger than his brother. His gray hair still has streaks of red. He's near the same height as Mark, a little over six feet, but not quite as heavy. Sean looks a little weary and disheveled in his wrinkled gray slacks and untucked blue Polo dress shirt. He says, "Please excuse my appearance as well as my tardiness. I was going to shower and change clothes, but I got tied up with a couple of business calls."

Mr. Henderson, who's wearing a lightweight gray sweater and black jeans, says, "Believe me, brother, these guys are not going to judge you on your wardrobe, so long as you have everything covered up." Then he says, "You've met Red and Leland."

Sean nods toward Red and Leland. They nod in return.

Mr. Henderson continues, "Since we're all here today, I thought it would be good to bring them up to date on what our partners and we have gotten done so far on our various projects in this area."

Sean takes a seat in a chair across from the sofa where Leland and Red are sitting as Mr. Henderson is walking over to his desk.

Sean says, "Well, guys, first of all, it's good to see you again. Mark has told me so many good things about both of you that I'm jealous. If you ever want to move to Pennsylvania, let me know. There'll be jobs waiting for you."

Mark walks back from his desk where he has picked up four packages of documents and photographs. He hands one each to Sean, Red, and Leland.

He says, "What these documents represent is a lot of work by a number of people. As you know, for some time now we've been trying to make several transactions take place at the right time without their being made public, and we all know how difficult that is in a small town, especially if there's money or land involved.

"As I told you last week, all of the parties to the various ventures represented by these documents agreed that the best course of action would be to first ensure that all of the land at issue here will be annexed into the Libertytown city limits. Fortunately, annexation in Alabama is much simpler if one hundred percent of the owners of the property to be annexed consent to annexation, so that's the route we took. To make that work, we first had to get consent from Allegheny Lumber, which owns the land where my lumber company sits. That wasn't a problem since Allegheny Lumber is owned by Sean, me, and the Henderson Family Trust.

"Next, my property company, Henderson Properties, which already owned fifty acres along Highway 74, needed to buy two more lots on Highway 74, which we did. Then we had to get the Brocks to consent to the annexation of the glass plant property, and, finally, Phil Bernstein had to give consent to annex his four hundred acres of farmland on the other side of Highway 74. Oh, and of course, Leland also had to give his consent. Well, today I can confirm that the annexation is all but done."

Leland feels Red's right knee lightly bump his left knee.

"As you also know, along with the annexation, we needed to get Southern Utilities to commit to extending its water and sewer services all the way out to the glass plant. You probably know that the glass plant has been operating all these years with its own well water system and wastewater system.

"As we've recently heard through the grapevine, the Brock family plans to shut the glass plant down in the near future because there's no one left in the family who has any interest in running the plant, and the Brocks know that the factory and the two hundred-plus acres that it sits on would be worth considerably more if the plant had city water and sewer service. So, they've been holding off on putting the property on the market until they know the status of the water and sewer situation, as well as status of the annexation; and they've using their influence to help us get those things done.

"The final piece that had to fall into place for our plans to work to their fullest extent was for the zoning of the land to change so that more houses and small businesses could be built on Highway 74."

Mark smiles and says, "Well, Sean and I can say now that all those pieces that I just described are in place. We have written approvals or commitments from all necessary officials and other parties."

Red and Leland look at one another. Red chuckles and slaps Leland on his thigh.

Mark continues, "What you two didn't know is that Sean and I were able to go to Dunham Fine Furnishings and get them to agree to something that we had been discussing with them, in one form or another, for the last two years.

"Let me put this part into context. As I've told you before, Allegheny Lumber has been the main lumber supplier for Dunham since back when my grandfather ran our company, and Dunham wants to keep it that way. Well, a while back, one of the Dunham brothers saw a future in creating a line of high-end furniture for upscale hotels and resorts. So, the Dunham company built an addition to their Lebanon County facilities and began making that new line of furniture.

"As it has turned out, that hotel furniture line has sold so well that their Pennsylvania factory can't fully satisfy the demand, and Dunham has no more room for expansion in their present location. So, they decided that the best approach would be to build a factory at another location devoted specifically to the hotel and resort furniture business. After considerable research, they decided, for several reasons, that the Southeast would be the best part of the country for the new factory.

"When Sean and I found out that Dunham was looking for a Southeast location, I had Sean and two of the Dunham brothers come down last year on three different occasions to check out the Libertytown area as a potential site for the factory, with our company to be the chief lumber supplier for the new factory.

"The Dunham boys were lukewarm about the idea at first. But Sean and I pointed out all of the potential benefits of this area, including using the glass plant location for the factory. After giving it a lot of thought, the Dunhams eventually bought into the idea of moving here if they could buy the glass plant property—which includes a two hundred thousand square foot main building, two large warehouses, and about two hundred twenty acres—at a decent price, and if that property were to get city water and sewer services and city fire department coverage.

"By the way, we didn't know when we first started talking to the Dunham brothers that the Brock family was already thinking about closing down the glass plant and selling the property. That was an unbelievably lucky break. And, of course, we've spent a lot of time discussing how our lumber company could work with Dunham to make sure that their Libertytown factory would be fully supplied with the same type and quality of lumber that their Pennsylvania factory has been receiving from our site up there for many years.

"Red, I know that Leland and you have already heard, in bits and pieces, a lot of what I've been saying. But what you haven't heard, and what Sean and I want to let you know today, is that everything is now in place for Dunham to buy the glass plant property. All they're waiting for are the official final approvals by the city, county, and utilities company on the annexation, the zoning, and the utilities. Once that's done, and we expect it to be soon, Dunham will enter into an agreement to purchase the glass plant property, and we'll start preparing our company for Dunham as a new customer, including expanding our capacity, hiring new employees, and installing some new state-of-the-art equipment."

Red says, "You're right, boss, we had no idea that the Dunham project was happening. But I still want to see everything nailed down on that before I get too excited about it."

Leland says, "I'm kind of like Daddy, boss, as far as still being a little skeptical. I'm not going to be comfortable about this until the Dunham contract with the Brocks is signed, sealed, and delivered. And then what about a contract between us and Dunham? When would that be done?"

Sean looks at Mark. Mark says, "That's already done. We've agreed on all the details, subject to Dunham establishing a factory in Libertytown. If they decide not to build here, our contract is automatically voided, and nothing happens. But, if Dunham goes forward with the factory as planned, our contract goes into effect the day that Dunham signs the deal for the glass plant property."

Mark continues, "And as soon as the Dunham purchase agreement is signed, both of you will be given new assignments and higher salaries, because your authority and your duties are going to immediately expand. From what we've learned from our Dunham sources, Brock will want a one-year shutdown period before Dunham can move in, and we expect that once the Dunham factory renovation and construction project begins, it'll take ten months to a year to complete, because they'll have to expand and reconfigure the main glass plant building as well as renovate the other existing buildings and construct a couple of more buildings. Along with that, they'll have to install their production and shipping equipment. So, all things considered, we'll have maybe twenty-two months, maybe less, to make all the changes that we need to, because Dunham will want us to be available as their lumber supplier for that factory as soon as production starts. As I said, that means that our work will start as soon as we know that the Dunham contract with Brock has been signed."

Sean says, "And of course, our Pennsylvania complex will be assisting however we can in your preparation for the Dunham startup."

Leland looks at Red. Red says to Mark and Sean, "Fellas, if I was still a drinking man, I might be making a toast right now."

Mark looks at his watch. "By the way, there was no way that all of this could have happened without Hollis Bailey and Phil Bernstein using their local political connections and calling in some favors. Phil should be here in about fifteen minutes. You two might want to thank him when he gets here."

Sean cautions, "But, remember that the news about the Dunham factory and your contract with them is still confidential, so be sure to keep everything to yourselves until they make the public announcement."

On the morning of the Tuesday after Labor Day, Danny's Diner is inundated with customers, so much so that Earline and Diane don't get a chance to talk about the previous day's lunch at Mr. Henderson's house until around ten o'clock. Just as Earline and Diane begin their conversation, the Moore sisters come in for their usual coffee.

Diane lays her hand on Earline's shoulder. "I'll take care of them."

Diane greets the Moore sisters with a friendly smile, and the sisters confirm that they each want coffee.

As Diane is setting their steaming coffee mugs onto the counter, Beth asks, "How'd your Labor Day go, Diane? Melanie and I took our kids down to Fairhope, and we all had a great time. What'd you and Leland do?"

"Leland, and his parents, and my mother and I had lunch with Mister Henderson at his house. It was a lot of fun. We had barbequed ribs and chicken, and his brother Sean from Pennsylvania and Mister Bernstein were also there. Earline and her sister Katherine catered the lunch, and then they ate with us. The food was great."

Diane senses that the Moore sisters are processing what they just heard.

Finally, Melanie says, "Well, that's sounds like y'all had a good time."

"Oh, we did." Diane notices Earline signaling to her and says, "Excuse me, if y'all don't need anything else right now, I need to talk to Earline for a minute."

Diane briskly walks to where Earline is standing in front of the picture window. On her way to Earline, Diane can hear the Moore sisters quietly talking to each other, but she can't make out what they are saying.

Earline, looking out the window, says, "You must have told them about yesterday. They looked like somebody poked them with a cattle prod."

Diane giggles softly. "Yeah, I did mention it. They asked what Leland and I did yesterday, so I told them."

"Did you tell them that y'all let the help eat at the main dining table with you?"

"I did."

Earline is smiling as she starts to walk toward the front door to take care of another customer who has just come in. After her first step, she stops and turns back to Diane. She says, "If only we could have heard what they were saying to each other just now."

Chapter Fourteen

On Friday, October 15, 1994, Mayor Steadman and the president of Southern Utilities are holding a press conference at City Hall where they are making an announcement about the annexation of the Highway 74 property and the expansion of the utilities service area and fire department coverage. The mayor also informs the audience that he expects that certain pending zoning changes will lead to the development of more residential properties on Highway 74, and that with the possibility of that new housing in mind, the city and the utilities company are working on a plan for the installation of fire hydrants along Highway 74, as well as additional streetlights.

On Saturday, November 16, 1994, there is another public meeting at City Hall. At that one Ralph Brock, president of Brock Glass Corporation, announces that his company has entered into a contract to sell its buildings and land to Dunham Fine Furnishings Corporation and that Brock Glass will be shutting down its operations effective October 13, 1995, and then transferring possession of the property to Dunham as soon thereafter as feasible.

Mr. Brock includes in his announcement the news that Brock Glass Corporation has negotiated with the union representing the glass plant employees and agreed to pay the employees their full salaries and benefits through December 31, 1995, as well as paying buy-out compensation to all employees who will have at least three years of services as of the October 13 shutdown date. Mr. Brock then turns his microphone over to union president Robert Faulkner who announces that the union has also agreed to offer a prorated retirement pension to all employees who will have accrued at least twenty years of service at Brock as of December 31, 1995.

Right after he listens to the announcements about Brock Glass, Judge Bailey leaves City Hall and comes into the diner for lunch. As usual, his necktie is loosened and his suit is rumpled. Diane comes to his table, and he tells her that he wants "a ham and cheese sandwich and some French fries."

"Judge Bailey, is it true that they just announced that the glass plant is going to shut down in October of next year?"

"Yep. Friday, October thirteenth."

"I think my mother is going to miss that place. She's been working there almost twenty years, and that's the only real job she's ever had."

Judge Bailey brushes from his forehead a few loose strands of his long gray hair. "We're all going to miss that plant. It's been a part of the community for about sixty years. Ralph Brock's great-grandfather Abraham started it when he came over from Germany in 1936 to get away from the Nazis. The story is that Abraham was a successful glass maker in Germany but had the good sense to get his family out of there before the persecution of Jews got any worse. I was told that they sneaked out of the country with all the money and jewelry they had, but left everything else behind."

"I didn't know Mister Brock is Jewish. Mama never mentioned it."

"Yeah, he's one of the few Jews in Libertytown. He's a member of a synagogue over in Carleton. Oh, and it was Ralph Brock's great-grandfather who changed the family name from Brach, spelled B-R-A-C-H, to Brock, spelled B-R-O-C-K, to look more American. Yeah, the great-grandfather was quite a man. He put all the money that he and his wife had into the glass company in the midst of the Great Depression, and he somehow managed to make the company a success even though he didn't know anybody here in Libertytown and he had to learn to speak English while he was building his company."

"How in the world did he wind up in Libertytown in the first place?"

"I'm not sure, Diane, but Mobile had a big Jewish population even back then, so that's probably where he started out when he got to America. And it was most likely some of the Jewish businessmen in Mobile who told him that here would be a good place to start a glass factory. Anyway, Abraham started his first glassmaking factory in a little cotton warehouse that had been around since the eighteen hundreds, and that business slowly but steadily grew to what it is now. That first location was not too far from where the plant stands now."

"Wow, Judge Bailey, that's an interesting story. I wonder if Mama knows all that."

"I don't know, but over the years I've learned that Libertytown is full of interesting stories that most people here have never heard."

As Diane walks away to give Judge Bailey's order to Theo, she looks back at him and says, "Maybe one day somebody'll write a book about Libertytown. I know you'll be in it."

At Diane's studio that night working on another painting, Beverly mentions her upcoming retirement from Brock Glass. "I guess I lucked out. I'll have twenty years at the plant as of June fifteenth of next year."

Diane turns away from the painting that she's working on. She asks, "Are you going to be able to get by on the retirement pay?"

"It'll be close, but I'll only be forty-two, so I could always get another job." Beverly laughs. "Maybe I'll go to work for Dunham. Wouldn't that be a twist?"

"Sure would be."

Just then Leland comes into the studio from his workshop. "Hi, Miz Beverly. I heard about the glass plant shutdown. I kind of knew that it was coming, just didn't know when. Are you going to be okay?"

"Oh, I'll be fine. Diane said that y'all would support me."

"That'd be fine by me, if you need us to. I'm about to get another raise."

"Diane says, "You are?"

"Yeah. I couldn't tell you before, because it wasn't for certain, but now it looks like we're going to be the main lumber supplier for the Dunham factory."

"But that's a long way off, isn't it?"

"It is, but it'll take us the better part of two years to get ready for it, because we'll have to expand our working space, install some new equipment, and hire and train additional personnel. So, my work is going to start increasing as of next week."

Beverly says, "We don't see enough of you now. How many more hours a week are you going to have to work?"

"I don't know that yet. I just know that my job is going to be covering some new areas. Daddy's also going to have his job expanded a good bit. He's going from being line supervisor to being chief of production. That means that a new line supervisor will be under him, as well as the shipping supervisor, and the milling works supervisor."

Diane asks, "Do you know yet what your new areas will be?"

"Well, for one thing, I'm going to be helping Mister Henderson plan and oversee the expansion of our company, and for another, I'll be the manufacturer liaison. That means I'll be the contact person for Dunham as well as other customers that are manufacturing companies. Right now, we only have two others, Airtight Storage Building Company and a company in Bay Minette that makes school furniture. But Mister Henderson says that with the new equipment we're buying and our additional crew members, we'll be able to take on some more manufacturing plants as customers. Besides that, Dunham is going to get bigger and busier as their hotel furniture market grows."

Beverly says, "Leland, you've come a long way in a short period of time."

"Well, it hasn't really been that short a period. You have to remember that I actually started working part-time at the company when I was sixteen and still in school, and even back then I worked full-time there in the summers."

"Yeah, I guess you're right. That means you've been working there for what, about eight years now."

Diane laughs and says, "And he's always been Mister Henderson's pet. That's what Daddy Johnson says."

Leland smiles and holds up his hands. "I can't deny that. For some reason, he's always treated me great. That's one of the reasons that I'll do anything for the company that he wants me to. I think I've done every job there at one time or another, everything from working on the production line to repairing machinery, to unloading logs, to loading lumber, to working in the milling shop, to sweeping floors and cleaning restrooms."

Diane wrinkles her nose. "You could have left that last one off. I can't imagine the restrooms in that place."

Leland smiles. "There're just like you'd think they'd be. But they always get cleaned up pretty quick. Mister Henderson's very particular about keeping everything neat and clean."

Leland looks around the studio and sees over a dozen paintings, some finished and some unfinished, leaning against the walls or propped up against various pieces of furniture. He says, "You two have really been busy. Is there another show coming up?"

Diane answers, "Yep. A few months ago, Melanie came up with the idea of an early December show, thinking that people would want to buy paintings for Christmas presents."

"That makes sense. Not something that I would do, but I can see how some people might buy a painting for a Christmas gift."

"And this time, I got Mama to agree to put up some of her paintings for sale."

Beverly says, "I guess that was good timing for me, considering my job's being eliminated."

Leland says, "That's all right. When we get our house built, you can sell yours and come live with us."

Diane asks, "Are you hinting at something, Leland Johnson?"

"Yep. We'll be starting on the house in March."

Diane runs over and hugs Leland, getting blue paint on his work shirt.

Beverly quickly comes out of her chair and wipes the paint off Leland's shirt with her turpentine rag.

Chapter Fifteen

THE CHRISTMAS ART SALE ON SATURDAY, DECEMBER 3, 1994, IS A BIG success. The gallery sells numerous paintings and prints, as well as pottery items and sculptures.

On Tuesday evening, three days after the December art sale, Diane is cleaning her kitchen when she receives a phone call from Melanie. They exchange hellos, then Melanie asks, "Can Beverly and you come by the gallery one day this week? We have checks for y'all, and Frank has a proposal that he wants to talk to you about."

"What kind of proposal?"

"He has an idea of how Beverly and you could make more money from your art. But if you don't mind, I'd rather for y'all to talk to him about it directly, because he has all the details."

"Mama's out in the studio right now, so I could ask her. What's a good day for us to come?"

"Well, we'll be open on Thursday, Friday, and Saturday afternoons, so any of those days would be fine."

"I'll check with Mama, but let's say Saturday afternoon, unless that's a problem with her. Any particular time?"

"Anytime between one and six."

"Okay. Will I see you at Danny's tomorrow?"

"No, Beth and I are going to be Christmas shopping in Mobile tomorrow, but we'll probably see you Thursday morning."

"All right. I'll let you know then if we can make it to the gallery this week."

After the call, Diane finishes cleaning the kitchen and walks down to the studio. Beverly is intently working on a painting of a little girl in a field of sunflowers.

"That's beautiful, Mama. I especially like the way you used that dark pink in the sky."

"Thanks. I'm almost to a stopping point now, and my hand's starting to cramp anyway from painting all these little flowers."

"I got a call just now from Melanie Pebworth. They want us to come by the gallery on Saturday afternoon and pick up our checks from the last show, and Frank wants to talk to us about what Melanie called a proposal."

Beverly does not say anything at first. Then she says, "Mark's going to take me to the country club for lunch on Saturday, but after that I could go."

"Wow, you and Mister Henderson are becoming good buddies, but I can't believe you agreed to go to the country club. I know how you feel about those country club folks."

Beverly winks. "That's why I'm going. It'll drive them crazy to see me there, being the low-class religious nut that I am. But with Mark taking me, they're not going to say anything to my face."

Diane says. "But they'll be buzzing like bees after y'all leave. I'd love to be there for that. So, how about if I pick you up around two on Saturday?"

"That'll be fine. Pick me up at Mark's house."

"Okay. Now, I'll help you clean up your painting stuff, and then we'll go make a pot of decaf. I'll go over and tell Leland that we're going to the house."

When Leland gets to the kitchen about half an hour later, he washes his hands in the sink and asks if there's any decaf left. Diane tells him to sit down then brings him a hot cup of coffee in one of her new white mugs with the Danny's Diner logo.

As she sets the coffee down, she asks Leland, "Did you know that Mister Henderson is taking my mama to the country club on Saturday for lunch?"

Leland smiles at Beverly, who's sitting across the table from him. "No, I hadn't heard that. Are you doing that just to spite those old biddies at the club?"

"How could you think that? I'm going there for the fine cuisine, and, of course, to annoy the old biddies."

Leland holds up his open right hand, and Beverly slaps it with hers. Leland says, "Good for you, Miz Beverly. It's about time you had some fun."

Diane says to Leland, "And Melanie called and said we can pick up our checks from the art show on Saturday."

Leland asks, "Did she say how much?"

"No. But I know that five of my paintings sold, and they sold all three of Mama's."

"Well, don't you two run off to the dog track with all that money."

Beverly says, "No danger of that. Remember, I'm about to be unemployed."

Diane says, "Mama, I wish you'd quit talking about that. Everything's going to be fine."

"Oh, I guess I know that."

Chapter Sixteen

THE NEXT DAY, LELAND TAKES A SEAT AT THE DESK IN HIS SMALL office down the hall from Mr. Henderson's and looks at the notes in his inbox. He sees a note from Sally, Mr. Henderson's secretary, that says Mr. Henderson wants to meet with Red and him as soon as he gets in from his meeting downtown. Sally estimates that Mr. Henderson will be in "around 9:45 or so."

Leland dials Red's cell phone number and tells him about the meeting. Red says he got the same message and that he'll come up to Leland's office at nine forty.

When Red gets to Leland's office, he asks, "Boss in yet?"

"Not yet, have a seat. Do you know why he wants to see us?"

"Nope. But it probably has something to do with the Dunham deal." Red sees that Leland has a thick document in his hand. "What're you working on there?"

"I'm going over last quarter's production report on the milling shop. I'm sure you know that shop is making the company a fortune."

"Yeah, Bernie runs a tight shop, and they're really good at what they do. All the guys in that shop are first rate."

Leland says, "I hope Dunham doesn't try to steal Bernie from us."

"I wouldn't worry about that. There's no way that Bernie's going to work in a factory doing the same thing every day. That would drive him crazy. He likes variety. Right now, his shop is making some big fancy custom windows to match those in a hundred-year-old Catholic Church in Mobile."

"Really. I'm gonna have to go down and take a look at those. That sounds interesting."

Just then they hear the heavy footsteps of Mr. Henderson as he's walking down the hall. He stops at Leland's door and asks, "Did you two get the message that I want to see you this morning?"

Red answers, "Yes, sir. Do you want us to come to your office now?"

"In about ten minutes. I've got to make a call."

While they're waiting to meet with Mr. Henderson, Leland asks Red if he'd heard that Mr. Henderson is having lunch on Saturday with Diane's mother.

Red says, "No. I hadn't heard that. Is she doing that just for spite? I mean, they could have lunch anywhere."

Leland smiles. "That's what *I* said."

Red thinks about it for a moment, then says, "You know, I kind of like the idea of those two being friends."

"I'm the same way. They're both good people."

The phone on Leland's desk rings. When he answers it, Sally tells him that Mr. Henderson is ready to meet with Red and him.

They walk into Mr. Henderson's large, well-furnished office and take seats in two of his leather chairs.

Mr. Henderson looks at the two documents he's holding in his right hand, then hands one to Red and one to Leland.

He says, "These are your new job descriptions. Red, as you can see, your new title will be Production Supervisor, and Leland you'll keep your current job title of Assistant to the President, but you'll have the added designation of Manufacturer's Liaison. These two job descriptions reflect what we've already talked about in terms of handling the expansion to accommodate the Dunham contract as well as taking care of whatever other new business comes up once we have the updated equipment and increased capacity.

"Red, your new salary will be seventy-two thousand, and Leland, yours will be sixty-eight thousand."

Red and Leland sneak glances at each other.

Red says, "This is awfully generous, boss. We appreciate it."

Mr. Henderson says, "There'll be some other employees whose duties and salaries are going to change, and we'll also be incrementally increasing our number of employees in addition to those we'll be hiring for the Dunham account, and you two are going to be helping me with all of those personnel matters."

Leland looks up from his job description. "Boss, I've been reading my new duties and responsibilities. Are you sure that I can handle this? You have to remember that I'm only twenty-four."

Mr. Henderson leans back in his tall desk chair. "Leland, when I was twenty-four, I was just getting home from a year of commanding an artillery unit in Vietnam." He stares at Leland, waiting for a response.

Leland squirms a bit, then says, "Yes, sir. I guess if you think that I can do it, then I'll be glad to take them on."

"The most important thing that I learned in the Army was how to know who I could trust to do what needs to be done. That's why I picked you two for these jobs. If anybody has a problem with that, they can take it up with me.

"Now, we're going to start next week on enlarging our workspace and our warehouse space, updating our current equipment, and buying additional equipment to meet the estimated demand from Dunham. Both of you know that it's going to be a good while before the Dunham factory will be operating at full speed. But we can't wait for that. Like I said, we'll start making those changes next week."

Mr. Henderson picks up a business card from his desk and hands it to Red. He says, "Sean wanted me to give this to you. It's the business card for his head of production, Dan Proznovsky. Sean and I have arranged for you to take a three-day trip up to the Pennsylvania complex where Sean will have Dan show you how they handle their Dunham account, including what equipment they use for that account.

Red writes a note on the back of Dan Proznovsky's business card and says, "Got it. That's a good idea, boss, about me going up there and seeing firsthand what they do. Just let me know when."

Mr. Henderson continues, "I will. I'll be sure to give you at least a week's prior notice. Now, you both know that I don't believe in working long hours. I believe in working efficiently. So, I don't expect that either of you will have to work that many more hours a week than you have been, except for the first few months, or possibly a little longer. But once the initial work is taken care of, your hours should be pretty regular. Any more questions?"

Red and Leland simultaneously say, "No, sir."

"Good. Because there's one more matter that I need to discuss with you two. Are you familiar with the old Liberty Hotel?"

They both nod yes.

"I've got a proposition for your construction company if it's still in business."

Red says, "Yes, sir, we're still working pretty steady with our company when we're not here. What do you need?"

"I want your company to do some consulting for me on renovating the old hotel."

Red says, "Don't you think we're too small to handle that kind of job."

"Now hear me out before you answer. A group of five of us formed the Liberty Hotel Company, LLC, and bought the old hotel building. We plan on renovating it and reopening it at around the same time or a little before the Dunham factory starts production. I want you two to do a study for me and prepare a list of written recommendations about how to make the necessary renovations to put the hotel back in business, including structural needs, plumbing, wiring, fire safety, utilities, everything. You'll be doing this along with our architect, Ron Anderson, who I know you've worked with before. And after our Liberty Hotel Company members have received and reviewed the recommendations, we'll all meet with Ron to go over everything again and make any changes that we think need to be made. After that, the four of us will meet with the contractor. Then, once the renovation starts, I want you guys to make periodic inspections to make sure that everything is going according to plan, and to make sure that the project is building code compliant, ADA compliant, and environmentally compliant."

Leland says, "We worked with Ron a bunch of times. He's good to work with, and he really knows what he's doing. Who's going to do the renovations once y'all decide what you need done?"

"Wolff Construction in Mobile. You know them. They've bought a lot of lumber from us for years, and they've used our milling shop on many occasions. You probably know that they've renovated several old hotels and apartment buildings. Phil Bernstein and I went and checked out four of the hotel projects that they did and liked what we saw. Wolff also came highly recommended to us by one of the big architectural firms in Mobile."

Leland says, "Yeah, we've worked with Wolff several times, too, a couple of times on apartment building renos. They do first rate work. But, if you've got them and Ron already lined up, why do you need us?"

"Because you two are obsessive compulsive nitpickers just like me. You won't miss anything, and you'll see to it that everything's done right the first time and on time."

Red thinks about that. He asks, "How's Wolff going to feel about two local small-time carpenters like us looking over their shoulders and inspecting their work? I mean, that's a huge company."

"Well, I talked with Don Wolff a few days ago, and he's fine with it. I told him that it was either going to be you two doing periodic inspections or me doing it. He said that he'd be happy to work with you guys."

Red and Leland look at each other and smile.

Leland says, "We'll need to have licensed plumbers and licensed electricians and hvac specialists and all kinds of other people work with us on this."

"Your contract will cover that. You'll hire whoever else you need for specific assistance and then bill us for the costs. None of those costs will come out of your consultation fee . . . Now, how about we meet at the hotel on Saturday afternoon around three o'clock, and walk through the building? I'll pick up a draft contract from our lawyer this week that you can take home and read, and if you decide you want the job, you can sign the contract and start immediately."

Red says, "I don't want to sound ungrateful, but how much are y'all planning to pay for this consulting that you want us to do?"

"We're thinking twenty-five thousand, but we can raise the amount if the renovation turns out to be more complicated than we think. We can discuss that on Saturday after we've done the walkthrough."

Red asks, "Are you at liberty to tell us who your partners are?"

"Sure. My property company, Henderson Properties, is a forty percent owner of the hotel company, Phil Bernstein owns ten percent, my brother Sean ten percent, Hollis Bailey ten percent, and Dunham Furnishings thirty percent."

"That's some heavy hitters. What made y'all decide to do this?"

Mr. Henderson holds up three fingers. "Three things. First, once the Dunham factory gets up to full speed, and once we start getting bigger and taking on new customers in addition to Dunham, it would be good for anybody coming to meet with either or both of us to have a decent place to stay.

"Second, we're going to turn the top floor of the hotel into three penthouse suites furnished with Dunham's top of the line hotel furniture, and we're also going to furnish the lobby and some of the lower floor rooms with Dunham products. That way, the Liberty Hotel will be a showcase for Dunham luxury hotel and office furniture.

"And third, downtown Libertytown needs a good hotel. When the Liberty was in its heyday, it did a hell of a business. Our group has done a study with the help of a business professor at South Alabama, and we believe it could do that again."

Red and Leland look at each other. Leland turns to Mr. Henderson and asks, "What do you estimate the project to cost?"

"First of all, we got the building dirt cheap from the City of Libertytown, because the City Council never could agree on what to do with the building after they bought it from the estate of the original owners. They were glad for us to take it off their hands. But, to answer your question, our estimate at this point of the total cost of the project, including the purchase price, is one point five million. That's taking into account the discounts that we'll get from using our lumber company and Phil's flooring company in Bay Minette as suppliers. And, of course, Dunham is going to supply most of the furnishings at a discount. But just to be on the safe side, we've budgeted $1.8 million."

Ron says, "I know that it's none of my business, but is John Lancaster's bank going to do the financing for the project?"

"No, there won't be any financing. The members of the company have already put the total budgeted amount into an interest-bearing Liberty Hotel Company account that we set up at the same bank in Pittsburgh that Allegheny Lumber uses. Of course, we've also set up a checking account here at John's bank that we'll be using for upfront expenses and for operating expenses once the hotel opens."

Mr. Henderson snickers. "You should have seen John's expression when he saw that our initial deposit was $250,000, especially since at that time he didn't have any idea what the Liberty Hotel Company was. To put him at ease, I told him in general terms about our project. He was all for it after what I told him, and he said that his bank and the Creek County Chamber of Commerce would help us in any way they could."

Ron looks at Leland and asks, "What do you think, son, should we do it?"

"Absolutely. I'm looking forward to it. I'd love to see that old hotel come back to life. I was just a little kid when it closed."

Chapter Seventeen

It's a few minutes after two on the following Saturday afternoon, and Diane is turning her car into the driveway of Mr. Henderson's house. She sees her mother talking to Mr. Henderson just inside the open front door. Then she sees Beverly kiss Mr. Henderson on the cheek and stroke his upper arm before she comes out the door.

Beverly walks down the porch steps and gets into the car. As she's buckling her seat belt, she looks at a smiling Diane and asks, "What are you so happy about?"

"Oh, nothing special. It's just good to see you."

"You saw me kiss Mark on the cheek, didn't you? That's what you're grinning about."

"Yes, ma'am, but only because I'm glad to see you so happy. By the way, how'd lunch at the country club go?"

"Just like we thought it would. When I walked into the dining room arm-in-arm with Mark, you've never seen so many bug-eyed women. I swear I don't know what it is with that high society bunch. It's like they think people like us are a different species."

"Yeah, sometimes it does seem that way. Did any of them come over and say hello?"

"A couple of the men came by and spoke to us, but none of the women even looked like they wanted to. The food was good, though."

"What'd you have?"

"A grilled chicken salad with Italian bread, and banana pudding for dessert."

"That does sound good."

Right at two-fifteen, Diane parks her Toyota in a space in front of the Main Street Gallery. When Diane and Beverly get to the front door of the gallery, they see that Frank and Melanie are engaged in an energetic conversation with a somewhat portly, middle-aged woman in a navy-blue designer pantsuit. The woman has a camera strap over her left shoulder and is taking notes on a small pad.

Beverly says, "Wonder who that is."

Diane says, "I've seen her before at the diner. She's from the *Creek County Courier*."

"Well, I hope that she doesn't want to talk to us."

"I don't know why she would, but she seemed to be a nice lady the times that I've seen her on TV."

Frank, Melanie, and the reporter all turn when they hear the front door opening. Frank says, "Y'all come on in and meet Miss Bonita Franklin from the *Creek County Courier*. She's doing an article on our gallery."

Diane and Beverly walk over to where Miss Franklin is standing and say hello. Then they stand there awkwardly, not knowing what to do next.

Miss Franklin smiles and says, "Hey, I know who y'all are. You're the mother and daughter from the Mother and Daughter Exhibit in June of last year, am I right?"

Diane says, "Yes, ma'am."

"I absolutely loved that exhibit. I still have some photos that I took of the gallery that night, including two or three of your exhibit. Would you like copies?"

Diane answers, "Oh, I'd love that. I could hang one in my studio. Thank you."

"That'd be very nice of you, Miss Franklin," says Beverly.

"Great. I'll get some copies made and send them to Frank. Have y'all done any other joint exhibits since then?"

Frank says, "They each had paintings for sale at our pre-Christmas event, but there was no designated Mother and Daughter Exhibit at that show. Their paintings were mixed in with everyone else's. But the paintings they had in that show were excellent, and most of them sold that day."

Miss Franklin looks at her watch. "I wish that I had known y'all would be here. I would have allowed some time to interview you. But I've got to run now . . . Do you think that maybe we could get together some time in the future for an interview?"

Diane says, "Oh, I don't know about that. We both kind of like our privacy. But thanks for asking."

Miss Franklin gives them each her business card. "If you change your minds, give me a call. I promise not to pry too much." Then she puts her notebook and pen into her camera bag, and Frank escorts her to the front door where she turns around and waves good-bye."

As they are waiting for Frank to return, Melanie smiles at Beverly and says, "I swear, Beverly, every time I see you lately, you're looking prettier. What's your secret?"

"You're too kind. But I have to give all the credit to Gloria at the Downtown Salon. Ever since I told her last year that I wanted to start looking a little more presentable for the sake of my daughter and grandson, she's taken me on as her personal project. I'll be sure to tell her what you said."

"My sister and I have always gone to a salon over in Carleton, but we may have to check out Gloria's salon."

"Well, I haven't been to many beauty salons, but I really like hers. She told me that she used to work in a fancy salon in Mobile, but she prefers having her own place. And she said she likes living in a small town."

Frank returns and says, "It's so good to see y'all again, and you both look so lovely today. Why don't y'all follow Melanie and me to our office."

After they're all four seated in the office, Frank reaches over and takes a red folder from the top drawer of a two-drawer wooden file cabinet near his desk. He removes two checks from the folder and hands one to Beverly and one to Diane.

"These checks are for your shares of the proceeds from the December show, after the deduction of our fifteen percent commission. Personally, I have mixed feelings about these checks, because I believe that you both underpriced your paintings, and I hate to see y'all get less than what I think you could have. On the other hand, y'all both still made a handsome sum. But I do suggest that in the future you consider pricing your paintings just a little higher. Melanie and I will be glad to help you determine what a fair price would be.

"That said, I have one more financial proposition to make. For the past few months, we've been experimenting with making prints of some of my and Melanie's more popular paintings and selling them, and there does seem to be a market for them. We found that we can have high quality eleven by fourteen prints made for just a few dollars apiece and then sell them for twenty dollars apiece. Now, that doesn't sound like much until you consider that there's no limit to how many prints you could sell, or any limit on how long you sell them. Our only cost is having our photos professionally processed on archival paper.

"And once you have the photo of your painting, you can also use it to make other items to sell, such as cards or buttons, or t-shirts, or whatever. Of course, if you sell the painting itself, you'll need to make sure that you retain certain reproduction rights.

"So, how about we just keep things simple and have y'all consider whether or not you would let us make photos of some of your paintings, then let us make and sell prints from those photos."

Beverly says, "I'd like to see Diane take advantage of your offer, but how much could she make if she did?"

"That would mainly depend on what price the market would support at the time."

Frank turns and points to a framed eleven by fourteen print hanging on the wall behind his desk. It's a picture of a panther in a jungle tree. "For example, it cost me roughly six dollars a copy to make that print, and we sell them unframed for twenty. So, using that as a guide, we could theoretically negotiate how much of that fourteen dollar net the artist would get and how much the gallery would keep."

Beverly looks at Diane then back at Frank. She says, "That doesn't sound like much, but, as you said, there's no limit to how many of each print you could sell, and since the gallery's taking care of the manufacturing and the selling, all the artist has to do is sit at home and wait for a check, which might be a little or might be a lot."

Frank nods. "Yes, that's a very practical way of looking at it, Beverly."

Diane gets up and looks at the print hanging on Frank's wall. She says, "I'd be willing to do it on a trial basis, with maybe three different paintings. What do you think, Mama?"

"I think you should give a try and see how it goes. What do you say, Frank?"

Frank looks at Melanie, then says to Diane, "How about I bring my camera equipment by your studio one day, and we can pick out three good candidates."

Diane responds, "That sounds great. Let's do it and see what happens."

Melanie is staring intently through the front window of the gallery. She asks, "Is that Mark Henderson across the street unlocking the front door of the old hotel?"

Frank looks toward the hotel. "Yes, I believe that it is."

Beverly also looks. She says, "That's him. He told me earlier today that he was going to take Red and Leland on a walkthrough of the hotel so that they could see what renovations need to be made."

Diane says, "Yeah. I think I remember hearing Leland say something about that the other day. If I remember correctly, he said that a group of investors were planning to renovate and reopen the hotel . . . That's Leland's truck pulling up now."

Melanie says, "I hope it's true that they're going to be renovating the hotel. I'm getting tired of looking at that dilapidated old building every time I'm here. What about you, Frank?"

"I'm with you, darling."

Leland parks his truck in front of the hotel, and Red and Leland get out and walk through the open front door. They see that Mr. Henderson and Judge Bailey are standing in the lobby, looking up at the ceiling.

Mr. Henderson speaks first. "Come on in, boys. You know Hollis Bailey. He's going to do the walkthrough with us as soon as Ron Anderson gets here. Ron called me right before I left my house and told me he'd be here about three-fifteen."

At 3:13, Ron walks in carrying a clipboard and a pen. "I'm sorry if I held y'all up."

Mr. Henderson says, "No problem, Ron. Let's get started."

For the next hour, the five men make a slow and careful inspection of the seventy-one-year-old, four-story brick building. Leland is taking notes, including the measurements of each space that they inspect. As they go from floor to floor, Ron, Red, and Leland learn from Mr. Henderson that the hotel originally had sixteen guest rooms on each of the top three floors, with the lobby, registration desk, café, manager's quarters, and ballroom on the first floor.

Mr. Henderson explains the new design will need to have the second and third floors retaining the sixteen-room design, with the top floor reconfigured to have one three-bedroom and two two-bedroom penthouse suites, with each penthouse suite having a bathroom for each bedroom, as well as a living room and a kitchenette with a dining area.

Judge Bailey says that the design of the first floor will need to be revised to have a coffee shop instead of the café that the hotel originally had. He goes on to say that the ballroom needs to be larger than before and be capable of being divided into two sections. As they're discussing the ballroom, Mr. Henderson tells Red and Leland that another reason that he wanted them as his construction consultants is because they're musicians. He says, "I want this ballroom to have the best sound system in the county, and I figure that you two can appreciate that because you've no doubt played some ballrooms with godawful sound systems."

Red says, "That's for sure. And we'll also need to make sure that the acoustics are as good as they can be."

Leland says, "Now, that part of our job will be fun. We've already been researching sound systems and acoustics, because we're going to build a small music studio next to my workshop after we move the workshop to its new location behind the house that we're building."

Mr. Henderson nudges Judge Bailey and says, "I knew we picked the right men."

While they're standing at the front door after completing their initial walkthrough, Mr. Henderson looks at Red and Leland and asks, "Well, boys, are you still in?"

Red extends his open right hand toward Mr. Henderson and says, "Definitely in. This looks like it's going to be something this town can be proud of, and we'd love to be a part of it."

Mr. Henderson shakes Red's hand and then Leland's. He hands Red the draft contract that he just took from his inside coat pocket and says, "Take this home with you, make whatever changes you need, fill in a dollar amount that you think is fair, and bring it to my office on Monday."

As Red and Leland say their goodbyes to Judge Bailey and Ron, they notice that everyone seems to share Red's enthusiasm for the project.

A few minutes into the drive back home, Leland says, "Daddy, I don't know what we did to deserve it, but things have sure been looking up for us lately."

"Son, just remember what I've always tried to teach you. Every good opportunity you have is another chance to give back more than you receive."

"Yes, sir."

Chapter Eighteen

MR. HENDERSON COMES INTO HIS OFFICE AT A FEW MINUTES BEFORE eight on the Monday after the Liberty Hotel walkthrough. He finds in his inbox the draft contract that he gave to Red the Saturday before, and he reads through the few suggested revisions that Red has handwritten in the margins. He sees no problem with any of Red's revisions. He notices that the contract amount that Red has inserted is twenty-two thousand dollars. When Sally brings him a cup of coffee at eight-thirty, Mr. Henderson thanks her for the coffee and hands her the draft contract. He gives her instructions on what changes to make and tells her to print out three copies of the contract after she's made the revisions.

Shortly after nine, Red Johnson raps on Mr. Henderson's door. When Mr. Henderson looks up from his desk, Red says, "I got a message that you wanted to see me, boss."

Mr. Henderson motions for Red to come in and have a seat at the small mahogany worktable on the right side of his office. Mr. Henderson gets up from his desk chair and walks over to the worktable with the contract copies in his right hand. He says, "Red, please have a seat here and read over this contract to see if the revisions we made are what you wanted. If they are, I need your signature on the line under the name of your construction company. I've already signed all three copies, so once you sign them you can take your copy with you."

Red says, "Yes, sir" and begins reading the contract. A few moments later, he says, "Everything looks good, but I noticed that you changed the amount from twenty-two to twenty-five thousand."

"Got a problem with that?"

Red smiles. "No, sir. Guess not." Then he signs and dates each of the three contracts and folds in two the one that he's taking with him. Red hands the other two to Mr. Henderson and says, "I'm really glad that you're including Leland and me in this project. I know you didn't have to do that."

"I'm just doing what's best for the project."

"Yes, sir. Anything else I can do for you?"

Mr. Henderson rises from his chair and says, "No, I won't keep you any longer. I know you're busy, and we've got a lot more to do before the Christmas break."

"Yes, sir. We're all busy. And I can tell already that we're going to stay busy for quite a while."

Mr. Henderson slaps Red on the back as he walks back to his desk. He says, "You're a good man, Red."

Red waves at Sally as he walks back to the production line.

On Monday night at Red's house, Leland and Red are sitting at the worktable in Red's home office, making out a schedule for their part of the hotel project. They decide that the best approach will be to fully inspect and draw up recommendations for each floor, one at a time beginning with the first floor, and then come back after completing that process and look at the building as a whole to make sure that everything they intend to recommend is compatible with the overall design.

As part of their work plan, they're making a list of the names and phone numbers of the plumber, electrician, lighting contractor, hvac contractor, structural engineer, glass installer, elevator technician, and others that they intend to consult with as they carry out their assignment. Leland suggests that they also ask for Theo Bellos's help with the design and equipment needs of the coffee shop. Red agrees.

Red prints out three copies of their list of specialists, one for each of them and one for Ron Anderson with whom they'll be meeting at the hotel at 5:30 the next afternoon.

When Red and Leland arrive at the hotel at 5:24 on Tuesday, they see Ron Anderson's car parked in front of the hotel and notice the front door standing open. Red parks his truck next to Ron's Volvo, and he and Leland walk inside.

Ron says, "Hi, guys. Quite a mess, huh?"

Red answers, "Yeah, and it's cold in here, too. I'm glad we wore our work jackets and gloves. But, you know, Ron, from what we've seen so far, this building is in very good shape from a structural point of view.

Ron says, "Yeah, from what I can tell the exterior walls and the roof are solid. That's a relief."

Red hands Ron his copy of the list that Red and Leland made the night before of other people that they intend to call upon as they go through the inspection process.

Ron studies the list. "This looks good, Red. I know all these people, and they're all good at what they do. They should be a big help. I'm glad y'all aren't shy about asking for advice."

Red says, "Nope, that's how you learn. And you know that Leland and I are also going to rely on your expertise when we come up with any design questions. And, as Mister Henderson said, you'll have the final word before our recommendations go to the hotel company for their review."

"Yeah, that's the best way because I'm the one who'll have to draw up the blueprints and write our formal report to the company members. So, I need to be completely satisfied with everything we recommend before I submit it to the members for their approval."

Red and Leland stand with Ron for about fifteen minutes in the lobby of the hotel as they discuss with Ron their schedule for the upcoming weeks and how they'll coordinate with him as the project goes forward. Leland says, "Actually, Ron, we intend to stay here a couple of more hours tonight and get started. You're welcome to stay."

Ron slides his copy of Red's list onto his clipboard and says, "Not tonight, boys. I'm not dressed for it. Just let me get out of your way. Here's my business card with my cell phone number on it. Call me if I can help along the way."

As Ron is walking toward the front door, Red looks at the business card and says, "Thank you, Ron. We'll try not to call after midnight."

"My wife will appreciate that."

They're walking down the main hall of the first floor, shining flash-lights on the floor and up the wall and onto the ceiling when Leland asks Red, "Daddy, does this hotel remind you of some you've seen in Western movies?"

"Kind of. With the echoes in here, it's almost like I'm hearing a Marty Robbins song in my head."

"I know what you mean. Something like 'The Night I Shot the Bandit at the Liberty Hotel.'"

Red thinks for a minute. Then in his best Marty Robbins voice, he sings, "I rode all through the desert and a thousand miles of hell, until I caught the bandit at the Liberty Hotel . . ."

At a few minutes after eight, Red tells Leland to turn off the inside lights except for the one above the door, and he reaches into his pocket for the key to the hotel door. While Red is locking the door after they're both outside, Leland is standing under a streetlight looking at their three-page list of recommendations.

Leland laughs. "Good lord, Daddy, if this keeps up, we're going to have fifty pages of recommendations."

"Nah, I think that once we get everything sorted out, it'll be more like twenty. For the first few weeks, we'll be throwing all kinds of ideas around, but as we get more familiar with the building, we'll learn what makes the most sense and toss out the rest."

On the way home, Red says, "I just thought of something, Leland. Will you tell Mister Henderson tomorrow that somebody needs to start moving out all that trash that's piled up inside the hotel. And be sure that he knows we'll have to be there to coordinate it, because we don't want anything thrown out that needs to stay."

"Okay, Daddy. And I'll call Zach Cannon and have him put a couple of dumpsters in the back parking lot."

A little while later, when Diane hears Leland unlocking the front door of the trailer, she goes to meet him. He holds up his hands and says, "Sorry, babe. Better let me shower before you get too close."

Diane takes a whiff and says, "Good idea. You smell like you've been locked in a damp basement."

After his shower, Leland comes out from the bathroom in his pajama bottoms and a white t-shirt and goes to say hello to Bret, who's asleep on the little bed that Leland built for him. When he hears Leland's voice, Bret lifts his head and begins to talk to "Dada" in a sleepy combination of words and noises. Leland leans over the edge of the bed and says, "I'm not sure exactly what you said, Bret, but Dada's glad to see you, too." Then he picks up Bret, kisses his forehead, and tucks him back in.

While Leland is eating his dinner of fried chicken and mashed potatoes, he gives Diane a report on how their first night of hotel duty went. "That place is so cool, babe. Mister Henderson gave Daddy copies of a bunch of old photographs of the hotel that he got from the historian at the *Courier*, and we're using those pictures to get a better sense of what the hotel looked like back in the day. The plan is not to make the Liberty completely identical to what it used to be, but to save as many historic details as we can, so as to keep that old timey look."

"I like that idea. It wouldn't be anything special if it looked like every other hotel."

Chapter Nineteen

CHRISTMAS COMES ON A SUNDAY IN 1994, SO MR. HENDERSON DESIG-
nates Friday the twenty-third and Monday the twenty-sixth as the company's Christmas holidays. He invites Red, Jeanette, Leland, and Diane
to have a Christmas Eve dinner at his house at five o'clock.

As Red drives his pickup into Mr. Henderson's driveway on Christmas Eve, Jeanette looks out at the lighted Nativity scene in the front yard
and the Christmas decorations on the front porch. She says, "Look how
pretty the porch is with all those angels."

A little later, Leland pulls into the driveway and parks his truck
behind Red's. Diane and Bret get out and walk hand in hand across the
yard to get a better look at the Nativity scene. Bret points at Jesus in the
manger and loudly proclaims, "Baby."

Diane says, "That's right, Bret. That's baby Jesus."

Bret points again and says, "Baby yees."

Diane and Bret walk up the front steps to where Leland is waiting for
them. Leland picks up Bret and says, "My Bret sure is smart."

Bret says, "Bret mart."

Red is inside the front door waiting. He laughs and says to Leland,
"Better be careful what you say around that boy if you don't want it
repeated."

Jeanette is in the foyer talking to Beverly, who has prepared the meal
that they're about to eat. She says, "Beverly, why didn't you let me know
you were cooking for us. I would have been glad to help."

"Oh, that's all right. Mark was my kitchen helper today. He's in the kitchen now, slicing the ham."

Red starts walking toward the kitchen. "I've got to see this." When he walks into the kitchen, Mr. Henderson looks up from the ham and says, "Merry Christmas, Red. Come on in and help me get everything ready."

"Be glad to. But I didn't know you were a cook."

"Red, I've been a bachelor for ten years now. Who do you think fed me?"

"I always thought you had a cook."

"No, not always. I did for a while, but it seemed silly to have a cook for just me. I found that I prefer fending for myself."

"Well, what can I do for you?"

Mark tells Red where the dishes are and shows him the serving cart to use to take the food out. The two of them manage to get all the plates, utensils, and food to the dining table without any problem.

Once the serving cart is at the table, Jeanette and Beverly take over and see to it that everything is put in its rightful place. While they're doing that, Mr. Henderson is getting a report from Red and Leland on how their hotel inspection is going. Mr. Henderson learns that they expect to complete their inspection and recommendations by the middle of January, and that they will be meeting with Ron shortly after that so that Ron can start preparing a formal report for the hotel company members. Leland says that they would have been able to finish sooner except that the hvac man and the plumbing company won't be available until the first week of January.

Mr. Henderson says, "No problem. We won't be able to start the renovation until the first week of March anyway, because Wolff Construction won't be available until then."

"Leland and I could start some of the preliminary work as soon as the plans are approved, if that'll help," offers Red.

Mark thinks that over. "That's not a bad idea. As soon as you can get a good idea of what the lumber needs will be, you can start by writing up a preliminary lumber order and then getting the lumber placed on the right floors of the hotel when our trucks bring the lumber to the site. You can do the same thing with the flooring, the paint, the fixtures, and anything else that we can go ahead and order. We'll just need to be sure that the hotel has burglar alarms and security by the time that stuff starts coming in. So, why don't you plan to start work on the preliminary orders as soon as possible, and I'll amend your contract to cover your time."

Red says, "You don't have to do that, boss. We don't mind putting in a little extra time."

Mark puts his hand on Red's shoulder. "Red, a very wise man, my father, once told me that there's no such thing as extra time."

Once they're all seated at the dining table, Diane quiets Bret and situates him in the high chair that Leland brought into the house from his truck. Beverly asks everyone to bow their heads and gives thanks to the Lord for His son Jesus, for the food they are about to eat, and for the love and affection that they all have for one other. Bret hears everyone else at the table say "Amen" at the end of the blessing, and he adds his "men" and claps his hands.

A few minutes into the meal, Leland turns to Beverly and says, "This is pretty good ham, Miz Beverly."

Beverly says, "Mark baked it for us last night."

Leland turns to Mr. Henderson. "This is pretty good ham, boss."

"Thank you, Leland. What do you think about the ham, Bret?"

With his mouth full of mashed potatoes, Bret manages an "Umm."

After dinner is over and the table is cleared, everyone retires to the family room. Red wants to light up a cigarette, but he knows that Mr. Henderson doesn't allow smoking in his office or his home, so he excuses himself and goes out to the front porch. Leland excuses himself and follows Red.

Once they're outside, they notice that there's a string of Christmas lights shining from the ceiling of the porch. Leland says, "This is really nice, isn't it? You know, this is the first Christmas since Diane and I got married that I haven't felt stressed about money."

Red lights up his Marlboro and takes a slow draw. He blows a puff of smoke toward the ceiling and watches it rise. He says, "I know that's a good feeling, but you've earned it. You've worked your butt off this past year."

"No more so than you."

"Well, I feel pretty good, too. It's been a good year for both of us. And best of all, we're both healthy, and I'm still sober."

Leland studies Red's face as Red blows a smoke ring into the air. He has never felt closer to his father.

For the next five minutes, Red and Leland sit on the front steps saying nothing, just looking at the stars through the barren branches of tall oak trees and enjoying the moment. Then Red puts out his cigarette on the concrete porch floor, field strips it, and puts the pieces into his jean pocket. He stands up and says, "Let's go inside before they think we've abandoned them."

After they get up from the steps, Red puts his right arm over Leland's shoulders, and they walk in together. Bret runs up to his daddy with his arms held high, wanting to be picked up. As soon as he settles into Leland's arms, he closes his eyes and starts to doze off.

On the way home, Leland says to Diane, "I'm so lucky to have you and Bret."

Diane leans against Leland and says, "And I love you, too, Leland."

Chapter Twenty

It's a cold Tuesday on January 17, 1995, when Red and Leland meet with Ron Anderson at noon at the offices of Anderson Architects, PC. Ron is sitting at a drafting table in his office when they come in. Leland hands Ron an expandable manila folder that contains all the Liberty Hotel inspection/recommendation documents that Ron hasn't already been provided.

Leland says, "This should do it, Ron, as far as our recommendations. If you have any questions while you're writing up the report, you can call Daddy or me."

Ron starts flipping through the items in the folder. He looks up from the folder and says, "This looks good to me. Matter of fact, everything that y'all have brought me so far has been great. Very clear and very well thought out. And I like the way that along with each recommendation, y'all include a detailed rationale for it.

"Now, I've already written up everything that y'all brought me before, so it shouldn't take me but a few more days to finish the draft report and this preliminary blueprint that I'm working on here. So how about I call you, Red, once I finish the draft report and blueprint. You can look them over to make sure that I got everything right, then we'll go down to the hotel together, and I'll take some photographs to include as part of the final version of the report . . . You know, I feel good about this project. I can tell already that the hotel is going to be someplace exceptional."

"I especially can't wait to see the penthouse suites when they're finished," says Leland. "That three-bedroom suite is going to take up about forty percent of the top floor. But there's one more thing that you need to do for the project, Ron, so that we can start bringing in materials in advance of the construction. Is there any way that you could get some kind of security system installed within the next couple of weeks?"

Ron answers, "Sure, I can do that. There's a security company over in Mobile who can set up a temporary system for us. And they can set up a temporary system in such a way that it can be incorporated into the permanent system when it's installed. Don't worry, I'll make sure that we have a security system in the building before the materials start arriving."

Red looks at his watch and stands up. "Thanks, Ron. You're the best, man. Now, we've got to get back to our real jobs before we get fired."

Ron laughs as he rises to shake hands with Red and Leland. "Mark would fire everybody else in the company before he would you two. He brags about y'all all the time."

Red opens the door for Leland, and they head to the parking lot.

When they get to Red's truck, Leland asks, "Daddy, do you really think that Mister Henderson brags on us all the time?"

"It wouldn't surprise me. He always gives credit where credit's due, whether it's us or anybody else. That's his way."

On Thursday, February ninth, Red and Leland receive word at work from Mr. Henderson's secretary that there will be a meeting of the Liberty Hotel Company members the next afternoon at three o'clock.

At ten to three on Friday, Red and Leland meet in front of Sally's desk in Mr. Henderson's outer office. The door to his inner office is closed. Red asks, "Is he tied up, Sally?"

"Not for long. He's meeting with the other Liberty Hotel Company members right now, except that his brother couldn't make it in person, so he's on the speaker phone."

As Red and Leland look around for somewhere to sit in the outer office, they see Ron Anderson coming through the door in a dark gray suit with a black briefcase in his left hand.

Ron asks, "Is he ready for us, Sally?"

"Not quite yet, Mister Anderson. Why don't y'all just have a seat over there in those chairs?" Then Sally points to a credenza on the right side of the room. "And there's fresh coffee on that credenza."

In a few minutes, Red, Leland, and Ron are sitting in adjacent chairs, each holding a steaming Styrofoam cup of coffee. Ron says, "I went over our report one more time right before I left my office, and I don't think that they're going to want to make many changes from what we're recommending. Everything looks good. But, knowing Mark, he's going to want to make some small changes just to keep us on our toes."

Red smiles and nods.

At ten after three, Sally's intercom buzzes, and she picks up her phone. She smiles at Ron and says, "They're ready. Just go on in."

After the members stand and welcome Red, Leland, and Ron, everyone takes a seat around the long mahogany conference table in the center of the office.

Mr. Henderson says, "Let me put you at ease right off, Ron. Great job on the report. We've all had time to review it and discuss it, and we only see a few things that we'll need to change. By the way, guys, my brother Sean is on the speaker phone. We faxed him a copy of the report yesterday morning, so he'll be in on our discussion."

The voice on the speaker phone in the middle of the conference table says, "Afternoon, everybody. You don't know just how much I wish I was with you. It's twenty-two degrees here. Tell them about it, David."

David Dunham, who is sitting next to Mr. Henderson says, "He's right. It was about twenty-five when I left from Harrisburg Tuesday night." David looks at the speaker phone and loudly says, "It's fifty-two here, Sean."

Judge Bailey laughs and says, "Well, Mark, now that we've gotten all the weather reports, why don't you lead the discussion on Ron's report."

"First of all, I want to say again great job, guys. Everything is clearly laid out. When Judge Bailey and I did a walkthrough Tuesday night, with the report in hand, there was no doubt about exactly what was being recommended. And as I just said, we only have a few things that we think need further consideration. So, I'll start with the coatrooms for the ballroom. Ron, I understand why you recommended two coatrooms for the ballroom, because the ballroom can be divided into two sections. But what would you think about putting the two coatrooms right next to each other near where the two sections meet in the center of the ballroom?"

Ron looks at Red and nods. Red says, "We did consider that layout, sir, but we had to take into account that when the ballroom is sectioned in two, each section will have its own entrance door, and the lock on the center entrance door will be set so that it can't be opened from the hallway. That's why we thought that separating the coatrooms and having them situated close to the two side entrance doors would work better. And that way they'll both still be directly accessible from the hallway whether the ballroom is sectioned off or not."

Mr. Henderson takes another look at the ballroom diagram in his report. He says, "Thanks, Red. We'll take your explanation into consideration before we make our final decision. Next question, why did you recommend that a freight elevator shaft be installed at the far end of the hallways. There's no way that a freight elevator would look as good as a passenger elevator. So, that would detract from the style of the rest of the hallway."

Ron says, "First, let me explain why a freight elevator is needed at that end of the halls. It's because, otherwise, the only freight elevator in the hotel will be at the very front of the building, which is quite a distance from the far rooms. And we found out that the design of the building wouldn't accommodate another freight elevator anywhere other than at the far end without taking out a room on the second and third floors and also making one of the penthouse suites smaller.

"Now, there is an alternative design that Red and I have looked at. That would be to have a service elevator, rather than a freight elevator, at the far end of the building. A service elevator looks essentially the same as a passenger elevator, but is capable of carrying heavier loads, just not as heavy a load as what a freight elevator can handle."

David Dunham says, "That sounds like a good compromise to me, Mark."

Judge Bailey says, "Me, too."

Mr. Henderson puts his elbows on the table and looks directly at Ron. "Ron, if I didn't know better, I might think that you put that freight elevator in your design knowing that we wouldn't approve it, but also knowing that we would agree to a service elevator as an alternative. I'm thinking that the service elevator was what you actually thought was best the whole time, but you wanted us to feel as though we had made an executive decision on something. Am I right?"

Ron smiles. "I refuse to answer that question on the grounds that I might incriminate myself."

Everyone laughs, and the mood of the meeting immediately lightens. From that point on, the members make only three small changes to Ron's proposal, and then, after a short discussion, they approve what Ron recommended for the locations of the ballroom coatrooms.

In closing, Mr. Henderson tells Ron to draw up the final blueprints to include the changes that were affirmed today by the members. After that, he adjourns the meeting but asks Red and Leland to stay around for a few minutes.

Judge Bailey, Phil Bernstein, Ron Anderson, and David Dunham leave, and Mr. Henderson has a few final words on the phone with his brother. After he says goodbye to Sean, he places his hotel documents into a manila folder and says to Red and Leland, "Excellent job, men. Now, I'm going to be meeting at the hotel with Don Wolff as soon as Ron draws up the final blueprints and gives us the initial materials and equipment list. I want you two to be there with Ron and me when we talk to Don. I'll give you a couple of days' notice."

When they see Mr. Henderson look at his watch, Red and Leland gather their materials and rise from their seats to get back to their sawmill work."

Chapter Twenty-one

IT'S ABOUT 8:20 ON THE MORNING OF APRIL 17, 1995. BETH IS ON THE top front step of her house tightening the laces of her new white Nike walking shoes. She sees Melanie walking toward her with her arms spread above her head.

Looking skyward, Melanie says, "This is a great spring day, sis. It's good to be young and alive."

"What in the world's gotten into you?"

"I don't know. I just woke up feeling good."

"I'm glad you did. I didn't sleep that well last night, because our cat kept whining and howling about something. I'll probably be all right once we've walked a bit. But you're right, this is going to be a beautiful day."

After they've walked a few blocks, Beth asks Melanie how the gallery is doing.

"Everything's going great. Our revenues are up more than thirty percent over last year at this time, and our donations are up right at twenty-two percent."

"What about those prints of Diane's paintings? How's that going?"

"We had fifty prints each made of three of her paintings in early February, and we've already sold a total of twenty-eight, and that's just from walk-in customers. We haven't had a show since December."

Beth thinks about that for a moment. "So, it's possible that those prints could sell out by the end of the year."

"Yeah, I can see that happening. That's why I'm going to try to get

Diane to let us make some prints of at least two more of her paintings before our next show, which is in about a month."

"Do you think she'll do that?"

"I'm going to ask her when we get to the diner."

At about a block before they get to the diner, Beth points toward a two-story white house across the street and asks Melanie, "Can you believe the bright red color that the Parkers painted those shutters?"

Melanie looks at the shutters and makes a face. "That is a tad vibrant. But you know Marie Parker is from an Italian family from somewhere up North. That red was probably her idea."

"Well, I think it's vulgar."

They walk into Danny's at a few minutes before nine. They wave to Judge Bailey, who's having coffee and a jelly donut at a corner table. Melanie says hello to Mrs. Margaret Roberts and Mrs. Jessie Givens, two of the town's most respected senior women, who are having breakfast at a window table near the entrance. Mrs. Roberts and Mrs. Givens are both dressed in fashionable dark dresses.

Beth says to Mrs. Roberts, "It appears that you two are heading out to somewhere fancy."

"Unfortunately, honey, it's to a funeral over in Headland. A high school classmate of ours passed away from breast cancer."

"Oh, I'm so sorry to hear that. Who was it?"

"Janet Bromley, she was Janet Crowder when we were in school."

Melanie asks, "Was she related to Harry Crowder? We know him."

"His great aunt. You know, it's gotten to where it seems like we're losing somebody we know every week. Now, I know that it can't really be that often, but it sure feels like it."

Mrs. Givens looks up from her scrambled eggs and says in a plaintive voice, "You girls take the advice of two old ladies and enjoy life while you're young."

Beth says, "Yes, ma'am, we will. Y'all be careful on your drive over to Headland."

After the sisters take a seat at the counter, Melanie whispers to Beth, "Well, that certainly put a damper on my mood."

Diane walks over to the sisters and says, "Good morning. Y'all want coffee?"

Beth nods. Diane turns around to the coffee urn and fills two mugs. When she places the coffee in front of the sisters, she asks, "Something wrong? Y'all are awfully quiet."

Beth says, "We're fine, but Melanie has a business question for you."

"What's that, Miz Pebworth?"

Melanie takes a deep breath and releases it. Then she smiles and says, "Diane, the sales of the prints that we made of your three paintings are going so well that we want to know if you'd be willing to let us make prints of two more of your paintings."

Diane shrugs her shoulders and says, "I don't see why not. Just come by the studio sometime and pick out a couple. I wouldn't mind making a few more dollars now that we're building our house."

Beth looks surprised. She says, "You're building a house? Is it going to be where your trailer is now?"

"No, we bought the lot next door. Actually, we kind of traded lots, and the house is going to be on the lot next door."

Melanie asks, "On which side of your present location is your new lot?"

"On the town side."

"Beth asks, "What are y'all going to do with your trailer and your studio building?"

"Well, the trailer goes with the lot, but we can live in it until the new house is finished. The workshop building is going to be disassembled and moved to a spot behind our new house. Leland and his daddy built the shop in such a way that it could be disassembled and then reassembled somewhere else."

Beth says, "That was smart."

"Yeah. Leland's always surprising me with how smart he is. But he's always been smart, even in high school. He even helped me with English my last semester so that I could graduate early."

Melanie looks at Beth, then at Diane. "We heard that it was *you* who tutored *him*."

Diane smiles. "I can see how people would think that, but, no, it was him who helped me. When do y'all want to come by the studio?"

Melanie says, "I'll have to talk to Frank. He'll be taking the photos. But, speaking of photos, I've been meaning to ask you if Bonita Franklin ever sent you the photos she took of your Mother and Daughter Exhibit? She called Frank and got your address."

"She sure did. She sent us three real nice pictures, and I've got one framed and hanging in our trailer and another one hanging in the studio. Mama's got the other one at her house."

"That was nice of her to send you the photos. Now, as for the photos for your prints, I'll let you know when Frank can come by and take those."

"That'll be fine."

As the sisters are walking back home, Beth asks, "Can you believe that they're building that fantasy house we were joking about a few years ago?"

"I know. Do you think there could be more to Leland and Diane than we first thought."

"I don't know. Maybe. But what about Diane's mother? Talk about a surprise."

Melanie says, "I haven't made up my mind about her yet. She's a very talented artist, but she still seems a little odd to me."

As they reach the corner of Main and Union, Beth notices that there are cars parked in front of the old Holman house. She gets Melanie's attention and points. "Look down there. I wonder if the Holman house has sold."

"Let's go look."

As they approach the house, the sisters see a man and a woman carrying boxes through the front door. The man and woman are followed by a blonde girl of about eight years.

Melanie says, "It does look like someone's moving in. Do you recognize anyone?"

"Only Michelle the real estate agent. Let's go ask her if the house has sold."

Michelle sees the sisters coming. She waves. The couple, who are now coming back down the front steps, also see the sisters. The woman's face lights up as she starts walking briskly down the sidewalk toward the sisters. She's an attractive young redhead in faded blue jeans and a loose-fitting Air Force Academy t-shirt.

Under her breathe, Beth asks Melanie, "Recognize her?"

"No, but she's acting like she knows us."

"Well, everybody knows us."

When the woman gets near the sisters, she reaches out as if to hug Melanie, and Melanie awkwardly asks, "Do I know you?"

"Of course, you do. It's me, Emma."

Melanie looks confused. Then she smiles and says, "Of course, it's you. I'm sorry. I didn't recognize you at first. How've you been? Is that your husband?"

Emma turns to see the man approaching them and holding the right hand of the little girl in his left hand.

Emma extends her right hand toward the man as he gets closer to her. The man takes her hand in his and says, "Hello. I'm Brad Crawford. You must be the Moore sisters that I've heard Emma talk about so much. It's good to finally meet you after all these years."

Emma says, "And this beautiful girl is our daughter Melanie."

Melanie smiles at the girl. "Another Melanie."

Emma touches the face of the little girl. "I named her after you, my best friend in high school. We're going to have to get a picture of you two together."

Beth, who has been quietly taking everything in, asks, "Are y'all moving into your old family home?"

"Yes. Bradley will be transferring to an eighteen-month assignment on a base in Turkey in a couple of months. So, we've taken the house off the market, and Mel and I are going to move in here as soon as her school year is over in Texas. We're going to stay here until Brad gets back to the States."

Beth asks, "What are you going to do with the house once he gets back?"

"Not sure. We'll either put it back on the market or rent it out. Either way, we're going to get it back into top shape while Mel and I are here."

Melanie asks, "How far along are you on the moving?"

"Oh, we just got started today. We brought a few things with us, but it'll be near the end of May before Mel and I move here. We plan on having everything here by the end of the first week of June, except for what Brad will need while he's still in Texas."

Melanie says, "Again, I'm so sorry that I didn't recognize you. I feel bad about that."

"Well, I am forty pounds lighter and a redhead instead of a blonde."

Beth says, "Well, I think you look great."

"Why thank you. Nice of you to say so. And you two look spectacular, as always."

Melanie says, "Thank you. Where are y'all staying tonight?"

"Mobile. We'll head back to Texas in the morning," answers Bradley.

Emma says, "We came here today to meet with Michelle, our agent, and to get the utilities transferred to our name and arrange for a telephone account, and also to see what appliances we need to buy and what repairs need to be made to the house. Like Brad said, we're about to leave, but Mel and I will be back the weekend after next to do some more preparation, so give me your phone number and I'll call you when we're back in town. I can't wait for us to spend some time together."

Melanie gives Emma her gallery business card and says, "Looking forward to it. I'll have to tell you about this art gallery that I help run. By the way, how are your parents doing?"

"They're doing fine. They really like living in Florida. But they're anxious to get this house off their hands. I told them that if it didn't sell right away after we moved out that Brad and I would buy it and rent it out until he retires. We're planning on moving to this area when Brad retires."

Beth says, "Well, I'd much rather have y'all living in our neighborhood than some outsiders we don't know anything about."

Once the sisters are back on the Main Street sidewalk, Melanie says, "Boy, Emma is a completely different person. She's not the shy, chubby teenager from my past."

Beth smiles. "No, she's not shy or chubby. And she's going to shock some of the women who used to know her back in the day, even make some of them jealous. They'll remember her the same way we did, a timid, overweight, kind of nondescript teenager. But you know that means she's going to have to maneuver her way through everyone getting used to who she is now."

"You're right. I just hope that she doesn't expect me to take her around and re-introduce her to everybody. I've got enough on my plate right now."

"Yeah, I know what you mean."

Chapter Twenty-two

On the afternoon of September 9, 1995, Mr. Henderson, Beverly, Red, and Jeanette are all standing on the front porch of Leland and Diane's recently completed house, waiting to see the inside for the first time since the house has been finished.

The new house is a one-story white three-thousand-square-foot Craftsman style with a porch that extends across the front. It has light blue shutters and a dark blue front door. A matching white two-car garage sits next to the house, and there's a covered walkway between the side door of the garage and the kitchen door.

Above the garage is Diane's new art studio, which is a change from their original plan of reattaching Diane's studio to Leland's relocated workshop. To Diane's delight, three months into the construction of the new house, Leland decided that building the studio above the garage was a feasible revision to the construction plans. So, Red and he added the new studio and had Leland's contractor install plumbing, electricity, and an hvac unit for the studio. Then Red and Leland removed the cabinets, worktables, and light fixtures from the previous studio and installed them in the new location.

Leland is standing at the front door of the new house looking at the anxious faces of those waiting to go in. He takes his key chain from the right front pocket of his jeans and asks, "Are y'all ready?"

The group answers loudly in the affirmative.

Leland unlocks the door and opens it wide. Diane is the first one in.

While she's standing at the door to the family room looking at the newly painted walls, all the others are coming in behind her and going in various directions throughout the house.

Jeanette especially likes the kitchen. "This reminds me so much of my grandmother's kitchen in her farmhouse, except for the modern appliances, of course. I'm glad that y'all went with traditional white, and I like the black granite countertops." She tries one of the stools next to the island in the center of the kitchen. "And I love this island that Red and Leland built, with all that storage space."

Mr. Henderson slaps Leland on the back. "This is great work, men. I can't wait to see this house when all the furniture is in place."

Diane says, "That's going to be the fun part for Mama and me. We've already made out our shopping list. We don't have much furniture at all in our trailer that'll work in here. The best piece we have so far is the double bed from Mama's guest room that she gave us."

Mr. Henderson says, "Well, once you get your list made out, and before you buy anything, come by my house. I'm having the living room, family room, dining room, and foyer repainted and redecorated, starting next week. You two can have any of the old furniture that's being replaced."

Diane looks at Leland then at Mr. Henderson. "But that's some very expensive furniture you're talking about. I don't know if we'd feel right taking it."

"It'll be my housewarming gift to you. I'd love for you two to have whatever you can use for this house."

Beverly praises Red and Leland for the fine work they did on the interior. Red thanks her then says, "Now, you have to remember that most of this was done by the construction company that Leland hired, but Leland and I did all the trim work and all the cabinets. And we also refurbished three doors that we salvaged from the old hotel and used for three of the bedrooms."

Leland tells Beverly, "We found the doors in the basement of the hotel, and they looked pretty funky, and even after we got them to Daddy's workshop, we weren't sure they'd be usable. But after I stripped them down and sanded them, they looked great. We had first planned to paint them white, but the oak looked so good that we decided to stain and varnish them instead."

Mr. Henderson walks over to look at one of the bedroom doors. "This looks very good. I'm glad you decided not to paint over the oak."

Jeanette puts her arm around Diane, who's holding Bret's hand. She says, "Y'all are going to love living here."

Diane smiles and nods. "Especially after seven years in that little trailer."

Leland says, "Well, I'm going to miss that trailer. It got us through some tough times."

Mr. Henderson puts his hand on Leland's shoulder. "Don't worry, son. It won't take you long to get used to the extra space, especially all the closets that you and Red built in."

"That was Diane's idea. She wanted lots of closet space."

Jeanette asks Red, "How long will it take to move Leland's workshop over here?"

"Not too long. We had the concrete company pour the foundation for the workshop when they poured the foundations for the house and the garage. And the construction company will take care of installing the utilities."

Mr. Henderson says, "That reminds me, Red. Do you remember when I first bought my house and had you expand and upgrade the bathroom for the master bedroom?"

"Yes, sir."

"I need some more cabinet space in there. Could you build me a matching cabinet for the opposite wall of where you built the one that I have now?"

"I'm sure I could. I'll come by and measure and take some pictures."

Leland says, "Shouldn't I be the one to make the cabinet for you, boss? You know, to kind of in a small way thank you for the furniture that you're giving us?"

Mr. Henderson smiles. "Sure, but I was going to pay Red. However, if you want to do it as a favor, I'd appreciate that."

Red says, "We'll do it together. Leland's workshop is not set up yet, so we can do it at my shop, and I won't charge anything, either."

"Why thank you, Red, just let me know when you want to come by and look at the bathroom."

Jeanette says, "I know it's none of my business, Mister Henderson, but it sounds like you're going to be making a lot of changes in your house. Any particular reason?"

"Yeah, I've got a family event planned, and I want the house to get dolled up a bit before the event. And since I know next to nothing about interior design, Beverly and her friend Emma have offered to be my designers."

Diane asks, "Who's Emma, Mama? Do I know her?"

"Do you remember Emma Holman, who used to babysit you sometimes when you were little?"

"Of course I do. I really liked her, but I thought that she moved somewhere out of state."

"She did. Her husband's in the Air Force, and they were living in Texas. But Emma and her daughter Melanie moved back here at the end of May to stay here for about a year and a half. They're going to live in her old family home and fix it up while her husband is stationed in Turkey. By the way, her last name is now Crawford. Anyway, I ran into Emma the other day at the paint store. She told me about moving back temporarily. While she was telling me about how they were redecorating the old homeplace, she happened to mention that one of the changes they were making to the living room was based on a design that she had come up with when she was studying interior design.

"When I heard that, I asked her more about her interior design training, and then, of course, I recruited her to help me with Mark's house. I called Mark right then from the paint store and asked what he was willing to pay to have a professional interior designer help me. You know how Mark is, he said 'Whatever's fair.' So, I made a deal with Emma right there in the store. She said it would help her, too, because she would use the money that she makes decorating Mark's house to spend on her house."

Just then, Bret breaks free from Diane and starts running across the kitchen. Diane walks after him saying, "Come here, Bret, let me show you to your new room." Bret doesn't pay any attention to her. He runs out from the kitchen and into the dining room with Beverly and Diane chasing him. Then he runs back to the kitchen where Leland scoops him up.

After an hour or so of thoroughly examining Leland and Diane's new house, the group goes over to Mr. Henderson's house to have a fried chicken dinner that Beverly has prepared. There, the conversation continues about the new house. In the midst of the group's discussion, Beverly gets a commitment from Diane to have this year's Christmas Eve dinner at the new house.

After they've eaten dinner, Mr. Henderson asks Red and Leland to come with him to the library to talk over some business. The three of them get comfortable in the library, and Mr. Henderson begins, "I went down to the Liberty Hotel today to check it out, and things are looking very good. And they're about a month or so ahead of schedule, which is good because the members of the hotel company want the hotel's grand opening to be on July fourth of next year.

"I also talked to David Dunham last night about their factory project, and he says that the factory could potentially be ready for business as early as the middle of November of next year. David said that they'll be able to start renovating the glass plant buildings earlier than they originally thought because, as you know, Brock is going to shut down production in mid-October so that they can have more time to move out the leftover inventory and all their equipment. That's also why Beverly will be able to retire two months earlier than expected. Anyhow, David told me that he and Mister Brock agreed that after Brock starts clearing out the plant, Dunham can start their renovations so long as they won't be in the way of the Brock employees."

Red says, "Sounds like things are really cooking, boss, because the city, the county, and the utilities company are all ahead of schedule, as well."

Mr. Henderson says, "Let's keep our fingers crossed that nothing slows down progress. And our company can help things move along for Dunham by getting an early order for the lumber they'll need for the renovations and for those additional buildings that they'll be constructing. They can warehouse that lumber in one of the empty warehouse buildings on the glass plant property. I'll give David a call about that on Monday, so that they can work up an initial order for us and also arrange for security at the warehouse where they'll be storing the lumber."

The following weekend is spent by Diane and Beverly on getting Diane's new studio organized and ready to use. Immediately after completing that task, they get back to working on their paintings for the upcoming December art show.

As planned, Brock Glass Company ceases production on October thirteenth and begins to clear out the factory building and the warehouses. Three weeks later, the first members of the Dunham construction crew come to town to assess the plant building and begin preliminary work for the renovation. The foreman of the Dunham crew also prepares an initial lumber order that Red immediately begins to fill.

Chapter Twenty-three

On December 8, 1995, Frank, Melanie, and three gallery volunteers are putting last minute touches on the displays for the next day's show. One of the volunteers, a college art student named Judy Graddick, is hanging five of Diane's paintings on the same wall on which Diane's paintings hung the year before. After she hangs the last painting, Judy stands back for a better view of the display. She says to Frank, who is working at the panel next to hers, "My goodness, Frank, every single one of these paintings is just great. I bet they all sell."

Frank says, "When you finish hanging those, come over here and look at these paintings by her mother. They're just as good."

Judy makes an adjustment to one of the paintings that she has just hung. Then she walks over to where Frank is hanging the last of Beverly's four paintings. She says, "You're right. I never would have thought that there were two artists this good living in Libertytown. Where'd they come from?"

"From right here, believe it or not. While you were away at school, Melanie discovered them both and convinced them to start participating in our shows. The exposure and reception they've gotten has been good for both them and the gallery."

The next day at four o'clock, Frank unlocks the gallery door. He opens the door a few inches and sees that there is a line of at least twenty people waiting to come in to see the exhibit. When Frank is spotted by an elderly couple standing at the front of the line, he opens the door wide and motions them in. As he is welcoming the other people in line into the gallery, Frank can see cars parking across the street and more people walking down the sidewalk toward the gallery.

Leland stops his pickup in front of the gallery at a few minutes after four and lets Diane out. Then he goes searching for a parking space. As he is exiting his truck at a parking spot on the next block, he sees Mr. Henderson and Beverly walking down the sidewalk toward him. He calls out, "Hey, you two want some company?"

Beverly waits for Leland to lock his truck door, and then she walks over to him and gives him a hug. As the three of them are walking to the gallery, Mr. Henderson asks Leland if Diane is already there. "Yes, sir. I dropped her off at the front door and then went to park."

"That was a gentlemanly thing to do. I probably should have done that."

Beverly pulls Mark's arm toward her. "Just remember to do that in the future."

When they get to the gallery, it is already crowded. There are people at every section of the exhibit, and Leland can see that several of them are already talking to Frank about making purchases. Leland says, "Boss, if you plan on buying anything, you better not wait too long."

"Don't worry, son, I've already put my order in with Frank. I'm buying two of Beverly's pieces to hang in my library along with those two of Diane's that are already in there."

Beverly says to Leland, "He wouldn't let me give them to him."

Leland winks at Mr. Henderson. "That's cause he knows you can use the money."

Diane is standing in front of her exhibit talking to a young couple when she sees Leland and waves to him. Just as Leland gets to Diane, she is approached by a young woman in tailored black slacks and a dark gold silk blouse. The young woman extends her right hand toward Diane and says, "Missus Johnson, I'm Emily Dunham. I love your work. Could I have a few moments with you to talk about a business proposition?"

Diane takes her hand and says, "Glad to meet you, Miz Dunham. This is my husband, Leland. And, sure, I'd be glad to talk with you if we can find someplace quiet enough."

"We can use Frank's office. I've already asked."

Leland whispers, "Go ahead," and the two young women walk toward the gallery office.

They walk into the office and settle into two of Frank's chairs. Diane turns to Emily and asks, "You did say your name is Dunham, didn't you? Are you related to the Dunhams who are going to build a factory here?"

"I did, and I am. My husband is David Dunham. He's here in the gallery somewhere."

"My husband Leland met your husband a while back. He really likes him. They're working on some kind of deal together."

"It's good that Leland likes David, because it was David who asked me to talk to you."

"What did he want us to talk about?"

"Your art. You probably don't know it yet, but David and I bought all five of your pieces tonight."

Diane blushes. "Why, thank you so much. That was really nice of y'all."

"You're welcome, but it was our pleasure. We love every one of your paintings. That's why I want to talk business with you."

"What kind of business?"

"I know that you're probably not familiar with our company's products yet, but we have been making in Pennsylvania, and we'll soon be making at our new factory here, a line of high-end furniture to sell to upscale hotels and resorts."

"I did hear something about that from Leland."

"Well, as the company's chief interior designer, I help the buyers of our furniture design the interiors into which the furniture is going. And my designs almost always include original paintings. So, here's my proposal. I'd like to contract with you to sell us during the next twelve months six original paintings of subjects and sizes to be agreed upon by you and me. At the end of that period, you and I will decide whether we want to terminate the contract or extend it. And if we decide to extend it, we can also modify it as needed."

"That sounds interesting. What size paintings do you think you would you need?"

"Most would be eighteen by twenty-four, and our offer is to pay you twelve hundred dollars for each painting, and we'd reimburse you for your cost of materials. We can arrange for different prices for other sizes."

"So far that sounds great. What subjects are you thinking about for the paintings?"

"What if we start with landscapes, still lifes, and flowers? In other words, nothing different from what you've already been painting."

"I think I might like to do it, but do you mind if I talk to my husband before I make up my mind?"

"Of course not. Here's my business card. Just call me when you're ready to talk again."

Emily hands Diane a light gray business card on which the Dunham logo is embossed in dark gold ink. Then Emily reaches into a folder that she's carrying and hands Diane a two-page document. "This is a draft of the contract that I'm proposing. We've used this format with other artists, but we can always make whatever changes you and I agree on."

Diane takes the contract and looks at it. Then she folds it twice and puts it into her small black purse. She says, "Thank you so much for buying the paintings today, and I'll get back with you right away about the contract."

Emily and Diane walk side by side to where Leland is still standing. Emily smiles when she sees that Leland is now talking to her husband David. She says, "Well, you two seem to already know each other. Diane and I were just getting acquainted."

David says, "That's what I told Leland. I said that I hoped you were in there trying to get a commitment from Diane to do some paintings for our customers."

Emily says, "Well, Leland, now that everyone else knows what I want, how do you feel about it?"

"It sounds pretty good from the little that I've heard from David. But I'll need to know the details before I can form an intelligent opinion."

David gives Leland an understanding nod, then he points toward the other side of the lobby and asks, "Who's that with Mark Henderson?"

Diane turns to look. "That's my mother. They're friends."

Emily says, "Your mother's very pretty."

"Thank you. I'll tell her you said so. Did you see her paintings, Beverly Randall?"

"I did. They were very good. I bought two. Do you think that she might also be interested in being a contract artist?"

"I'll have to ask her. Then I'll let you know."

David takes Emily's arm and says, "Time for us to go. We've got to catch the flight home."

Emily says to Diane, "You have my number and email address, Diane. Please let me know what you decide."

"I will. Y'all have a good trip home."

As soon as Emily and David have left for the door, Frank comes up to Diane and says, "Did Emily Dunham tell you that she bought all of your paintings?"

"She did, and I told her that was very nice of her."

"I think that she may want some more."

"Well, she left me her business card. I'll talk to her soon."

Frank reaches to shake Leland's hand. "Leland, I'm so sorry I didn't say hello to you just now, but I guess I was too excited about Diane's good fortune."

Leland shakes Frank's hand. "That's okay, Frank, I understand."

Beverly comes up to Diane and puts her arm around Diane's shoulders. She says, "Frank told me you sold out tonight. That's great. I'm so proud of you."

"Well, Mama, it was all to one lady, so I'm not sure what that means."

"It means that someone really likes your work."

Later that evening, Beverly, Diane, and Leland are sitting in Mr. Henderson's newly repainted and redecorated family room where Mr. Henderson is brewing a pot of decaf at his coffee bar. Diane gets up and walks around the room to look at all the changes that have been made since she was last there. Then she asks Beverly to show her the other rooms that Emma and she have redecorated.

When they get back to the family room Diane says to Mr. Henderson, "I've never seen a house this beautiful, and I still can't believe the expensive furniture that you gave us for our new house. I don't know how we can ever repay you for that."

"I'm sure we'll think of something someday. And remember, Leland's going to have to refurbish most of that old furniture. It's pretty worn down. Also, he's already added that cabinet for me in the master bath. But, enough about that, let's look at your draft contract with Dunham that Leland told me about."

Diane hands the contract to Mr. Henderson who sits in his recliner and looks it over. Then he hands it to Red for his review. After Red hands him back the contract, Mr. Henderson recommends to Diane that she have Dunham include a clause whereby Diane would retain the right for some designated time period to make and sell prints of all paintings covered by the contract. Red nods in agreement and recommends an additional provision that each of Diane's paintings have a small brass plate attached to the frame, stating the title of the painting and the name of the artist. Mr. Henderson gives his thumbs-up approval of Red's recommendation.

Diane says, "I really appreciate you taking the time to help me on this, Mister Henderson. You, too, Daddy Johnson."

Mr. Henderson says, "Glad to." Red reaches over and gently squeezes Diane's hand. He says, "You just don't know how proud I am of you."

The doorbell rings, and Mr. Henderson excuses himself. There are voices at the front door, and soon Mr. Henderson escorts Emma and her daughter, Melanie, into the dining room. Beverly stands up and walks over to Emma. She gives Emma a hug and says, "What a nice surprise."

Emma looks around the room and asks, "Anybody need a babysitter?"

With a stunned look, Diane gets up and walks over to greet Emma. "I can't believe that I'm seeing you again after all these years. And you look so good."

Emma smiles, "Not so fat anymore, huh. And you are just beautiful yourself." Emma motions for Melanie to come over. "Mel, I want you to meet an old friend of mine, Miz Diane."

Melanie extends her right hand and says, "Glad to meet you, Miz Diane."

Diane gently shakes Mel's hand. "Glad to meet you, too, Mel. Come have a seat."

Diane introduces Emma to Leland, Red, and Jeanette. Jeanette says, "I hear from Beverly that you're the brains behind the transformation of Mark's house."

"Thank you, but it wasn't all me. Miz Beverly and Mister Mark had a ton of ideas. It was my job to figure out a way to make everything they wanted fit together, and I am proud of the way everything turned out."

Beverly says, "Emma, you need to drop by Leland and Diane's new house and give them some ideas on decorating it. They could use some help."

Diane says, "Boy, could we. Right now, we have stuff stacked every-where, because Leland and his daddy are still working on a lot of what will be going into the house. But I'm not about to ask you to take your time to help us. I heard that you've got your hands full right now redeco-rating your family home."

"After how good Beverly has been to me since I've been back, I'll be glad to help. But I'm afraid I won't have time to do any hands-on redecorating. What I can do is come by one day and see if I can help y'all get started in the right direction. You and I can make a list of things you could do."

"Do you and Mel have any plans for Christmas Eve?"

Emma looks at Mel. "Not yet."

"Good. I'll get back to you about joining us for Christmas Eve dinner once we settle on a time."

On the following Monday evening, as soon as she gets home from work, Diane calls Emily Dunham. After a short, pleasant discussion, they come to an agreement that generally follows the terms of the draft contract, but which gives Diane a three-year, non-exclusive license to make and sell prints or other reproductions of each painting that Diane sells to the Dunham company and provides that there will be a brass nameplate on each of Diane's paintings. Emily likes the brass nameplate idea and makes a note to herself to use engraved brass plates on all their paintings.

During that phone call, Emily tells Diane that she failed to mention the other evening that the twelve-hundred-dollar price for her paintings would be for unframed pieces, since the Dunham company will be making frames to coordinate with the décor in each setting. Diane says how much she appreciates that, because otherwise she was going to have to ask Leland to make the frames, and she already has him refurbishing furniture and building a shoe rack for her closet. After the discussion about a contract for Diane, Emily asks Diane about the possibility of a contract with Beverly.

Diane says, "I talked to her about it, and showed her the draft contract. She told me that she was very appreciative of Dunham offering me a contract, and also appreciates your interest in her work, but that she'll be too busy for the foreseeable future to enter into a contract herself."

"I understand, but please let me know if she changes her mind."

Chapter Twenty-four

On the Monday after the December art show, Diane parks her car in the lot behind the diner. She is humming one of Leland's songs to herself as she gets out and starts walking toward the front door. Just before she reaches the door, she sees Melanie and Beth about half a block away, walking toward the diner. She waves to them before she heads inside.

A few minutes later, the Moore sisters come in and take their seats at the counter, Diane comments, "I've never seen you two here this early. Are y'all going somewhere else when you get back home?"

Beth says, "We've got to take Mother to the Mobile airport. She's going to Atlanta for a few days to visit her family."

"That's nice."

Melanie asks, "Nice of her to visit her family, or nice of us to take her to Mobile?"

Diane smiles. "Well, both I guess."

Melanie says, "Sorry for being snippy. I just can't wake up this morning. Do you have any truck driver coffee?"

"I'll get you the extra dark roast. What about you, Miz Lancaster?"

"Good gracious, girl, when are you going to start calling us by our first names?"

"I don't know. I respect y'all so much that I'd be a little uncomfortable doing that."

Melanie says, "Don't be silly. Please call us by our first names. We'd prefer that."

Diane takes a deep breath. "Well, okay. What about you, Beth, what do you want this morning?"

"The usual. I wasn't up as late as Melanie."

Diane turns around to the coffee urns to fill the sisters' orders. As she's filling the second mug with Melanie's extra dark roast, she hears her name being called. When the mug is full, she turns back around and sees Emma Crawford and Melanie standing just inside the door. Diane carefully sets the hot mugs in front of the sisters, who have also turned around to see who's coming in. Then she walks around the end of the counter to go speak to Emma. When Diane is near enough, Emma reaches out and pulls her close and wishes her good morning.

Diane says, "Y'all come on in and have a seat."

The Moore sisters are watching Diane and Emma. Beth asks Melanie, "Did you know they knew each other?"

"Nope."

Emma and Mel sit at a table away from the door to avoid the cold draft. When Earline comes over to take their order, Diane says to Earline, "Take good care of them." Then she says to Emma, "Let's talk in a few minutes." She pats Emma on the shoulder and goes back behind the counter to serve another customer, a young sheriff's deputy who looks as though he might have been up all night.

After she takes the deputy's order for pancakes and coffee, Diane asks the Moore sisters if they need more coffee. Melanie moves her mug toward Diane and says, "Hit me."

Diane refills Melanie's mug.

Beth quietly asks Diane, "How is it you know Emma?"

"Believe it or not, she was my babysitter for a while when I was real young."

Beth raises her eyebrows. "Well, who would have thought that? Did you already know that she was back in town before you saw her just now?"

"Not for long. I found out at Mister Henderson's house the night of the December art show. Emma and Mel dropped by while some of us were having coffee there."

When she sees the surprise on Melanie's face, Diane says, "Oh, I guess y'all didn't know. My mother and Emma redecorated some of Mister Henderson's downstairs rooms. He invited us over to have coffee and look at what had been done."

Beth looks at Melanie. Melanie says, "Well, it's about time somebody updated that mausoleum. How does it look?"

"Prettiest place I've ever seen. You need to go by there."

Beth says, "We will. I've got to see it. You know, I saw a big van out in front of the house when I was driving by one day about a month ago, but I didn't give it much thought."

Melanie looks at Beth. "That's not like you. I would've thought you'd stop the car and run over to see what was going on in there."

Beth says. "I know. I must have been in a hurry."

Diane asks, "Will y'all please excuse me. I've got to tell Emma something."

Beth says, "Sure. Tell her we said hi."

Diane waves to Mel as she approaches the table. Mel and Emma are having waffles and milk. Diane asks "Is everything all right? Can I get y'all anything else? By the way, the Moore sisters say hi."

Emma waves to the Moore sisters. "We're fine. These waffles are great. What did you want to talk about?"

"The invitation is still good for Christmas Eve dinner. That way, you can get a free meal, and I can get some advice about decorating the house."

Emma looks at Mel. Mel smiles and nods yes.

"What time?"

"Everybody should be there by no later than five o'clock. We'll eat at around six."

Emma asks Diane to write down her address and phone number, which Diane does on a paper napkin. She hands the napkin to Mel, who looks at it then gives it to her mother.

Christmas Eve morning of 1995 is unusually nippy, so Leland

lights the gas logs in the family room for the first time since they were installed. When the flames appear, Bret points and excitedly yells, "Fire." Then he walks over to the fireplace and holds out his hands to feel the warmth.

When Diane hears Bret yell "Fire," she scurries into the family room. When she sees that it is the fireplace that has Bret so excited, she breathes a sigh of relief and says, "That looks so pretty. You know, this is the first time I've seen the logs lit. What do you think, Bret?"

"I like it, Mama."

The doorbell rings, and Bret runs to answer it. He opens the door and sees Grandpa and Grandma Johnson. He jumps up into Red's arms and holds onto his neck. Red carries Bret into the family room and sits him in Leland's recliner.

Leland says, "Y'all are awfully early. It's only 10:15."

"Your mother insisted on coming over this morning to see how she could help Diane."

Diane says, "Come on in the kitchen, Mama Johnson. I can sure use your help. I've never cooked for this many people before."

Red says to Leland, "The house looks a lot better than when I was over here last week. I can see you've been busy moving furniture in."

Leland nods his head. "Yeah, but it's about to wear me out. Diane keeps changing her mind about where she wants things."

From the kitchen comes, "I heard that, Leland."

Red looks around the room again. "That sofa y'all got from Mr. Henderson really looks good in here."

"It does. You did a super job on the upholstery. But, man, that thing is heavy. I should have waited for you to help me move it. I had to slide it in here on some torn down pasteboard boxes."

Red lifts one end of the sofa. "This *is* heavy. It must have a lot of bracing in it because it's made for commercial use. Next time, call me. Don't hurt yourself."

"Believe me, I will."

"Got any coffee? I can't stay. I'll just have a cup and then run over to the sawmill. Then I'll come back this afternoon."

"What are you going to be doing at the sawmill today? There won't be anybody else there."

"That's why I'm going today. I've got to make some adjustments to the new equipment that was installed last week. It's best to do that when everything else is shut down."

"Well, be careful. Don't cut any body parts off. Do you want me to go with you?"

Red stares at Leland. "No, I can handle it. Just shut up and get me some coffee."

"Yes, sir. Have a seat on our new sofa, and I'll bring your coffee."

By four o'clock, Jeanette and Diane have everything ready for dinner except for the two pecan pies that are still cooling. Diane says, "If you'll cut those pies for me when they cool off, Mama Johnson, I'll go clean up now and put on some fresh clothes and be right back."

"Take your time, sweetheart, I've got it under control."

Just as Diane leaves, Leland comes through the back door with grease on the front of his work shirt. Jeanette says, "Good gracious, Leland, go get cleaned up and put on some clean clothes. Your company's going to be here soon."

Leland looks at the kitchen clock. "You're right. I didn't realize what time it was. I need to get on it." He heads for the bedroom.

Red returns at 4:40 in starched blue jeans and his new black corduroy shirt.

Diane walks in from the bedroom and says, "You look handsome Daddy Johnson, with your red hair and that black shirt."

"Thank you, baby. I think I'll wear this outfit next time I'm on stage. With my black cowboy hat, and maybe some shades."

"That'll look good. And I want to hear you and Leland play again."

At 4:55 the doorbell rings, and once again Bret runs to answer it. This time it's Mr. Henderson and Beverly, carrying gifts for Bret to place under the tree. They put four gaily wrapped boxes near the tree, and Beverly says, "Bret, how about helping us by putting these presents in the right place under the tree."

Bret says, "Yes, ma'am." He then carefully picks up each of the four gift boxes, in turn, and looks for a place under the large fir tree to put it. After he puts the last box under the tree, he claps his hands and proclaims, "All done."

Beverly says, "That's my Bret" and musses his dark hair.

While Bret is carrying out his gift placement duties in the family room, Mr. Henderson is in the kitchen asking Jeanette if there's anything that he can do to help.

"Oh, no. But thank you for asking. Neither of the other two men around here has offered to help us."

Mr. Henderson laughs. "You don't want those two in your kitchen. Cooking is not within their skill set."

"Yeah, you're probably right. But they could at least *offer* to help before I run them out."

At exactly five o'clock, the doorbell rings again. Once more, Bret runs toward the door. When he opens the door this time, he sees Emma and Mel. Mel says, "Hi, Bret. Merry Christmas."

Bret looks at Mel and yells, "Merry Chimmas." Then he runs into the kitchen, laughing and calling for his Mama.

By six o'clock the food is on the table, and everyone is seated. Beverly asks them to bow their heads, and then, as she did the Christmas before, she gives thanks to the Lord for His son Jesus, for the food they are about to eat, and for the love and affection they all have for one another. This time when they all say "Amen," Bret joins in right on cue.

While they're eating, Emma asks Diane if the sofa in the family room is the one that they got from Mr. Henderson. When Diane confirms that it is, Emma says, "I can hardly believe it. It looks brand new now, and I love the fabric that you picked out."

Diane says, "I can't take any credit for the sofa. Red and Leland finished it before I ever saw it."

"Who did the upholstery?"

Leland answers, "Daddy."

"That is a flawless job, Mister Johnson. Where did you learn to do upholstery?"

Leland says, "Prison."

Emma looks startled, but when everyone else starts laughing, she realizes that Leland is joking. She says, "That was mean, Leland. Talking about your father like that."

"Stick around. He'll get me back."

After the meal, when all the guests are sitting in the family room having coffee, Diane says, "I'm so glad that y'all came over tonight. I can't remember a better Christmas Eve."

Mr. Henderson says, "Tonight reminded me of the Christmas dinners my family used to have when I was growing up back in McKeesport. And since we're all here together, I have an announcement to make about another family matter."

Jeanette asks, "What's that?"

"You're about to have a new family member in the very near future."

There's a murmur around the table as everyone looks at Diane, who says, "Oh, no. Don't look at me."

Beverly laughs as she reaches over to hold Mr. Henderson's hand. She says, "Mark, look what you've done. Just come on out and say it."

"The new family member is going to be me. I've asked Beverly to marry me, and she has graciously accepted my offer."

Diane looks at Leland, who is smiling. Leland says, "So that's why you needed another cabinet in the master bath. I kind of suspected that was what it might be, or at least I was hoping that was it."

Red lifts his glass of iced tea and says, "Congratulations, you two. *I* never suspected it, but I'm glad to hear it."

Emma smiles and looks around the table. "You know, even though I'm not part of this family, I feel like I am tonight. Is there a date for the wedding?"

Beverly says, "February seventeenth. Mark's mother and brother are coming down to stay with him for a few days, and we're going to get married at my church while they're here, and then we'll have a reception at the house. The wedding is going to be family only, but you and Mel are more than welcome to come to the reception at our house after the ceremony. We'd love to have y'all."

Emma looks at Mel and says, "We'll do that."

Leland says, "Well, I, for one, am looking forward to this wedding. Two of my favorite people are getting married. That is so cool."

Diane, who is sitting next to Beverly, takes Beverly's hand in hers and says, "Me, too. I just know y'all are going to be so happy together."

Mr. Henderson says, "And there's one more thing. On the night of the fourth of July, Beverly and I are going to be the first ones to have a party in the Liberty Hotel ballroom. We're going to throw an Independence Day party for our company employees. So, Red, you and Leland need to start practicing. Your band is going to be the first act to perform at the new ballroom."

Red looks at Jeanette. "That sounds good to me, honey. That ballroom has one fine sound system." Then he turns to Mr. Henderson. "Oh, one more thing, boss, can I call you Mark now?"

"Not until February the seventeenth, and even then, not at work."

At the end of the night, Mr. Henderson motions Leland into the kitchen.

"Yeah, boss, what is it?"

"I've got a check for you."

"For the trailer?"

Mister Henderson nods and hands Leland a check written on the Henderson Properties account. "This is payment for the trailer. I've got a bill of sale back at the office that I had our company lawyer draw up for us. You and Diane will need to sign the bill of sale before a notary and then get it back to me as soon as you can."

Leland takes the check and looks at it. "Wait a minute, this is more than we talked about."

"What the hell, it's Christmas Eve."

Chapter Twenty-five

CHRISTMAS 1995 IS ON A COLD MONDAY. THE MOORE FAMILY ARE having their Christmas dinner at the elegant home of Horace and Sarah Moore. John and Beth Lancaster, George and Melanie Pebworth, and their three children are there. Grandfather Moore and his wife Abigail are not. They are spending Christmas week at the Cove Eleuthera in the Bahamas.

The family is sitting around the long Chippendale dining table when Sarah picks up a silver dinner bell and signals for their cook Shantell and her helper Denise to bring the food and drinks. Shantell and Denise carry the dinner in on large silver platters and serve each member of the family beginning with Sarah and Horace.

Once dinner is on the table, Shantell asks Sarah if they need anything else, and Sarah says, "Not until dessert, Shantell, thank you."

While they're eating, Melanie asks, "Mother, do you remember me telling you about Emma Crawford coming back to town to fix up the old Holman place?"

"Yes, dear. I do remember that."

"Well, I was driving by the Holman house this morning, and I saw her working in the yard, so I stopped and chatted with her for a few minutes. And you'll never believe what she told me."

Sarah puts down her fork and leans over the table. "What did she tell you?"

"She said that she ate dinner last night at the home of Beverly Randall's daughter, Diane, and found out that Mark Henderson and Beverly are getting married in February."

Sarah raises her eyebrows. "My, that's interesting. I would have thought that Mark could do much better than her."

Horace looks up from his plate and says, "Now, what do you mean by that, Sarah? Beverly's a fine person."

"Oh, I was thinking about the social class difference."

Horace smiles and shakes his head.

Beth, who had already heard from Melanie about the engagement, says, "I don't know about social status, but that will certainly be a huge step up for Beverly in terms of financial status." She turns to her husband. "John, what do think Mark Henderson's net worth is?"

"Honey, you know I don't discuss our customers' finances."

"Okay, then what's his company worth? That should be a matter of public record."

"Oh, all right . . . Let me see, his company here is a division of Allegheny Lumber Mill and Millworks, which is headquartered in Pennsylvania, and from what I can tell from articles that I've read in business magazines, their overall organization is probably worth around a hundred fifty million."

Sarah inhales a deep breath. "My goodness. I had no idea."

Horace taps his fork against his wine glass. "Okay, that's enough talk about other people's money. Let's eat."

Sarah says, "No, no, Horace. I've got to know more." She looks at John and asks, "Who owns Allegheny Lumber whatever you said?"

"Well, I'm still not all that comfortable talking about Mister Henderson's finances, but since that's also a matter of public record, I guess it won't hurt to tell you. The company is owned one-third by Mark Henderson, one-third by his brother Sean, and one-third by a family trust fund that provides for their mother and is also available for schooling and college tuition, and travel abroad, and such things as that for her grandchildren and great-grandchildren. Mister Henderson's father and the two sons established the trust fund not too long before the father died in a plane crash some time ago. Mister Henderson and his brother also control the assets of the family trust."

"Wait a minute. John, are you telling me that Mark Henderson is worth fifty million dollars?"

"No, ma'am. I'm saying that's about what his share of the lumber company is worth. He also has other business and personal assets. Now, please forgive me, Mother Sarah, but I've already said more than I feel comfortable saying about Mister Henderson's finances. He's very protective of that kind of information."

Sarah looks at Horace then back at John. "I just can't believe that scruffy old Mark Henderson is worth fifty million dollars. My goodness, I've seen him walking around town in wrinkled overalls and an old khaki work shirt. And now, on top of that, he's going to marry that religious kook, Beverly Randall."

With a wry smile, Beth says, "Now, Mother, you heard what John said. The fifty million is only a part of his fortune."

Melanie adds, "And Beverly's not a religious kook, Mother. I've gotten to know her pretty well, and I think that she's a very smart, talented person. She might be a little unpolished and a tad eccentric about her religious beliefs, but she's far from being a kook."

With a stern look, Horace says, "Now, come on, that's just about enough everybody. Let's have no more money talk and no more gossip. Let's please enjoy our dinner together."

George says, "Thank you, Horace. We just need to be grateful today for how blessed we all are as a family and not be concerned over what someone else has or doesn't have. I mean my company just had one of its best years ever, and I'd rather think about that tonight."

"I'm with you, George," says John. "My bank is doing great right now. We're about to open another branch in north Carleton. And I do have to admit that a lot of our success is attributable, in one way or another, to things that Mark Henderson has done or is doing."

Sarah glares at John, and then at George, and then at Horace. She snatches the napkin from her lap and excuses herself from the table. She walks from the dining room into the library where she sits at her

Chippendale desk with the napkin still in her hand and mulls over what she has just heard.

As Sarah is sitting at her desk tapping her long red fingernails on the desktop, Daphne, Beth's younger daughter, comes into the library and softly asks, "What's the matter, Grandmother? Are you okay?"

Sarah forces a smile. "I'm fine, dear. I just need a minute to sort something out. Why don't you go on back to the dining room. I'll be in there shortly."

"Yes, ma'am."

At around nine o'clock on the morning of the Wednesday after Christmas, Melanie is sitting in a wooden swing on her front porch bundled up in her new black hooded puffer coat, a red wool scarf, and her black woolen cap. She's waiting for Beth to come out from her house to join her for their morning walk.

Melanie sees Beth coming out her front door in her dark gray hooded puffer coat and takes one last swig of her hot chocolate that is now luke-warm. She places the half-full cup under the swing. When she and Beth meet on the sidewalk, they feel a steady winter breeze blowing down Main Street in their direction.

Beth pulls her dark blue Auburn woolen cap down over her ears. "We must be crazy, being out in this cold."

Melanie answers, "You know why we're out here, because it seems that every time we stay home from our walks, something interesting happens that we miss."

"That's true. Remember that time we stayed home and then found out later that the Burkes had gotten drunk and had a shouting argument in the middle of Main Street."

Melanie laughs. "I do remember that. By the way, whatever hap-pened to the Burkes and why in the world were they both drunk at nine o'clock in the morning?"

"Lord knows why they were drunk at that time of day, but I heard from their former housekeeper that they moved shortly after that big argument to a swanky retirement village in Boca Raton."

"I hope they don't get thrown out of *there* for fighting in the street."

"Last I heard they were still down there."

After they've walked a few blocks toward downtown, Melanie says, "You know I still can't get it out of my head that Mark Henderson is worth over fifty million dollars, maybe considerably more than that."

Beth laughs. "Hey, you're not the only one. I was afraid that Mother might have a stroke the other night. She may never get over finding that out. Personally, I have no problem with him being obscenely rich. I just can't understand why he's not marrying some hot twenty-five-year-old trophy wife."

"Now that part I can understand, because he's about the most unconcerned person I've ever met when it comes to social status or impressing other people. He seems impervious to that sort of thing. And as much as I hate to say it, I think that he and Beverly are probably a good match."

They walk another block. Beth asks, "How old is Mark anyway, fifty-three? That means that when he retires in another fifteen years or so, Leland will probably take over as head of the lumber company. And have you thought about the fact that Beverly Randall, who's about forty-two, is almost certainly going to outlive Mark and someday be the richest woman in Creek County?"

"Of course I've thought about all that, and for some reason that I can't explain, it gets under my skin."

Beth looks at Melanie and laughs. "It's because you're a spoiled shallow woman, just like me."

Melanie opens her mouth as if to say something but doesn't.

After they've walked a little farther, Melanie says, "You know what just occurred to me, Beth. Beverly won't have to wait until Mark dies. As soon as they get married, she'll already be the richest woman in Creek County."

"You're right. I hadn't thought of it that way. Now *I'm* annoyed. A few days ago, I was kind of enjoying the fact that Beverly was going to have to rely on you and Frank to help her sell her paintings now that the glass plant has shut down, and she would be needing the money. And now we find out that she won't be needing anything from any of us. And by extension, neither will Diane."

When they get to the diner, the sisters immediately look for Diane. They see her serving waffle plates to Judge Bailey and Phil Bernstein. Diane sees the sisters and smiles at them. They smile back and go over to hang their coats on the tall coatrack at the end of the counter before they take their seats.

After the sisters have been there a few minutes and Diane is serving them coffee, Beth asks, "Diane, do you realize that when your mother marries Mark Henderson, she's going to be the richest woman in Creek County?"

Diane looks surprised. "Really? Is Mister Henderson that rich?"

Melanie says, "He sure is."

"Well, I doubt that Mama even knows that. But it wouldn't matter to her. She's just not made that way."

Beth says, "But that also means that you'll be the only child of the richest couple in Creek County. That'll make you the sole heir to their wealth."

"Well, I don't want to think about either one of them dying. I hope they both live to be a hundred."

Beth and Melanie look at each other, then Beth lays her hand on top of Diane's and says, "You're a good daughter, Diane."

On the way home, Beth asks, "Sis, did you ever wonder what it would be like to have a naïve, innocent mind like Diane's? I mean, she's a smart girl, but she doesn't seem to comprehend what's about to happen to her life, with her art career flourishing like it is, and her mother marrying Mark Henderson."

"No. I've never wondered what it would be like to have a mind like that."

Chapter Twenty-six

It's eleven o'clock on the morning of February 15, 1996, two days before the wedding. Beverly is sweeping dead leaves off the front porch of Mark's house and talking to herself about the terrible weather that came into south Alabama the night before from the northwest. "Why aren't we getting married in June like everybody else?" she asks herself. Then she immediately smiles and says, "Nope. I don't want to wait till June. I'm not getting any younger."

At 5:40, Beverly is in the library dusting furniture. She hears Mark's truck come into the driveway, then hears the truck door shutting. In a few minutes, Mark comes through the front door into the foyer, carrying his briefcase and a thick folder. He calls out, "My goodness, Bev, this frigid weather reminds me of home."

Beverly walks up the hall from the library to the foyer. She hugs Mark and kisses him on the cheek. "Well, now I know why you left."

"I saw that you swept all those dried leaves off the porch. It looks much better now."

"I'm going to check the upstairs porch afterwhile. It probably has leaves on it, too."

Mark puts his briefcase and folder on the sofa in the foyer and takes off his coat and lays it on a shelf in the foyer closet. He retrieves a faded University of Pittsburgh sweatshirt from the closet and says, "Let me get a cup of coffee in me and put on this sweatshirt, and I'll help you with the upper porch."

Beverly says, "Okay, that would be great. You know, I'm a little nervous about it, but I'm really looking forward to meeting your mother tomorrow. I'm looking forward to seeing Sean again, too."

On his way to the library to unload his briefcase and papers, Mark says, "So am I. And I know that Mother's going to love you to death. She likes strong, independent women. Now, she may not be obvious about it, because that's not her way, but she'll like you." He takes off his dress shirt as he walks to the kitchen.

Beverly is looking at a photo of Mark's mother that's sitting on a shelf in the library. "Your mother is very attractive. She must have been beautiful as a young woman."

Mark pokes his head from the kitchen doorway. "She was. When we have time, we can try to find that old photo album of mine that's full of family pictures. It's around here somewhere."

Still looking at the photo of Mark's mother, Beverly says, "She looks tall in this picture."

"She's about five seven or so. She used to be a little taller when she was younger."

"How old is she here?"

"Maybe seventy-one. She's seventy-six now, but still looks about the same. She takes very good care of herself. Walks almost every day and does yoga a couple of times a week."

"I hope I look this good at seventy-one."

Mark finishes his coffee then tugs the wrinkles out of the Pitt sweatshirt that he has slipped on. "I'm sure you will. But what else can I help you with today besides the upstairs porch?"

"Other than that, I think we're in good shape, except that there are some big boxes in the foyer closet that you need to move to the attic so that we can use that closet for hanging coats."

"Yeah, I've let that closet get pretty cluttered. I'll move those boxes after we take care of the porch."

Mark and Beverly walk up the stairs together to one of the guest bedrooms. They walk across the room, and Mark opens the door to the upper porch. When Beverly turns on the porch lights, they see that the wind has blown dried brown leaves into little piles that are scattered among the porch furniture. Mark lays down the plastic trash bag that he's holding and reaches for the broom and dustpan that Beverly is carrying. "Why don't you stay inside, Bev. I'll take care of this. Just have some hot chocolate ready when I finish."

"Okay. While you're sweeping up the leaves up here, I'll get those boxes out of the foyer closet and straighten up the closet. You can carry the boxes up to the attic when you get a chance."

Mark steps out onto the porch and starts sliding furniture away from the leaves. "Okay, but don't forget about my hot chocolate. I'm going to need it after being out here in this cold wind."

In about twenty minutes Mark walks into the foyer and sees Beverly sitting on the floor with a cup of coffee beside her and a pile of documents in front of her.

Mark picks up Beverly's coffee cup and takes a sip. He asks, "What are you doing, Bev?"

"Just poking around in this stuff that fell out of one of the boxes. I'm sorry, I didn't mean to be nosy, and I'm also sorry that I haven't gotten around to making your hot chocolate."

Mark says, "Oh, that's all right," then he sits down on the floor across from Beverly and starts picking up some of the documents and looking at them. He laughs. "There are some things in here that I've been looking for." He holds up a small white booklet. "Like this program from my college graduation ceremony at Pitt. The other day, I was trying to remember the names of two of my classmates who I haven't seen in about thirty years."

Beverly asks, "Can I see that?"

Mark wipes the dust off the program with the palm of his hand and hands it to Beverly. She looks at it for a few moments and says, "This is interesting. Believe it or not, this is the first college graduation program I've ever seen."

Mark gets up from the floor. He says, "Well, why don't you just sit there and look over it while I go make us some hot chocolate."

Mark walks to the kitchen and opens the cabinet where he keeps his hot chocolate mix. He heats a small pitcher of milk in the microwave. Just as he finishes pouring the hot milk into two tall mugs, Beverly walks in with the graduation program in her hand. "This program says that you have a Master of Business Administration. I didn't know that."

As he's mixing the hot chocolate in one of the cups, Mark says, "No reason you would. It doesn't come up in a conversation very often."

"But that's something you should be proud of. Where's your diploma?"

"I'm not sure. Probably in one of those boxes."

"Well, I guess when we get around to looking for your family photo album, we can also look for your diploma."

Mark hands Beverly her mug of hot chocolate and says, "Okay, if you're that interested, we'll look for it sometime. But be careful with this cup, it's hot."

Mark later takes the three boxes from the foyer to the attic, and Beverly vacuums the foyer for the second time. They move to the library where Mark lights the gas logs in the fireplace and relaxes in his recliner, where he starts to read a contract that he's taken from his briefcase. After she drinks her hot chocolate, Beverly stretches out on the wide sofa and closes her eyes. With her eyes still shut, she adjusts the throw pillow under her head and asks, "Do you know how much I love you, Mark?"

"I don't know, a million?"

Beverly laughs. "No, at least a billion."

"Wow, that's a lot. I don't know if I deserve that."

"How much do you love me?"

"Oh, at least a couple of dozen."

Beverly rises from the sofa smiling. "Okay, smarty, I'm going home. I'm tired and I'm sleepy."

Mark gets up from his recliner and walks over to Beverly. He holds her tightly and gently kisses her lips. She tastes like chocolate. He says, "I'll be glad when *this* is your home."

"Me, too. But it won't be long now."

After Beverly leaves, Mark sits in his recliner with a fresh mug of hot chocolate and reads a few more of his work documents. Then he puts the papers back into his briefcase and picks up his college graduation program from the coffee table where Beverly left it. He carefully reads through the names.

After he reads through the program, he closes it and places it on the end table next to his recliner. He takes a sip of hot chocolate and lies back in the recliner. He lets out a sigh then softly quotes Shakespeare to himself, "All the world's a stage, and all the men and women merely players; they have their exits and their entrances, and one man in his time plays many parts. . ."

Mark closes his eyes and thinks of the classmates whose names he has just read. His thoughts then turn to Vietnam, and he recalls the faces of the young soldiers with whom he served. He feels a mixture of pride and great sorrow as he pictures the three brave men whom he lost in combat. He wonders where the others are now.

Then he thinks of Stella and Virgil, and his eyes moisten.

Mark dries his eyes with his shirt sleeve and takes a deep breath. He studies the silent flames of the gas logs in the fireplace. A feeling of solace comes over him as he sees the faces of Beverly and Diane in his mind's eye. He lifts his mug in a toast to his good fortune and drinks the last of his hot chocolate. He rises from his recliner and sets the empty cup on his desk. Then he turns off the gas logs and the lights as he leaves the room. He slowly walks down the dark hallway toward his bedroom.

Chapter Twenty-seven

At around 4:15 the next afternoon, Mark is sitting at his desk at the sawmill when Sally buzzes him and tells him that Sean is on line two. Mark picks up the phone. "Hello, Sean, where are you?"

"We're about an hour or so away."

"How's Mother?"

"She fine. A little tired, but otherwise good."

"So, she never changed her mind about not flying."

"She not only insisted that I drive her down, but that we come in her Mercedes." Sean chuckles. "She's giving me a dirty look now, so I have to say what a great traveling companion she is. Actually, it's been a pretty good trip, and this car *is* more comfortable than my Land Rover, so I guess I shouldn't complain."

"Well, tell Mother that I can't wait to see her. I'm going to be heading home in a few minutes, so I'll be there waiting for you and Mother. You'll like the changes we made in the house. Beverly and a friend of hers redecorated the downstairs for me."

"I'm glad to hear that. It was looking a little worse for wear."

"It looks good now. Drive carefully."

After his call from Sean, Mark calls Beverly to tell her that his mother and brother will soon be arriving in Libertytown. Beverly tells him that she'll get dressed and meet him at the house.

A few minutes after Mark gets home, he hears Beverly opening the front door. She finds him in the kitchen making coffee and gives him a quick kiss on the back of his neck. He's still in the light blue dress shirt and wrinkled khaki slacks that he wore to work.

"I'm so nervous, you wouldn't believe it," Beverly says.

Mark looks at Beverly. She's wearing a red turtleneck sweater, black jeans, and stylish black leather boots. Against her red sweater is a tiny silver cross hanging from a delicate silver chain.

Mark says, "Don't be nervous. Mother's going to love you. Want some coffee?"

"No thanks. Are you sure she's going to like me? I mean, I'm sure she's used to hanging around with high society folks."

"Just relax. There's no doubt in my mind that she'll like you more than those dull society women. Just have a seat. They'll be here shortly, and you'll see."

In about ten minutes, the doorbell rings. Mark takes Beverly by the arm and starts walking her toward the front door. Beverly says, "I don't care what you say, I'm still nervous."

"It'll be fine."

When Mark opens the door his mother rushes in and wraps her arms around him. She kisses his cheek and asks, "Where's your bathroom?"

Mark looks at Beverly. "Beverly, please show Mother the way to the bathroom."

"Of course," says Beverly, as she gently takes Missus Henderson's upper arm. "Please come with me, Missus Henderson."

Mrs. Henderson looks into Beverly's face as they begin the walk down the hall. "So, you're Beverly. You're very pretty, Beverly, and please call me Joanne."

"Why, thank you, Joanne, for the compliment. Mark can tell you that last night I was looking at a photo of you and told him that I thought you were very attractive."

"Did you say 'for such an old lady'?"

Beverly laughs and says, "No." Then she shows Joanne a door to their right. "That's the bathroom door. Let me know if you need anything."

Beverly walks back to join Mark and Sean in the foyer. "I like your mother, Mark. She told me I was pretty."

"Well, you are, sweetheart."

"Somehow it meant more when I heard it from your mother."

Mark shakes his head and says, "Well, I'm going to help Sean with their luggage. Why don't you and Mother wait for us in the family room?"

Beverly goes to the family room and takes a seat on the new brown leather Empire sofa next to Mark's new brown leather recliner. She picks up a magazine from the coffee table. She puts it back without opening it.

Joanne walks in and asks, "Where're the boys? Getting our luggage?"

"Yes, ma'am. Would you like something to drink?"

"Thank you, I would. I'd like a glass of ice water."

"Well, have a seat, and I'll get it for you."

"I think I'll walk around the room a bit first to get the kinks out of my back."

Beverly returns in a few moments with the water. She sees Joanne standing at the bookcase where Virgil's photograph is displayed. "He was such a handsome boy. Such a shame that he died so young."

Beverly sets the glass of water on a coaster on the coffee table. "It was. Mark still misses him terribly."

"And then he lost Stella not long after that." Joanne turns to Beverly and softly says, "I'm so glad he found you. I didn't like thinking of him alone in this big house."

"Well, I'm certainly glad that we found each other. He's something special."

"Yes, he is. Both my boys are."

Beverly again takes a seat on the sofa. Joanne picks up her glass of ice water from the coffee table and sits in an overstuffed leather chair across from Beverly. She takes a sip of water. "That's feels good. My throat was dry. Thank you."

"You're welcome. How was the trip down?"

"I enjoyed it. I hadn't ridden through the South since I came down here for Stella's funeral. And we spent the night at a nice motel in Charlotte, North Carolina. I've always liked Charlotte."

"I've never been to North Carolina. What do you think of Libertytown?"

"I like what I've seen. It reminds me of some of the small towns in Pennsylvania."

"I grew up in Dothan. It's more of a mid-sized town."

"I know."

"Mark told you I grew up in Dothan?"

"No, dear, I'm not sure how to tell you this, but I had you checked out by a friend of mine who has a detective agency."

Beverly grins broadly. "No, you didn't."

Joanne's eyes twinkle as she smiles. "Oh, yes, I did. I had to assure myself that you weren't someone just interested in Mark's money. But don't worry, dear, you checked out fine. The detective who did the investigation told my friend that you may be the most upright person that he ever investigated. Of course, there *were* those nine months or so that you spent in a commune in California, but you were only a teenager then, so we can discount that."

Beverly shakes her head. "Yeah, I was such a dumb kid back then."

Joanne nods. "Don't worry. Now that I've met you, I think we're going to be the best of friends."

"You know, I get that same feeling. It makes me feel a little silly about how nervous I was about having to meet you."

Mark comes into the room announcing, "Everything's been unloaded and put in the proper bedrooms. Of course, Mother, I gave you the best guest room."

"That's only right, darling, I did give you birth."

Mark looks at Beverly, who's smiling at Joanne's comment.

Sean walks in with a cup of coffee and stretches out in Mark's recliner. He says, "You were right, Mark. The house looks great. Mother, did you know that Beverly recently redecorated the first floor here?"

"No, I didn't know that. But I did notice how wonderful the foyer and this room look. Beverly will have to show me the rest of the downstairs."

"I'd love to, but I have to give most of the redecorating credit to a friend who helped us with it. Her name is Emma. She's a trained interior designer. You'll meet her at the reception here tomorrow night."

The doorbell rings. Mark goes to let in Leland and Diane. He brings them into the family room and says to Joanne, "Mother, this is my new daughter-to-be, Diane, and her husband, Leland."

Diane walks over and takes Joanne's hand. "I'm so glad to meet you, Missus Henderson."

"And I'm glad to meet you, Diane. You're very pretty, just like your mother. She and I have been getting acquainted. I'll have to get her to tell me all about you, since I'm going to be your new grandmother."

"And I'll have to get her to tell me all about you, too."

Beverly says to Joanne, "Leland's been working for Mark for years at the lumber company. He's now Mark's assistant."

"Well, Leland, how do you like the sawmill business?"

"Love it, ma'am. And I especially like working for Mister Henderson."

Sean adds, "Leland and his father, who also works at the sawmill, are helping with the restoration of that old hotel that I showed you on the way in."

"The Liberty Hotel. I love that name," says Joanne.

Leland says, "Yes, ma'am. We're proud to be a part of that project."

The small talk continues as they have a dinner of homemade vegetable soup and grilled cheese sandwiches. After thirty minutes or so, Joanne sleepily announces that it's her bedtime. She excuses herself and asks Beverly to show her to the guest room, but to take the long way around so that she can see all the downstairs first.

Beverly comes back after taking Joanne upstairs to her room and suggests that they all call it a night so that Sean can also get some rest.

Sean and Mark exchange good nights while Beverly walks Leland and Diane to the front door and bids them good night. When she comes back into the family room, Mark is standing in front of the fireplace. Beverly stands behind him and softly says, "Well, Mark, tomorrow's the day."

Mark turns around and reaches for Beverly. "Indeed it is. I was beginning to wonder if it would ever get here."

"Me, too."

Chapter Twenty-eight

February seventeenth is a pleasant winter day. That afternoon, Mark and Beverly ride with Sean and Joanne to the True Believers Church of Libertytown on County Road 12 just outside of town. As they approach the simple white country church with the tall steeple, Joanne says, "This church looks just like something from a movie. It's beautiful."

Beverly says, "This is a special place to me. It's where I truly found myself."

Mark gently squeezes Beverly's hand. "When you walk into the sanctuary, Mother, you get a sense of calmness. There's nothing fancy about the church inside or out, but as Bev says, it does feel like a special place."

Joanne says, "Well, it's special today for certain. This is the perfect place for a simple wedding for two special people."

"We'd better hurry and get inside before this talk gets any mushier," says Sean.

Mark reaches over the seat and thumps the back of Sean's head. Everyone laughs as they exit the car.

The four of them walk up the front steps of the church. Pastor Robert Downs opens the door and says, "Welcome to our modest house of the Lord." Pastor Robert is a middle-aged man of medium height and an athletic build, dressed in a charcoal gray suit. He has neatly combed light brown hair and a ruddy complexion. He shakes each person's hand and says a few words to each as they enter the church.

As he shakes Joanne's hand, she says, "This is a beautiful church you have, Pastor Robert."

"Thank you, ma'am. We're blessed to have a generous congregation who help us keep our church in such fine condition. And Sister Beverly is one of our most dedicated members. She's always there when we need her."

"I'm sure she is. And she speaks very highly of you." Joanne looks around, then asks Pastor Robert, "Where would you like my son and me to sit?"

"Well, since it's only the immediate families, everyone can fit in the front row. That would be more intimate, anyway. Why don't y'all go have a seat down there while I greet these other folks coming in now."

Pastor Robert returns to the front door where Jeanette and Red are coming in, followed by Leland, Diane, and a wide-eyed Bret. Pastor Robert greets them, then leads them to the front row of pews.

After everyone is seated, Pastor Robert stands at the pulpit and in a resonant baritone begins, "I see that everyone is here now. Let me first say that I've never seen a more attractive group of people. And I really appreciate Mark and Beverly granting me the honor of presiding over their wedding in our humble little church." He turns to the organist and says, "Sister Nell, if you will, please play the betrothed in now. They're waiting back in my chambers."

Sister Nell nods to Pastor Robert and begins to play Dean Martin's "Everybody Loves Somebody." As Beverly and Mark enter the sanctuary from the pastor's chambers, Mark blows a kiss to his mother, and Joanne begins to tear up. "Everybody Loves Somebody" was her husband's favorite song, and when they were teenagers, he dedicated it to her on a local radio show. Sean whispers to her, "That song was for you, Mother."

Joanne whispers back, "I know. That was sweet of them."

Beverly takes her position at the altar in her dark rose long sleeve knotted shirtdress. Diane smiles at how beautiful she looks. Mark stands across from Beverly in his pinstriped navy suit and looks into her blue eyes.

Pastor Robert solemnly recites his simple wedding sermon, and Mark and Beverly exchange rings. Pastor Robert declares them man and wife, and Mark gives Beverly a quick kiss before she grabs him in a bearhug as the family members applaud.

That night at the reception, the newlyweds and their family members welcome Emma and Mel, the Moore sisters and their husbands, Judge and Mrs. Bailey, Phil Bernstein, Theo Bellos, Earline and her sister Katherine, Ron Anderson, and numerous of Mark's employees from the sawmill, most of whom brought their spouses.

About an hour into the reception, Phil Bernstein gets Mark's attention, and that of Judge Bailey, and motions them into the foyer where they see a very tan, dark haired, well-dressed young man whom neither Mark nor Judge Bailey recognizes.

Phil puts his arm around the young man's shoulders and says, "Gentlemen, this is our new hotel manager, Mister Raymond Dadurno. He has twelve years' experience in hotel-motel management on the Gulf Coast, and I convinced him that the Liberty Hotel is the place he needs to be. If you two have no objection, he'll start on May first and hire a staff, order supplies, and do whatever else he needs to do to get the hotel ready to open by the end of June."

Mark says, "Raymond, don't look so nervous. The Judge and I gave Phil the authority to search the Gulf Coast for a talented young hotel manager, and if you have his blessing, you also have ours. Welcome to Libertytown."

"Judge Bailey extends his right hand to Raymond. "Welcome to Libertytown, Raymond."

Raymond visibly relaxes as he shakes Judge Bailey's hand and says, "I'm really looking forward to this opportunity. Mister Bernstein took me through the hotel last week, and I think that y'all have done everything right in the design and the concept of the hotel. I've never seen such attention to detail. I'll be honored to be a part of the team."

Mark calls Red, Leland, and Ron Anderson into the foyer and introduces them to Raymond. He says, "These are the guys who are responsible for that attention to detail you noticed."

Raymond shakes hands with each of the three and tells them how much he's looking forward to getting the hotel open for business. Red gives Raymond his business card and tells him that Leland and he will be glad to help him move into the manager's quarters whenever he's ready.

Mark motions to Theo to come into the foyer. While Theo is making his way there from the far side of the family room, Mark says, "Okay, Raymond. Now I've got some news for *you*. Theo's nephew Angelo, who worked in Theo's diner until he started college, just graduated from South Alabama with a degree in hospitality and tourism management, and he has agreed to run our coffee shop. With that in mind, Theo and Angelo set up an LLC that the hotel will contract with to operate the coffee shop. Under that agreement, the hotel will provide space, equipment, utilities, maintenance, security, insurance, advertising and so forth, and the LLC will provide the staff, food supplies, etcetera for the coffee shop."

Raymond says, "That sounds like a smart way for a small new hotel to handle the situation. But, as Mister Bernstein and I have discussed, what we'll also need to do is develop a business plan that starts out with a coffee shop that, as food demands increase, will evolve into a soup and sandwich shop. And then, at some point down the road, we'll want to explore the option of having an in-house café with a full-service menu."

Mark looks at Judge Bailey who turns to Mr. Burnstein and says, "I believe that you made a good choice, Phil. This boy thinks like a businessman."

When Theo gets to the foyer after negotiating the crowd and speaking to several people along the way, Mark introduces him to Raymond, who shakes hands with Theo and tells him he understands that he and Angelo will be contracting to run the hotel coffee shop.

Mark tells Theo what Raymond just said about developing a business plan for the evolution of the coffee house into a soup and sandwich with the possibility of someday making it a full-service cafe.

Theo turns to Raymond. "Tell you what, Raymond, I think Angelo would really go for that. He loves the restaurant business, and I know he would welcome the opportunity to expand the coffee shop into a sandwich shop, and then a café at some point. As Mister Henderson knows, Angelo worked in my diner for two years before he left for college, and then he worked his way through college as a cook at Charlie C's Steak and Seafood House in Mobile. So, he knows the food service business from a real-world perspective and not just from studying it in college. As far as I'm concerned, we can write up that business plan as soon as Angelo moves back to town."

"Just give me a call when he gets settled in, and we'll knock out the plan."

Mark says, "All right, gentlemen, now let's get back to the party. It's almost time for Red and Leland to play some music for us. Raymond, you come with me, and I'll introduce you to some of the folks here."

Red and Leland go into the library and unpack their acoustic guitars from their cases. After they tune the guitars, they take them to the area of the family room that Mark and Beverly have cleared out for them. They each take a seat on their respective wooden stools, and Red gives out a loud whistle. Once the crowd has quieted down to the point where they can hear him, Red says, "Folks, the newlyweds have asked Leland and me to play a few songs for you tonight, and we hope you enjoy them. We're going to start off with Leland singing "Everybody Loves Somebody," an old Dean Martin hit which I understand has special meaning to Mark's Mother. So, Miss Joanne, this is for you."

Joanne winks at Red and bows her head in appreciation.

Leland and Red entertain the group for about another forty minutes, finishing their set with one of their original compositions, "Right Love, Wrong Time." At the end of that final song, Red says, "That's a song that Leland and I wrote a couple of years ago that got recorded last year by Leon Dickey on what has been a pretty successful album called 'Country Boy.' And, by the way, it just so happens that our song has been nominated this year for a Grammy Award for best country song. So be sure to tune into the Grammy Awards show on February twenty-eighth on CBS and look for us in the audience. Leland and I are pretty sure that the winner is either going to be 'Go Rest High on That Mountain,' a Vince Gill song, or LeAnn Rimes's 'Blue,' but we're still going to be out there in Los Angeles all decked out with our fingers crossed."

Applause and whistles fill the room.

Diane, who's standing right in front of Red and Leland, looks at Leland and mouths, "Really?"

Leland smiles and shrugs his shoulders. Then he nods in the affirmative.

Diane rushes up to Leland and hugs him. "I'm so proud of y'all."

"Thanks, babe. But it's just a nomination. It's not an award."

"Hey, a nomination for a Grammy is a big deal. Only five country songs a year get nominated."

"Well, yeah, since you put it like that . . ."

Mark makes his way to Red and says, "As you know, I know next to nothing about music, but even I can tell that's a great song you guys just played."

"Thanks, boss. We think it's one of our best. But we were still shocked to hear about the nomination. By the way, if we ask real nicely, will you give Leland and me a couple of days off to go to Los Angeles for the awards show? Leon's record label has offered to pay all of our travel expenses if we go."

"Only if you agree that if you win, you'll mention our company when you make your acceptance speech."

"You got it, boss."

After the reception is over and everyone else has left, Mark and Beverly sit in the library with Sean and Jeanette. Jeanette is having a glass of white wine. The other three are drinking hot chocolate.

Sean says, "Hell of a day, brother. I've never seen so many people in such a good mood."

Beverly slaps Mark on the thigh and says, "Yeah, even those Moore sisters seemed to be enjoying themselves. Well, sort of, anyway."

Mark chuckles.

Jeanette takes a sip of her wine and looks at Beverly. "I really liked your minister, Pastor Robert. I can see why you're so fond of that church."

"Yes, ma'am. He's a good man, and he's given me good counsel more than once."

"Would you mind if my wedding present to you and Mark was a donation to your church."

"Not at all. I can't think of a gift I'd like better."

Mark says, "Thanks, Mother."

Jeanette finishes her wine and looks at the empty glass. She sets it on Mark's desk. "Well, I've drunk my wine, and now it's time for bed." She gets up and goes to each of her sons and kisses him good night. Beverly gets up to walk Jeanette to her bedroom. When they reach the bedroom, they embrace and say good night to one another.

While Beverly's gone, Sean bids Mark good night, slaps him on the back, and retires to his bedroom.

Beverly is greeted by Mark at the library door when she comes back downstairs. He gently kisses her on the lips and says, "Can you believe that we'll finally be spending the night together."

Beverly pulls him to her and whispers, "You know, this all seems like a dream to me. I didn't know I could be this happy."

"This is only the beginning, sweetheart."

Chapter Twenty-nine

MONDAY MORNING OF THE WEEK AFTER THE WEDDING IS WET AND cold. It's a few minutes after nine when Earline and Diane see the red-cheeked Moore sisters burst through the front door of Danny's Diner.

Earline says, "Man, they look cold."

"They sure do. Let me go take care of them."

Diane walks over to the sisters and says, "It's looks like y'all could stand some hot coffee. Have a seat and I'll get it for you."

Melanie and Beth take their usual seats at the right end of the counter and sit there rubbing their hands together. Melanie says to Beth, "I can't stop shivering."

Beth snickers. "What exactly is wrong with us, going out on a day like this."

"I don't know, but we've still got to walk back home."

Beth looks out the front window. "The sun's broken through now. It won't be so bad going back."

Diane sets a steaming mug of coffee in front of each of the sisters. "Y'all are tougher than I am, being out there in this weather."

Beth says, "Not tougher, just dumber."

"Amen," agrees Melanie.

Diane says, "Well, y'all just sit here and get warm, and let me know if you want a refill. I'm going over to take care of Judge Bailey now. He looks cold, too."

As Diane is walking to Judge Bailey's booth, she sees that he's taking off his black leather gloves and rubbing his hands together. Diane smiles and says, "Good morning, Judge. What can I get you? Something warm, I bet."

"Good morning, Diane. First, please bring me a hot cup of coffee as soon as you can, and then bring me a waffle with a side of bacon. And some maple syrup."

"Yes, sir. Be right back."

Diane goes back behind the counter. She hands Judge Bailey's order to Theo and goes to check on the Moore sisters. Beth says to her, "We'll take you up on those refills, Diane."

Diane pours them each another mug of coffee and says, "It sure was nice of y'all to come to the reception Saturday night."

"It was our pleasure," says Melanie. "And you were right about the house. It looks beautiful now. I know your mother is going to love living there."

"Oh, she is. She's the happiest I've ever seen her. She's like a different person. She's so relaxed now, being newly married on top of being retired. I feel so good for her. She deserves to be happy."

Beth says, "She did look different the other night, like she didn't have a care in the world."

Melanie asks Diane, "Are you and she still painting together?"

"Oh, yeah. She took a few days off before the wedding, but we'll be getting back together this afternoon when I get home. Actually, she'll probably already be there painting by then. She's working on a picture of their house for Daddy Mark's library."

"You're calling him Daddy Mark now. That's sweet," says Melanie.

Diane laughs softly. "I'm still not sure he likes it, but it feels right to me."

Beth asks, "Did I hear correctly the other night that a song that Red and Leland wrote has been nominated for some kind of award?"

"Yeah, they were nominated for a Grammy for best country song of the year. Isn't that something?"

"It sure is. And didn't Red say that they were going to be on television?"

"They are. They're flying out to Los Angeles to be on the show on the twenty-eighth of this month."

Melanie says, "That's next week."

"It is. They'll be flying out next Tuesday morning."

"Are you going with them?" asks Beth.

"No. Mama Johnson and I are going to watch the show on television together at our house. And I can't wait till Bret sees his daddy on TV. He'll have a fit."

The sisters finish their coffee, pay their bill, and bid Diane goodbye.

"You were right," Melanie says to Beth on the walk back home. "It feels about ten degrees warmer now."

"Yeah, it's gone from horrible to just miserable. What do you think about Leland and his dad getting nominated for a Grammy?"

"It's surreal. I've never known anybody before who got nominated for a Grammy. But that *is* a good song they wrote. Do you think they made any money off it?"

"Oh, I'm sure they get royalties from the album. I'll have to ask John what kind of royalties songwriters get."

Two hours after they get home, Melanie gets a call from Beth.

"I asked John when he got home about how much Red and Leland might have made from their song. He told me that he had heard more about the nomination on the radio and was also curious about that. So, he called a friend of his in the music business in Atlanta and asked what he thought. His friend said that based on what he had heard about the album, it would probably wind up selling around two hundred thousand copies, and that would mean that Red and Leland would get around fourteen thousand dollars in royalties, maybe a little more."

"Interesting."

"But John said that they would continue to get royalties on the song as long as the album is still in production, and, also, if anybody else records the song, they'll get royalties from that other recording as well."

Melanie thinks for a moment. "Well, fourteen thousand dollars is not that much."

Beth says, "No, it's not. It'll barely pay for their trip to Los Angeles."

Chapter Thirty

Red and Leland land at LAX on Tuesday morning and take a taxi to the Four Points by Sheraton where Leon Dickey's record label has made a reservation for them.

When they get to the Shrine Auditorium on Wednesday evening, Red and Leland are led by an usher to the seats designated for them. Leland is wearing black jeans with a black western style sport coat over a red cowboy shirt. Red is similarly dressed except that he's wearing a yellow cowboy shirt. They're both wearing black cowboy hats and black snakeskin cowboy boots.

After they're settled into their seats, Leland turns to Red and says, "This is really something, isn't it?"

"Just take a good look around and let it soak in, Leland. We may never be back here."

"What are you going to say if we win?"

"Well, if we win, I'm going to thank the Academy for honoring us and thank Leon Dickey for putting our song on his album, and then I'll say hello to Mister Henderson and all the guys back at the Allegheny sawmill in Libertytown."

"We're not going to win, are we Daddy?"

"No. I'm pretty sure it's going to be Vince Gill."

Back home, Diane and Jeanette are intently staring at the television set in the family room of the new house. Bret is lying on the floor in front of the TV looking for Daddy.

"There they are," says Jeanette. Right at the bottom of the screen."

"Bret, do you see Daddy?" asks Diane.

Bret excitedly jumps up and points at the screen. He yells, "There's Daddy and Granddaddy on the telebision."

About an hour and a half into the broadcast, there's an announcement that the award for best country song is coming up right after the commercial break. Diane wakes up Bret and sits him next to her on the sofa. She says, "Pay attention, Bret, they're going to show Daddy again."

Sure enough, as the presenter recites the nominees for best country song, the camera goes to Red and Leland who are sitting tensely in their seats, and once again Bret shrieks, "There's Danny and Granddaddy on the telebision."

"And the winner is . . . 'Go Rest High on that Mountain,' songwriter Vince Gill."

"Shoot," says Diane.

"Shoot," says Bret, who immediately starts laughing.

"Well, I'm still proud of my boys," says Jeanette.

On Thursday night, Diane and Jeanette pick up Red and Leland at the Mobile airport. They look a little worn down as they place their suitcases into the trunk of Diane's Toyota, but when Jeanette asks if they had a good time, Red says, "The best. We even got to meet Leon Dickey and Vince Gill after the show, and they were both as nice as they could be."

Leland adds, "And this Nashville A&R guy came by and congratulated us and asked if we had any songs that hadn't been recorded yet. So, naturally, Daddy reaches into his coat pocket and whips out a demo CD that's got five of our songs on it."

"Always be prepared," says Red, with a big grin on his face and a forefinger to his right temple.

Bret, who has been napping in the back seat, wakes up and reaches for Leland. He groggily says, "I saw y'all on the telebision two times," then falls back to sleep.

They ride home with Bret sleeping in the back seat between Red and Leland.

When Leland gets home, he checks the phone for messages and finds one from Bonita Franklin, the cultural arts reporter for the *Creek County Courier* whom Red and he had met at the Main Street Gallery. She wants to know if she could interview Red and Leland one day soon about their experience at the Grammy Awards Show. Leland writes down the phone number that she left and puts it in his wallet. He makes a mental note to get with Red and call her back on Friday afternoon.

Leland and Diane are cleaning up the kitchen after dinner when Leland gets a call from Red. Red tells Leland that since he got home, he's gotten three calls from A and R guys at different record labels, and he'll be mailing each of them a demo CD. Then they schedule a time to call Miss Franklin.

When Red and Leland get to work on Friday morning, they each find a message that Mr. Henderson wants to meet with them in his office at nine o'clock. When they get to Mr. Henderson's office just before nine, Sally tells them that she saw them on the Grammys show, and they looked very handsome. As Red is thanking Sally for the compliment, Mr. Henderson's office door opens, and he waves them in.

"I need to meet with you two about the Dunham account as well as a potential new account with a furniture maker in South Georgia. But, first, I've got to tell you how proud I was to see you guys on television being nominated for a prestigious award. And Beverly was just giddy about the whole thing. And I'm sure that you don't know this, but one of the announcers described you two as sawmill workers from Liberty-town, Alabama. That made my night."

In the cultural events section of the next week's issue of the *Courier* is an article describing Miss Franklin's telephone interview with Red and Leland about their experience at the Grammy Awards Show. After Diane reads the article to Bret, she says, "Now, that was a very nice article, wasn't it Bret honey?"

"Yes, ma'am."

Chapter Thirty-one

At 3:50 in the afternoon on Independence Day, 1996, the tem-perature in Libertytown is ninety-six degrees. Red parks his pickup behind the Liberty Hotel near the loading dock. He and Leland exit the truck with their guitar cases. They're dressed in the same black jeans and cowboy shirts that they wore to the Grammy Awards Show. They enter the hotel ballroom by a side door that Raymond has left unlocked for them. Red sets his guitar case down, then turns around and locks the deadbolt behind them.

Leland sets his guitar case down on the newly waxed ballroom floor. He says to Red, "It feels good in here. It's stinking hot outside, and I've got soft since I started working in an office so much."

Red says, "Yeah, it is hot out there, but it'll be cooler when we load up after the show."

Leland walks out to the middle of the ballroom floor to look at the stage where their band set up their drums and sound equipment the night before. He takes a long look around the ballroom and says to Red, "They must have put up the Fourth of July decorations this morning. This really looks great, doesn't it? How about those American flag curtains they hung up in the back of the stage."

"Yeah, everything looks good," says Red as he surveys the room. He puts his right hand over his heart. "Makes me feel patriotic."

"I know you're kidding, Daddy, but there is something about celebrating freedom that makes you feel good. And I think this is going to be a good show, even though we only had about a forty-minute run-through last night."

"We'll be fine. We all know those songs. We've played them a thousand times. But you know what, you're right about celebrating freedom. Sometimes we just don't appreciate what we've got."

"Yes, sir, I was thinking about that last night when I was watching 'Saving Private Ryan' on TV."

"Good movie," says Red as he starts walking toward the door to the hallway. "How about we talk to Raymond for a few minutes while we're waiting for Cecil and Gary. I want to ask him how things are going."

Leland follows Red into the lobby. Leland looks down and says, "I really like the way this white marble floor turned out."

"It's Alabama marble from Talladega County."

"That's what Mister Henderson told me. He called it 'Sylacauga marble.'"

Red says, "Yeah, I've heard it called that before." He points down the hall. "There's Raymond coming this way now."

Raymond sees Red and Leland and salutes. When he gets to them, he shakes their hands and says, "I can't wait to hear your band tonight. What I heard of your rehearsal last night sounded great."

"Yeah, we're pretty good if you like an old-fashioned honky-tonk sound," says Red.

Raymond says, "You know, I've heard that term all my life, but I'm still not exactly sure what it means. How would you define what honky-tonk music is?"

Red smiles. "Well, Doyle Brice, an old ex-bandmate of mine, used to say that honky-tonk was music that makes you want to drink beer and dance with a fat girl. I think that sums it up pretty good."

Raymond laughs. "Only in Alabama would you hear that kind of definition."

Leland raises his right fist into the air. "Here's to Alabama. Wouldn't want to be anywhere else tonight."

Red asks, "What about the hotel, Raymond? How's the first week going?"

"Pretty well. Very few glitches, almost no complaints from the guests, and a lot of compliments."

"I like the way y'all named the coffee shop the 'Liberty Bell Coffee Shop.' How's it been doing?" asks Leland.

"It's running smooth as silk. You can tell that Angelo's been around the restaurant business all his life. He's the reason that I don't believe it'll be long until the coffee shop develops into the 'Liberty Bell Soup and Sandwich Shop.'"

Raymond turns toward the front door and leads Red and Leland to the middle of the lobby where he puts his hand on top of a six-foot wide, round mahogany table sitting directly under the antique chandelier. He asks, "Did you notice this new table? Dunham delivered it this morning."

Red and Leland lean down and closely examine the table.

Red runs his hand along the edge of the table. He says, "Man, this is some quality craftsmanship. Those Dunham folks really know what they're doing."

"I've already had several compliments on the table as well as the chandelier."

Leland looks up at the Waterford crystal chandelier, then back at Raymond. "That's a beautiful chandelier. And what about the marble floor? What do folks think of it?"

"Everybody loves this floor. And I think they're going to like the red oak floor in the ballroom, as well."

Red nods and says, "That is a nice floor in there. That red oak was Ron Anderson's idea. He'd used it before in a performance arts center in Biloxi." Red looks around the lobby. He says, "You've got quite a place here, Raymond."

"Hey, you two had a lot to do with it."

Leland says, "All we did was make recommendations and check on the construction every once in a while. You've got to give Wolff Construction and their subs all the credit for the quality of the renovation. And I don't believe anybody could have done a better job than they did."

Raymond tells Red and Leland that *South Alabama Living Magazine* is coming by in a few days to photograph the hotel and interview

Raymond and Mister Henderson for an article to come out in the next issue.

"That certainly won't hurt business," says Red.

Leland taps Red on the shoulder and says, "Hey, there's Cecil and Gary coming in the front door," Red turns around to see two men with longish brown hair in black jeans and gray cowboy shirts with white pearl snaps. The men both look to be in their late forties. The one carrying a Fender guitar case is tall and thin. The other man is shorter with a slight paunch pushing against his large silver belt buckle. He has two sets of drumsticks in his hands.

Red says to Raymond, "Guess it's time for us to start getting ready for the show. We'll see you in a little while."

"Let me know if you need anything."

Leland leads his bandmates into the ballroom and onto the stage. In a few minutes, Red comes into the ballroom and joins them.

The band spends the next twenty minutes or so completing their setup, tuning guitars, and adjusting the volume and tone on the amps and microphones. Red says, "Let me go out front and see how everything sounds out there."

Cecil does a drum intro, and Gary and Leland follow on guitars. Leland plays his black Stratocaster first, and then picks up Red's black Telecaster and plays a few bars on it.

Red calls out, "Cecil, turn the drum mic down a little. Gary, turn the bass amp volume up a little. Leland, back off a little on the treble on your guitar amp, and up the volume a little on mine. Once y'all do that, Leland, you test the vocal mics."

The band makes their adjustments, and Leland walks up to the right-side microphone stand that's holding a Shure SM58 and starts singing 'Help Me Make It Through the Night.'

Red says, "The volume's good, but back off on the reverb a little. This room has a lot of natural echo."

Leland adjusts the reverb dial for the right-side mic, then walks back to the front of the stage and sings into the mic on the left side of the stage. Red tells him that mic also needs less reverb. When he's satisfied with the sound, Red comes back onto the stage. He smiles and says, "Y'all won't believe how good the house P.A. sounds out there. Now, let's set the monitors, and we'll be ready."

Once the band members are satisfied with the monitors, they walk down the stage stairs and take seats at one of the two tables that have "Reserved for Band" signs on them. Red looks at his watch and sees that it's 4:25. He says, "They'll probably start arriving soon. We supposed to do the intro music at five unless the boss holds it off for a few minutes if folks are still coming in."

Just then, Mark and Beverly Henderson walk in, along with Jeanette and Diane. Gary and Cecil move to the other band table, and Jeanette and Diane take their seats. Beverly takes a seat at a nearby table reserved for "The Hendersons and Guests." Mark walks over and introduces himself to Gary and Cecil, who are looking very relaxed. Mark turns to Red and Leland. "Ready, guys?"

Leland replies, "Yes, sir. Do you still want the intro song to be 'Only in America'?"

"Yeah, you guys play that, and then I'll come up and welcome everybody and give my little spiel."

In a few more minutes, Gary and Cecil's wives come into the ballroom to join Gary and Cecil at the other band table.

Several sawmill employees, most with their spouses, come by and tell Mr. Henderson and the band how much they're looking forward to the show. One of the wives tells Red and Leland that she and her sisters had a watch party the night they were on the Grammys show. Emma Crawford also comes by to say hello, as do the Moore sisters and their husbands, as well as Judge Bailey and his wife, and Ron Anderson.

Leland squirms a bit in his seat. "I'm getting nervous now. We've never played anywhere where everybody in the audience knew us and would be seeing us the next day."

"Don't think about it," says Red. "Just sing to Diane, and I'll sing to Jeanette."

The band goes onto the stage at a few minutes before five. Right at five, Mr. Henderson points to Red and gives him the signal to start. Cecil kicks off "Only in America" with an upbeat tempo, and Red comes in on lead guitar in the key of E with the same licks that Brooks and Dunn used in their recording of the song.

As the band plays the intro song, Mr. Henderson comes up the left-side stage stairs. He walks up to the mic on that side and waves to the audience. When the band finishes the intro music, Mr. Henderson says, "Thanks, guys. That sounded great, and we're looking forward to hearing some more music as soon as I shut up."

Mr. Henderson looks over the near-capacity crowd and says, "It's so good to see so many familiar faces here this evening, and I'm glad to see that a lot of you brought your husbands and wives. Tonight, we're going to celebrate our freedom with country music and barbeque, because you can't get any more American than that. The music is going to be provided by Red and Leland Johnson and two friends of theirs from Montgomery, Cecil Banks and Gary Meadows. Just for tonight, we're going to call the band 'The Sawmill Boys.'" Loud applause, cheers, and whistles break out from the audience.

"I'm sure all of you know that I got married a few months ago, and for those of you who weren't able to make our wedding reception, I want to introduce you to my wife Beverly who is sitting right down there in the red dress. What most of you don't know about Beverly is that even though she looks like a high society lady, she's really not. She recently retired from working twenty years at Brock Glass Plant, and for the last fourteen of those years, she was an employee rep. That means that she knows how to put pressure on management. So, if any of you ever has a gripe with the way our company's being run, you might want to give Beverly a call and have her straighten me out." There is laughter and applause from the audience.

"The barbeque is being catered tonight by L.A. Barbeque in Summerdale, and, no, L.A. doesn't stand for Los Angeles, it stands for Lower Alabama. Beverly told me about L.A. Barbeque a while back, and I went over there the other day with her to try their food. Let me tell you, it's great. They'll start serving in about ten minutes, and you can find out for yourselves."

Mr. Henderson looks around the room again. "Our company is holding tonight's event for two reasons. First and primarily, it's to show our appreciation for all the fine work every one of you does. Secondly, it's to give you a chance to be part of Libertytown history as the first people to attend an event at this newly renovated Liberty Hotel ballroom." There's a murmur among the audience, and then loud applause.

"One more thing. Before we leave this evening, I'm going to try to come by and personally thank each one of you sawmill employees for your service to our company, which is something that I wish I could do every day." Mr. Henderson signals Red to start the music again, and, amidst the applause for his welcoming speech, he exits the stage to sit at the table with Beverly and David and Emily Dunham.

The band cranks back up with "Only in America" and then plays a forty-five-minute set of other country and rock-and-roll classics, after which the band members come back to their tables to take a fifteen-minute break with their wives.

Once they are all seated, Red says, "Guys, y'all sound great."

Jeanette says, "You sure do. And I'm so glad to see you two again, Cecil and Gary. And I love that Evelyn and Sue Ann came with y'all."

Cecil says, "Thank you, Jeanette. We had a good time playing at your retirement party, and it's great to be back down here playing with Red and Leland again. And this hotel is something else. I remember what it looked like before, and I can't believe how good it looks now."

Sue Ann, Gary's wife, says, "We're making the boys stay here tonight, instead of driving right back. This place is just too nice not to spend the night here."

"You can thank Mister Henderson for that," says Diane. "This is his baby."

At the end of their break, the band goes back on stage to play their second and final set. They start the set with "Help Me Make It Through the Night." As the song begins, Beverly stands up and reaches out to Mark, who lets her lead him onto the dance floor. While they're dancing, Beverly asks very softly, "Have you noticed how everybody's staring at us? I guess they're not used to seeing you this way."

Mark answers, just as softly, "No, they're not. At work, I'm not exactly Mister Fun."

Beverly pulls him closer. "Yeah, I was the same way. I guess we were just two lonely people who happened to wander into each other lives."

With a catch in his voice, Mark says, "That reminds me of something my son Virgil once said to me, after he found the girl that he intended to marry before we lost him. He said, 'Dad, love sure is funny. It just kind of sneaks up on you and grabs you by the heart.'"

Beverly lays her head on Mark's shoulder. She whispers, "So true."

The band concludes their second set with a raucous version of James Brown's "Living in America." As soon as the applause and cheers for that song start to die down, Red takes his mic and says, "Well, folks, that does it for us tonight. We hope that you enjoyed our show as much as we enjoyed playing for you."

Just as the audience begins to react to Red's comments, Leland holds up his hand to quiet them. He says into his mic, "Do y'all think we ought to ask the boss man to do this again next year?"

Cheers break out, and Mr. Henderson stands up to face the audience and give a thumbs up.

While Mr. Henderson is still standing, Leland leans into his mic and says, "And next year, some of you musicians out there need to be up here with us."

Mr. Henderson gives another thumbs up while the audience is whistling and applauding.

The party ends at around seven-thirty, and by the time it's over, Mr. Henderson has come to each table to speak to all of his employees who made it to the event.

On the way home after the party, Beverly tells Mark how much she enjoyed the evening. Then she tells him that while he was on stage at the start of the party, five of his employees came by and told her how much they appreciated him putting on the event for them.

"Well, they deserve some recognition, and I'm the world's worst about staying so busy that I don't spend enough time with the production employees."

"Believe me, honey, you're a long way from the world's worst about that."

"Thanks for trying to make me feel better, but I know I need to do more to show my appreciation, and you can help me with that, Miss Employee Rep."

"I'll be more than happy to, Mister Boss Man."

When the Moore sisters and their husbands leave the Liberty Hotel after the event, they drive over to downtown Carleton to have drinks at Ben's Tavern.

After they have been at Ben's for a while, John orders a second Miller Lite and, as the waitress walks away, he says to George, "I was really impressed with the band tonight, and I understand that they don't play together regularly. The two guys from Montgomery came down as a favor to Red."

Beth says, "I'm sure they got paid to be here."

"Yes, hon, but that's not the point I'm trying to make. What I'm trying to say is that for a group that doesn't usually play together, they were very good. Especially the harmonizing."

Melanie takes a sip of her white wine and looks at John. "But those were simple songs."

George, who's drinking coffee, furrows his brow and says, "What's with you two? I agree with John. That was a really good band, and not all of those songs were simple. The musicians were just good enough to make them sound that way. For example, that Nat Cole song they played, 'Unforgettable,' is a jazz classic, and it's not at all simple. And Leland did a very good job of singing it."

"Maybe so. You two know more about music that we do," concedes Melanie. "Maybe they were pretty good. But they're still just small-time musicians."

"Baby, are you forgetting that Leland and Red were nominated this year for a Grammy?"

"Well, they didn't win, did they?"

John shakes his head and takes a sip of his beer. Then he chuckles and says to George, "There's no use arguing with our wives, my friend.

They always have to get in the last word. It's in their breeding."

Beth and Melanie cannot help smiling at John's comments.

Later that night, Red and Jeanette come by to visit Leland and Diane at the new house. Earline has not left yet from having stayed with Bret. She and Diane are watching fireworks on the television in the family room. Red waves to them on his way to the kitchen where Leland has served Bret chocolate ice cream in a Sesame Steet bowl with a picture of Bert and Ernie on it. Bret has chocolate ice cream on his right cheek and on his Cookie Monster pajama top. Red smiles at Bret then takes a napkin and wipes the ice cream off his face. Red turns to Leland and says, "Great job tonight, son. You're sounding better than ever."

"Thanks, Daddy, but I just think that my voice is maturing. I can hear the difference between the way I sound on some of our recent demos and the way I sounded on some of our old demos."

"Maybe it's time you put out a record. You could make an album of songs that we've written together."

"Maybe someday down the road. But I'm way too busy at work to think about that right now."

From the family room. Diane shouts, "I agree with Daddy Johnson. You need to make a record."

"Okay, you two. I promise that once I'm not so busy at work, I'll see if I can do that."

"You heard him, Daddy Johnson."

"I did, baby, and we're going to hold him to it. I'm going to start working on some new songs for Leland's first album. What are we going to call it?"

"How about 'Maverick'?"

Chapter Thirty-two

On the afternoon of Sunday, July 7, 1996, Mark and Beverly Henderson come by after church to visit Leland and Diane. Diane greets them at the front door and tells them that Leland and Red are out behind the house reconstructing Leland's workshop building. Diane takes her mother by the hand and leads her into the kitchen. Mark stops on the way to the kitchen to say hello to Bret, who's on the family room floor watching the Braves game with his dog Otto.

"Mama," says Diane, "I want y'all to try this apple cobbler that I just made. I used a recipe that Earline gave me, and I think it's really good."

Diane takes the cobbler from her pie safe and cuts two slices that she transfers to two thick white saucers. She hands one saucer to Beverly and the other to Mark. Mark takes a seat at the kitchen counter and begins to eat his slice. Beverly is eating her cobbler while still standing. She asks Diane, "Aren't you going to join us?"

"Lord, no. I've already had two portions today."

"This is very good, Diane," says Mark. "It has just the right amount of brown sugar and cinnamon."

Beverly says, "Listen to him talking like he knows something about baking cobblers."

He chuckles. "I know zip about baking. My expertise is in eating."

Beverly eats another bite. "This is just as good as you said it was, Diane. I'm going to have to get a copy of that recipe."

Diane reaches into a cabinet drawer and pulls out a single sheet of white paper that she lays on the counter next to where Beverly is standing. "Here's a copy I made for you. Be sure to thank Earline next time you see her."

Red and Leland come through the front door singing one of the new songs that they've been working on. When they get to the kitchen they stop singing. Red says, "Hey, Beverly. Hey, boss. I didn't expect to see y'all here today."

Mark says, "I came by to run some things by you two. Have you got a few minutes?"

Leland answers, "Sure. We're taking a break to get some coffee and pie."

"Why don't y'all sit down at the dining room table and I'll bring the coffee and cobbler," suggests Diane.

Beverly adds, "Yeah, that way Diane and I can have some time together."

Red and Mark follow Leland, who turns on the lights in the dining room. Leland takes a seat in one of the side chairs and motions for Mark to sit at the head of the table. Red sits opposite Leland and looks at Mark. "What's up, boss?"

"Two things. The first is about the ten-acre lot that I bought from you, Leland, and the other ten-acre lot I bought next door to that one. As you know, I thought that with the Dunham factory coming here, that twenty acres would be a good location for a residential development. Now I'm trying to decide on lot sizes and housing restrictions. At first, I thought that two-acre lots would be the way to go, but since my property is only twenty acres, I'm leaning toward one-acre lots."

Red says, "Yeah, I think you ought to go with one-acre lots. That's plenty big enough for the size houses that you'll probably want there."

"I agree," says Leland. "And you'll probably get a better return on your money that way."

Mark thanks Diane for the coffee that she brings him. He takes a sip then asks, "What do you two think about a plan for fifteen residential parcels on the twenty acres? I'm thinking that would accommodate the set-asides for streets, utilities, and common areas."

Red says, "Sounds good, boss. That should work. You could draw up a draft layout and see if fifteen will work. And you could always make the lots smaller if you need to. When do you plan on starting the development?"

"As soon as I decide on the layout of the lots and the size restrictions on the houses. I'm thinking about having a minimum size of twenty-five hundred square feet and a maximum of thirty-five hundred, not counting garage space, and a requirement that each house has a two or three-car garage. Also, our homeowner covenants will require each house to meet certain design and construction criteria and pass an architectural review before it'll be approved for construction."

"Are you going to be the builder?" asks Leland.

"No. I'm just going to sell the lots and have a short list of approved builders."

"Have you decided on the builders yet?" asks Red.

"Almost. I've been asking around and I've got it narrowed down to six so far. You two can help me with that. Tell you what, I'll get you and Leland a copy of my list of prospective builders, and you can help me get it down to two or three, keeping in mind that Ron's going to serve as the reviewing architect, so it would be best if he agrees with your choices."

"No problem," says Red. "We could do that."

"Leland asks, "Are you going to try to design this project to appeal to the Dunham folks as your primary buyers?"

"Yeah. I expect that they'll likely be among our first buyers. That's why as soon as I get a draft layout drawn up, I'm going to share it with David Dunham to see what he thinks. And once we finalize the plan and the covenants, he can give his people advance notice of the development so that my property company can make pre-development sales if any of his folks wants to do that."

"What's the other thing you wanted to talk to us about?" asks Leland.

"Well, the other matter concerns our hotel company, but I thought that I'd tell you two just to keep you up to date on what's happening with the hotel. What I want to tell you is that within the last week, I've gotten three inquiries about buying the hotel. No offers, just inquiries."

Red asks, "Who'd you get inquiries from, boss?"

"Two large hotel chains that I can't disclose yet contacted me, and the third party was an investment group from Mobile."

"But the hotel's only been open a few weeks," says Leland.

"That's what intrigues me. I wonder what these folks know that we don't. I'm going to call a meeting of the hotel company members for later this month and tell them about the inquiries and see if any of them has any idea what precipitated the interest."

"Good idea," says Red. "But we'd sure hate to see y'all sell out this early."

"Don't worry about that. None of us got into this project for a quick profit. Our purpose was to help the community and the Dunham company. And I just can't see anybody wanting out this early. We're having too much fun with this project, especially David. He started bringing prospective furniture customers by the hotel to see how the rooms were furnished before the place even opened. But even though I know that we're not going to sell, I still want to find out what has stirred up so much interest from outsiders in buying the hotel."

Red laughs. "I guess that's one advantage to being a bunch of rich old men. Y'all don't have to sell if you don't want to."

Mark lifts his coffee cup. "Here's to rich old men." He sets the cup back on the table and says, "But, seriously, I'll let you know what we find out, and I'll also keep you abreast of anything else that has to do with the hotel. You've earned that much from us. And if either of you hears anything that might relate to what I've heard, please let me know."

Leland says, "We'll definitely do that, boss. I know it sounds a little silly, but Daddy and I feel like it's our hotel, too."

"That's because in a way it is. You guys put a lot of work into the project, and that creates an emotional attachment to it. You know, our family has a long tradition of buying and restoring historic buildings up in Pennsylvania, and it seemed like every time we brought an old building back to life, we would hate to just walk away from it. And even after we'd sold one of those buildings that we'd restored, we'd still make a point of driving by once in a while to check on it."

Red smiles and says, "We've been doing the same thing with the hotel. I went out of my way to drive by there yesterday."

Mark rises from his chair and says, "Fellows, I hate to leave so soon, but I've got some business calls to make back at the house. You've been very helpful. You've got me feeling better about which direction to go with the residential development."

Leland asks, "Do you have a name for the development yet?"

"Beverly suggested 'Dunham Place.' How does that strike you?"

Red and Leland look at one another. Red says, "I wouldn't have thought of that, but it's actually a pretty good name. What do you think, Leland?"

"I like it. Maybe David Dunham will build his house there."

Mark says, "No, he's got his eyes on the Holman house. I expect that he'll make an offer on it any day now."

"Yeah, I can see that. That's a nice place," says Leland, "and Emma has done a great job of renovating and landscaping it. And it's a good-size house, too, about four thousand square feet, maybe a little more."

Mark signals to Beverly that it's time to leave. He says to Red and Leland, "See you guys tomorrow."

After Mark leaves, Red says to Leland, "I get the feeling that the boss knows a lot more about building houses than he lets on."

Leland smiles. "Yeah, he knows more about everything than he lets on."

Diane comes into the dining room and asks Leland if he's okay with pepperoni pizza for supper.

"Of course. I'm always okay with pepperoni pizza for supper. What about you, Daddy? Do y'all want to stick around and have pizza with us after you and I reach a good stopping point for the day?"

"If it's okay with Jeanette, I'm all in."

Diane says, "Mama Johnson is fine with it. We're going to be up in the studio while y'all are working on the shop. Just give me a call on my cell phone when y'all are ready to call it a day."

"All right, babe."

At around 6:30, the four of them are sitting at the kitchen table eating pepperoni pizza and drinking Pepsis. Bret ate earlier, and he and Otto are asleep next to each other on the family room floor in front of the TV.

Red says, "Leland, there's something that I've been looking for the right time to tell you, and this is probably as good a time as any."

"What's that, Daddy?"

"Do you remember my friend Earl Gaines, the record producer?"

"Sure. I remember you telling me that he went out to Seattle to work with a bigtime recording company out there. It seems like that was about five years ago."

"It was something like that. Well, a couple of weeks ago, Earl called to tell me he was back in Muscle Shoals, and, of course, we got to talking about the music business. He congratulated me on our Grammy nomination and asked how our songwriting was going. So, I told him that I'd put together a demo of a dozen or so of our other songs and send it to him to get his opinion on them. Well, last night Earl called me and told me that he'd got our demo and listened to it twice. He said that he thought all of those songs had commercial potential, and he asked who the vocalist on the demo was. When I told him it was you, he asked if you'd ever cut a record, and I told him that you hadn't, but I thought you should. He agreed. He said that with a little coaching, you could be as good as any of the new country artists. I told him that we were both way too busy right now to do anything like that, but that I was going to try to get you to make an album of our songs once you weren't so snowed under. Then we got to discussing that idea some more, and the bottom line is that Earl wants us to come up to Muscle Shoals sometime soon and talk about you making a record there when the time's right. He went on to say that in the meantime we should keep writing new songs that could go on the record. What do you think about all that?"

A giddy Diane says, "I love that idea. I'd love to have a record of Leland singing songs that y'all wrote. Wouldn't you Mama Johnson?"

"Absolutely. I'd love to hear Leland singing on the radio."

Leland says, "Now, wait a minute, you two. Not only do I not know when I would have the time to make a record, we don't even know yet which of our songs Mister Gaines would want on it. I mean, there's a lot to think about on this."

Red says, "Well, assuming that we meet with Earl, and he lays everything out, and it all sounds like something that you could do, would you want to do it?"

"I'm pretty sure I would. But, if I did, I'd want you to be involved with making the record."

"Well, that would be up to Earl. Of course, if there was any way that I could help besides cowriting the songs with you, I'd certainly want to be involved. But you have to remember that I've only played on one album, and that was over twenty years ago when I was in Jack Jarvis's band, so I don't know how much I could contribute."

"I've still got that Jack Jarvis and the Jackrabbits album," says Jeanette. "Y'all did a good job on it."

Diane asks, "Can I listen to it next time we're at your house?"

"Sure, you can. I'll let you borrow it if you want. And Red can make you a copy if you like it."

Red says to Jeanette, "My point is that I'd love to be involved in the project, but I only want to do what's best for Leland, so I'm going to let Earl make that call."

Leland says. "Shoot, it'll probably be at least six months before we can even think about going to Muscle Shoals and making a record."

"That's what I told Earl. But he still wants to meet with us sometime well before then to discuss a concept for the album and decide what songs should be on it and what sort of instrumentation we would need and all that kind of stuff. So, I told him that we'd try to make it up there on a weekend day within the next few weeks."

"So long as he knows that we're coming up just to talk and not to commit to anything in particular."

"That's what I told him."

Jeanette says, "Diane, our Leland's going to be on the radio, and maybe even television."

"Yes, ma'am. I can't wait. And Bret will go crazy when he hears his daddy singing on the radio."

"Good lord," says Leland, chuckling. "Y'all calm down. We haven't even talked to the man yet. Not only that, we're probably going to have to write some more songs before we can do it."

Diane asks, "Can I design the album cover?"

Red says, "That's up to the label, baby. They have their own designers."

"Well then, when y'all talk to Mister Gaines, you be sure to tell him that I want to design the album cover."

"Yes, baby, I promise we'll tell Earl that you want to design the cover, but we're talking about one of the best music producers in the business, so, if it's all right with you, I'm going to leave all the decision-making up to him."

Chapter Thirty-three

THE TRIP TO MUSCLE SHOALS ON SATURDAY, JULY 27, 1996, IS A PLEAS-
ant change for Red and Leland, who have worked for two straight weekends on various side projects in addition to working long hours at the
sawmill. Red picks up Leland on Saturday morning at seven in Jeanette's
Mustang, and they arrive at Earl Gaines's office in downtown Muscle
Shoals at around 3:15 that afternoon. Earl's office is next door to a conference room on the second floor of a building that belongs to the law
firm of which his brother is a partner.

Earl greets Red and Leland at his office door. He is wearing faded
blue jeans and a purple University of North Alabama t-shirt. He says,
"Let's go sit in the conference room. My office is a mess right now. I've
got stuff piled up everywhere. I'm still trying to get myself organized."

Red peeks into Earl's office and says, "This is a nice office from what
I can see."

"It is. It used to be the office of one of Jake's partners who's retired
now."

"It must be good to have a brother with an office building," says Red.

"Yeah, this place is great. They've even got a breakroom and a fitness
room down in the basement. But I don't know yet how long I'll be here
because I'm almost through renovating and updating a little studio not
too far from here. The studio itself should be ready in a couple of weeks,
so we'll be able to record Leland's album there. But I'm not sure yet how

long it'll take to add the office and the conference room that I'm going to need. That said, this setup here is just fine for me until I get my own office finished."

Earl leads Red and Leland into the conference room where Earl takes a seat at the head of a long walnut conference table. Red and Leland take seats on either side of Earl.

Leland puts his notepad on the table and says, "It's really good to meet you, Mister Gaines, and I really appreciate you wanting to talk to us about the possibility of me making an album. I just hope we don't waste too much of your time cause it looks like you're pretty busy."

"Call me Earl, please, Leland. And you're right, I've got a lot going on right now, here and in Nashville. But I really wanted to talk with y'all because your songs are good enough and your voice is good enough that, with a little guidance from me, we could produce a first-rate country album and make you and Red some money.

"I'm sure that Red told you that I've been out on the West Coast working with pop acts and rap singers, and such as that, and the truth is that I was just ready to get back to my roots and make some good old country music and Southern rock. I've already done some work on three different albums since I got back a couple of months ago. Matter of fact, I'm working on a county album right now with Leon Dickey over in Nashville, and we want to cut one of those songs on the demo that you sent me, Red."

"Which one?"

"'Good Time with a Bad Girl.'"

"Yeah, that would be a good song for Leon," says Leland, nodding.

"Go for it, Earl" says Red. "I agree with Leland. Leon would knock that song out."

"Maybe if I do a good enough job of producing it, we can get y'all another Grammy nomination. I'll mail you a royalty agreement within the next few days. But right now, let's talk about making an album with Leland. The other eleven songs on that demo that you sent me would all fit into what I'm thinking of doing, so we only need three more. What I'm looking for are three more that are in the traditional country vein and are not just some more of this tepid 'new country' crap. And I think Leland's got the perfect voice for that traditional style. So, what have y'all been writing since I first talked to you about making a record?"

Red says, "We've got two songs in the works right now that should work for that kind of album, and another one won't be any problem, particularly since we've got several old-style songs that we worked on in the past and then set aside to get back to later. You know how that is. But don't forget, Earl, it's going to be a while before Leland's going to be available to cut an album."

Earl leans back in his chair and says, "Red, we've known each other for a long time. Trust me on this. I've got a plan that will accommodate the lack of time that Leland's got and still get us to where I want us to go. And, as I told you when we first talked about this on the phone, I really think that Leland's got something special, and I'd like the chance to help him take full advantage of what he's got."

Leland laughs. "You're embarrassing me, Earl."

"I'm serious, Leland. And Red can tell you that I've made enough money now that I can tell it like it is. I don't have to butter anybody up."

"That's a fact," says Red, looking at Leland.

"So, the bottom line is that I want to make a record with you, Leland, not just because Red is my good friend, but because it would be a fun project for me, too, and because what I've got in mind would be a damn good album."

"Are you sure that I'd be worth the trouble," asks Leland, "because I don't know much about making a record."

Earl looks at his watch. He says, "I don't have much time left to talk today, so let me just quickly lay out my plan for y'all. I've got access to some first-rate studio musicians who could lay down the music tracks whether you're here or not. We can use your demo, and the one that y'all are going to send me of the other three songs, to get the key, the tempo, and the feel and so forth for each track.

"So, what we can do is lay down a track for each given song with just the musicians and background singers, and then I'll send it to Leland to practice with. And, Leland, once you've rehearsed enough that you're ready to record, you'll come to the studio and knock out the vocal track at a time that would fit into your schedule. We could record the vocals for two or three songs a day that way, and we could do it on weekends so that it wouldn't interfere with your work schedule. And you could also call me beforehand with any suggestions you have about the instrumentation or background vocals after you listen to the music tracks."

Leland softly says, "You would do that for me? That sounds like you're going pretty far out of your way to accommodate me."

"Like I said, this is for me as much as you. Take my word, we're going to have fun doing this album."

Red asks, "Who's going to be paying for these musicians and singers, and production costs?"

"Red, just leave everything to me. I'll cover the upfront costs, and I've got at least two labels in mind that would fund the project once I can play them some of the finished tracks. So, y'all give this some more thought, come up with another three songs, and I promise you I'll get a record deal for Leland."

Leland says, "I know you're busy, Earl, and I hate to ask you this, but I have to because we promised my wife we would."

Earl looks at his watch. "What's that?"

"My wife is an artist, a very good artist, and she told me that she wants to design the album cover. So, she made me promise to ask you if that would be possible."

"I don't see why not, if she's that good. Tell you what, once we come up with a title for the album, she can send me her idea for the cover, and I'll see what I can do. How about that?"

Red says, "Earl, you're a good friend. Whether this album gets done or not, I appreciate what you're doing. Just let me know if I can ever do anything for you. If you want us to come up and help you with designing or constructing your offices, just let me know."

Earl stands up to shake hands with Red and Leland. Earl smiles and says, "I might take you up on that, Red. But the best thing y'all can do for me and yourselves right now is to keep writing good songs. The record industry can always use more good songs. Hell, the world can always use more good songs. But let's not think about what happens if we don't make the album, because we *are* going to do this album, and it's going to be good, very good. By the way, Leland, tell your wife that my working title for the album is 'Songs from Creek County.'"

Leland nods and says, "She'll like that."

Red says, "Thanks for your time, Earl. We'll get those three songs to you right away."

As they're taking the elevator down to the first floor, Leland says, "I really like Earl. Even if we never make an album, I'm glad I met him."

"Oh, we're going to make an album, son. If Earl wants to make an album with you, he's not going to let anything stop him."

Red and Leland eat a late lunch at a little café in downtown Muscle Shoals that's next door to a shop where Leland buys a black Muscle Shoals Sound Studio t-shirt. Then, at Leland's insistence, they drop by FAME Recording Studios, where Leland picks up a souvenir t-shirt for Diane.

Red fills up the Mustang at a Gulf station, and they leave Muscle Shoals at a little after five. They find a good blues station on the radio, and they sing along with it until it fades out just before they get to Birmingham. Leland looks for something else to listen to, and he finds a sports talk show that lasts until they get to Clanton where Red stops for gas and asks Leland to take over the driving so that he can take a nap.

When Red wakes up just north of Greenville, he turns on the radio and finds a classic rock station that they listen to until they get near Atmore. Then they find another classic rock station out of Mobile that they listen to until Leland parks the Mustang in his driveway at ten after eleven. Red gets out and stretches his back while he's walking around the front of the car to the driver's side. Leland pats Red on the back as they pass each other. "This was a fun day, Daddy."

"It sure was, son, but that was a long trip up there and back. Let's spend the night next time we go up."

"Fine with me. My butt's tired."

As Red is driving away, Otto comes running up to greet Leland. Leland scratches Otto's head then walks up the steps of the porch and quietly unlocks the front door. When he enters the house, he hears the TV and looks into the family room. He sees Diane in her pajamas sleeping in his recliner, and he sees Bret sleeping on the sofa with a throw pillow under his head. Leland walks over to Diane and takes the remote from her hand. She wakes up. It takes her a minute to realize where she is. Leland turns off the TV and helps Diane out of the recliner. Then he hugs her and kisses her cheek. She leans against him as he walks her to the bedroom. As he tucks Diane in, she asks, "Did you tell him I wanted to do the album cover?"

"Yes, I did. We'll talk about that tomorrow. Right now, I'm going to put Bret to bed."

Leland walks back into the family room and gently lifts Bret from the sofa. As he carries him to his bedroom, Bret wakes up and says, "Hey, Daddy." Then he falls back to sleep.

Leland tucks Bret in and walks through the house turning off lights until he gets to the kitchen. That's where he takes the Cheerios box from the pantry and makes himself a midnight snack.

After church the next day, Leland and Diane and Bret stop by the Henderson house to have lunch with Mark and Beverly. Beverly greets them at the door. She gives Leland and Diane a quick hug and then takes Bret by the hand and leads him into the house. "My goodness, Bret, you sure are getting big."

Bret grins and stands up even taller.

When they get to the kitchen, they see that Mark is slicing baked ham to go with the black-eyed peas and cornbread that Beverly has prepared.

Mark says, "That was good timing, folks. We just got out of our church clothes."

Once the meal is on the table and everyone is seated, Beverly says grace and then asks Diane what their preacher's sermon was on this morning.

"He talked about the importance of family and how family should always support each other, especially when times are bad."

Mark says, "Amen to that."

Beverly says, "Speaking of family, Mark, I've been thinking about something that your mother told me."

Mark smiles. "Nothing bad I hope."

"No, nothing bad. She told me that if I ever wanted to try to find out about my birth parents, she would get her detective friend to do an investigation for me."

"Is that something you want to do?"

"I've been thinking about it, but I haven't made up my mind yet."

Mark reaches over and gently takes Beverly's hand. "Well, you let me know if ever you want to do that. And I'm sure that I could find an investigator for you who's closer than McKeesport."

"I'll do that. I'll let you know. But as for right now, let's eat some peas and cornbread. What do you say, Bret?"

Bret says, "Yes, ma'am," and digs into his peas with a spoon.

After lunch, when everyone is gathered in Mark and Beverly's family room, Diane tells them about Leland's meeting with Earl Gaines. She makes a point of telling Beverly that she may get to design the album cover and that the working name for the album is 'Songs from Creek County.'

Beverly thinks about the title and says, "What you need is a picture that is representative of this area. How about your depot picture that we've got hanging in the library?"

Leland says, "I like that idea. We might even have to write a song about a train leaving Libertytown to go along with that picture."

Mark says, "Good thinking, Leland. You'd be making our painting famous, because they'll show the album cover every time you're on one of those late night TV shows. But seriously, I think it would be a shame if you didn't give this album thing a shot. You've got a renowned producer telling you he wants to make an album with you. Heck, even I've heard of Earl Gaines. Believe me, son, if you don't do this, you'll always look back and wonder what it would have been like to work with Earl Gaines."

"But, boss, you know better than anybody how busy I am right now."

"Tell you what, Leland. If you decide that this is something you really want to do, and I'm telling you right now that you should, I'll help you make it happen."

"Are you sure? I don't want to do anything that would hurt the business."

"You just tell me what you need, and we'll figure out a way to get it done that won't affect your job. How does that sound?"

"Sounds good to me. Thank you, boss."

Red says, "All right, Leland, we've got three songs to finish writing, starting tonight."

"And one of them has to have a train in it," says Diane.

Chapter Thirty-four

Diane is getting dressed on the morning of Monday, August 5, 1996, when she hears a loud rumble coming from the lot next door. She looks out the bedroom window and sees several large trucks hauling heavy equipment off the highway into the front yard of the trailer where they used to live. There is banging and clanging as the equipment is unloaded and then roaring as the engines are fired up. Diane thinks to herself: *That must be the road construction crew that Leland told me was going to be cutting streets through that property. I'm sure glad we're not going to be home while they're doing it.* She finishes getting ready for work, then goes into the kitchen where Bret is at the table eating scrambled eggs and grits.

"What's that racket, Mama?"

"That's some people working next door. Finish your breakfast, baby, and then go brush your teeth so I can get you over to Grandma Johnson's."

Bret says, "Yes, ma'am" and eats the last of his breakfast. Then he takes his plate over to the trash can and empties the leftover fragments. He sets the plate and spoon on the counter next to the sink and runs to the bathroom. A few minutes later, he runs out from the bathroom, through the foyer, and out the front door into the yard where he waits for Diane. Diane comes out from the house, locks the front door behind her, and takes Bret's hand to walk him over to her old Toyota that's parked next to the new burgundy Toyota Camry that Leland bought her a few days ago for their upcoming eighth anniversary.

As Diane is driving Bret to Jeanette Johnson's house to spend the day, he's singing the alphabet song from *Sesame Street* and keeping time by tapping the sides of his child restraint seat.

After dropping off Bret, Diane gets to Danny's Diner at a little before seven. She walks into the diner and locates her white apron. As she's tying her apron strings, she tells Earline and Theo that work is beginning on the new residential neighborhood next to their house.

Earline says, "Pretty soon, y'all are going to have neighbors for the first time since you've been married. How are you going to feel about that?"

"Oh, I love the idea of having some people nearby when Leland's not home. I'm always a little edgy when Bret and I are home by ourselves." Diane laughs softly. "Leland made me learn how to shoot his shotgun so that I'd feel safer when he's not there, but I don't want to have to shoot anybody."

Earline says, "But I bet you would if you thought that Bret might get hurt."

"Yeah, probably, but I'd rather not have to. You know, I heard that once the construction on the houses starts, the sheriff and the city police are going to be patrolling the area more often. I was glad to hear that."

"Seeing the police patrolling my neighborhood always makes me nervous. I don't know why. They've always been nice to me."

Diane says, "You see police officers and deputies in here all the time. You should be used to them by now."

"I'm not nervous about seeing them in here. It's just when they're patrolling my neighborhood."

Diane puts her arm around Earline's shoulders and says, "Don't worry. I'll come see you in jail."

"So will I," calls out Theo from behind the counter.

Earline shakes her head and walks over to the door to greet Mrs. Sinclair and ask her about the black pantsuit that she saw in the window of Sinclair Ladies Wear.

The diner is unusually busy that day and is almost full when the

Moore sisters come in at a little after nine. They take their usual seats at the counter, and Diane goes behind the counter to greet them and take their order.

"Just coffee, Diane," says Beth.

"I'd like a small glass of orange juice, then a cup of coffee," says Melanie.

Diane serves the coffee to Beth and the orange juice to Melanie, who says, "We keep hearing that David Dunham is looking to buy the Holman house. Has Emma said anything to you about that?"

"Oh, he definitely wants to buy it. He and Emily have been by there three times to look at it. I'd say that it's pretty certain that when Emma and Mel move out in January, Mister Dunham and Emily are going to be moving in."

Beth asks, "Do you know if there's a sales agreement yet? I'm curious what the selling price is."

"The last thing that I heard from Emma was that she had negotiated a tentative agreement and was waiting for her parents to approve it, because they still own the house, and the money would go to them. Emma didn't tell me what the offer was, but she said that if her parents approve it, Mister Dunham's going to go ahead and buy the house but let Emma and Mel stay there until the first week of January so that Mel can finish the fall semester before they move."

"I see," says Beth. "Looks like we'll have some Yankees moving into the neighborhood."

Melanie says, "Well, I don't have any objection to these particular Yankees, as long as they don't bring any more with them."

Diane excuses herself and goes to wait on Judge Bailey who has just sat down at a two-person table.

She brings him a mug of dark roast and says, "Judge Bailey, it seems like it's been about a week since I've seen you here."

Judge Bailey finishes hanging his blue and white seersucker coat over the back of the chair next to his, then he turns back to Diane. "Been over in Atlanta for a Federal trial."

"Did you win?"

Judge Bailey smiles. "Honey, I always win. But, as for my client, we're still waiting for the judge to render a decision. It's a complicated case, so it could be a while."

"What kind of case is it?"

"Securities. Do you know anything about securities law?"

"Not a thing. But I can bring you something to eat if that'll help you wait. What suits you this morning?"

"Scrambled eggs, sausage, and French toast. And bring me some maple syrup for the French toast."

Diane takes Judge Bailey's order to Theo, then she takes Melanie her coffee.

"Did we see you driving a new Toyota down Main Street last Saturday?" asks Melanie.

"Yes, you did. I was taking Bret to visit my mother."

Beth says, "That's a pretty car. What do you call that color?"

"It's called 'burgundy pearl.' Leland picked out the color. He said he bought me the car for our anniversary, even though it's not till November. I think he really bought it just to get me out of my old car before it completely falls apart. Anyway, I never saw the car until he drove up the driveway in it and told me it was mine."

"That was a nice surprise. But didn't I see your old Toyota in the parking lot today?"

"Yeah, I'm driving it one last time today. We're donating it to the auto repair program over at the high school, so I'm going to take the car by there after work this afternoon, and Leland's going to pick me up there. You know what, I'm going to miss that car. I've had it since high school, and Mama had it before I did. It's got way over a hundred thousand miles on it."

As she's drinking the last of her coffee, Melanie says, "Well, I don't think it'll take you too long to get used to your new car."

Beth pays their bill and gives Diane a two-dollar tip. Diane thanks Beth and goes over to a customer whom she had never seen before today. He is a well-dressed man who appears to be in his late thirties. Beside him on the table is a folded copy of the *Creek County Courier*.

The man has finished the breakfast he ordered earlier. When Diane gets back to his table, the man hands her a ten-dollar bill to pay for his breakfast and tells her the pancakes were very good. Diane tells him she'll be right back with his change. The customer smiles and tells her to keep it. Then he asks if she knows how far it is to the city limit of Carleton.

Diane says, "Let's see, it's seventeen miles from city limit to city limit, so it's probably between eighteen and nineteen miles from here to the Carleton city limit. Are you from out of town?"

"Way out of town. I'm from Sunnyvale, California."

"That *is* a long way. What brings you to Libertytown?"

"Business."

"Well, I hope you enjoy your time in Alabama. Is there anything I can do for you?"

The man rises from his chair, picks up his paper, and says, "No thank you, I've got to be on my way. You have a nice day."

After she gets off work, Diane drives her Toyota out to Libertytown High School where Leland picks her up at around 4:30. He asks, "How'd it go? Was the bill of transfer that I drew up for you okay with them?"

"Everything was great, except that I hated to part with my old car."

"I know you did. I'm glad we took a picture of you and Bret in it yesterday. We'll put that picture in our scrapbook."

"Leland, where's Sunnyvale, California?"

"I think it's somewhere south of San Francisco, why?"

"A customer in the diner this morning asked me how far it was to the city limit of Carleton. I told him it was about eighteen or nineteen miles, and I asked him if he was from out of town, knowing full well that he must have been. He told me he was from Sunnyvale, California. He said he was in Libertytown on business."

"Maybe it had something to do with the Dunham factory."

"Could be."

"I talked with the boss today about the new development going up next to us, and he said that he'd already gotten all his city and county approvals and had already presold two lots to Dunham executives. Maybe this guy was one of them. You know, I just have to believe that

Judge Bailey has been pulling some strings for the boss with the city and the county to get everything approved so fast."

"I don't know about that. I saw Judge Bailey today at the diner, and he told me that he'd been in Atlanta for a trial since the last time I saw him about a week ago."

"Well, if it wasn't him, it was somebody in his firm following his instructions, or it could have been Mister Bernstein. But, anyway, things are going awfully smooth, thank goodness."

"I like Judge Bailey, don't you?"

"Yeah, and he's a very good man to have on your side. Now, how about we go get Bret boy and take him to McDonald's."

"You mean take *you* to McDonald's."

Leland nods. "I do like their fries."

Chapter Thirty-five

LELAND SEES MR. HENDERSON IN THE OFFICE HALLWAY ON WEDNES-
day morning. He gets Mr. Henderson's attention and says, "Excuse me,
boss, was one of those Dunham executives who bought a lot at Dunham
Place from Sunnyvale, California?"

"No. Why do you ask that?"

"Diane told me on Monday that she had a customer from Sunnyvale
who said he was in town on business, and I speculated that it might have
something to do with the Dunham factory."

Mr. Henderson furrows his brow. "Let's go in my office and talk for
a minute."

Leland follows Mr. Henderson into his office and sits in one of the
chairs situated in front of Mr. Henderson's desk. Mr. Henderson takes a
seat in his leather desk chair and leans over the desk. "Let's you and I do
some thinking about Diane's out-of-town customer."

"Okay, what do you have in mind, boss?"

"Do you know of any kind of recent new business in town other than
Dunham? I mean, have you heard anything along that line?"

"No, sir. The only new business I've heard about beside Dunham is
what you told me about folks inquiring about buying the hotel."

Mr. Henderson leans back in his chair. "You may have something
there, Leland. Your mystery man could have been someone looking at
the hotel. I think what I'll do a little later today is call an old Army buddy
of mine who lives in San Francisco to see what he can tell me about

Sunnyvale. It's too early to call him right now, so why don't you go on back to your office, and I'll let you know later what I find out from him."

"Oh, there's something else, Boss. Diane's customer asked how far it was to Carleton from here. Maybe he was interested in something in Carleton, or between here and Carleton."

At around 10:15, Leland is double-checking his figures on the cost of buying a new logging truck when he gets a call from Sally telling him that Mr. Henderson wants to meet with him. Leland puts his logging truck documents back into the folder on his desk and walks over to Mr. Henderson's office.

Sally nods to Leland as he walks past her into the open door of the boss's office, and he nods in return.

Mr. Henderson is sitting at his worktable with a yellow legal pad in front of him. "Have a seat, Leland. I'll tell you what I found out from my friend Victor Vance in California."

Leland takes a chair across the table from Mr. Henderson.

Mr. Henderson taps his legal pad with his pen. "My buddy Vic gave me some interesting info. Maybe together we can figure out what it means."

"Okay."

"Vic was an Army intelligence officer who specialized in electronic intelligence gathering and analysis, and since he's been out of the Army, he's been an information management consultant. So, he tries to keep up with all of the goings-on in the computer technology world. That was one of the reasons he moved to Northern California. Anyway, he tells me that Sunnyvale is where a lot of the folks in the IT industry live.

"He also tells me that one of the mid-sized IT companies in that area is owned by an Egyptian family who want to set up shop somewhere in the Southeast to take advantage of the growing technology market in places like Dallas, Houston, Atlanta, Miami, Chapel Hill, and so forth."

"Did he tell you the name of the company?"

Mr. Henderson looks at his notes. "It's called Seshat Information Management, Incorporated. I phoned Missus Bachus over at the library and asked her to do a little research for me on what Seshat means, and she found out that Seshat was the Egyptian goddess of words, wisdom, and knowledge. Did Diane say that her out-of-state customer looked like a foreigner?"

"No. If he did, she didn't mention it. What are you thinking, boss, that there's a California technology company looking to move to Libertytown?"

"Or somewhere else in this area. Yeah, that's what I'm wondering."

Leland says, "Well, if they buy a building or any land in Creek County, they'll have to register the deed over at the Probate Office."

"I've been thinking about that, too. I want you to take a trip over to Carleton to look at the property records in the Probate Office, but let's first try to figure out where they might want to locate. Judging from what Diane's customer asked her, they may be looking at a site that's on or near highway 36 between downtown Libertytown and the city limit of Carleton. So, our first question is where might that be?"

Mr. Henderson runs his right forefinger down his notes and stops at a note near the bottom of the page. "I asked Vic how much land Seshat would need for an office complex, and he said at least three acres, but probably not much more than that. So, why don't we first see if we can find out if an out-of-state buyer has recently bought some acreage between here and Carleton."

"Do you know anybody at the Probate Office?"

"No, but I know someone who does. I'll get in touch with Hollis Bailey and ask him to call the Probate Judge's Office and arrange for someone on Judge Roper's staff to help you go through the property records to see if a deed has been filed recently on some land on or near Highway 36 between here and Carleton. Now, we have to bear in mind that even if there was a recent purchase, the deed might not have been filed yet."

"Do you want me to go over there today and check?"

"Might as well. It wouldn't hurt to find out if a deed *has* been registered. I'll let you know if today's a good day once I talk to Hollis."

Mr. Henderson buzzes Sally and asks her to call Judge Bailey for him.

"Leland, I'll give you a call after I hear from Hollis. But before you go to your office, tell me what you've found out about a new logging truck."

"I've found out that the cost of new logging trucks has gone up considerably since the last two we bought. But I've got the purchase narrowed down to two Kenworth dealers, one in Alabama and one in Georgia. They both have what we want in their inventory. I'm going to see if I can get them to bid against each other before I make a final decision. In any case, I figure we'll have a new truck within the next two weeks, and I can get our company lettering painted on it within two or three days after we pick it up."

"Sounds good, because we need to start confining that old Ford truck to short runs."

"That's for sure." Leland gets up to leave. "I'll let you know when I nail down the purchase of the new truck."

Just as Leland reaches the door, he hears Sally buzz Mr. Henderson and tell him that Judge Bailey's on line one. Leland stops in the doorway and waits to see what Judge Bailey has to say. He hears Mr. Henderson ask Judge Bailey for his help with access to the probate records.

Mr. Henderson hangs up his phone and looks over at Leland. "Hollis says you can go right on over to the Probate Office. He's calling there now to get someone to help you review the records. Give me a call if you find anything interesting."

"Yes, sir."

At 11:10, Leland parks his truck in front of the Creek County Probate Office. He enters the building and locates Judge Angela Roper's office. He introduces himself to her executive assistant who leads him to the Property Records room. He spends the next hour with a flirty young clerk named Carolyn Moody who remembers him from the article in the *Creek County Courier* about the Grammy nomination. Even though Miss Moody is apparently very proficient at her job, she and Leland find no indication of a recent property transfer anywhere in the area in which Leland and Mr. Henderson are interested. Miss Moody even goes so far as to check with the County Tax Assessor's Office to see if they have any information that might be helpful before she tells Leland that there doesn't seem to be any indication of a recent land purchase in that area. Leland thanks Miss Moody for her time and help and tells her that he might be back one day soon to check the records again.

Miss Moody smiles and says, "Any time."

As he walks to his truck, Leland feels slightly disappointed but not completely surprised at not finding what he was looking for.

Leland hears his name called and turns to see a carpenter friend of his leaving the Probate Office. Leland and his friend exchange a few words about their current projects before Leland gets into his truck. He turns on his air conditioner, tunes into the *Paul Finebaum Show*, and heads for home.

As soon as he's out of town and back on Highway 36, Leland calls Mr. Henderson on his cell phone and tells him that he was unable to find any helpful information at the Probate Office. Mr. Henderson says he understands and tells Leland to go by the Liberty Hotel when he gets back to town and pick up some information that Raymond Dadurno is putting together for him.

About halfway between Carleton and Libertytown, Leland sees a large white sign to his left on a rise next to the highway. The sign is advertising pastureland for sale. Leland pulls his truck onto the shoulder of the highway and writes down the name and phone number of the real estate broker who's referenced on the sign.

Chapter Thirty-six

Leland gets back to Libertytown from Carleton at around 12:20. At 12:25, he pulls his truck into a parking spot in front of the Liberty Hotel. He exits his truck and walks into the hotel lobby where he sees Raymond Dadurno standing behind the front desk next to the desk clerk who's registering two guests. Raymond sees Leland and points to his office. Both start walking toward the office door.

Raymond opens the door for Leland and motions him inside. Leland takes a seat in a chair in front of Raymond's desk, and Raymond sits down in his desk chair. Raymond opens a desk drawer and pulls out a sheet of hotel stationery. He hands the sheet of paper to Leland who sees that typed on the paper is a list of three names followed by a note about credit cards. Raymond says, "This is the information Mister Henderson asked for. Let him know to call me if he needs anything else."

"Will do. Now, exactly what am I looking at here?"

"Mister Henderson wanted to know if any guests from California had checked in within the last couple of weeks. He also wanted to know if any of them used a company credit card."

"Did he tell you why he needed this?"

"Nope."

"You're not violating any privacy rights are you, giving us this?"

"No. It's legit. Mister Henderson's one of the hotel owners. He has the authority to review the accounts, and he told me to show you what I find."

Leland reads each name and the city next to the name. He sees that one guest lists Palo Alto as his home address, one lists San Diego as her address, and one lists Sunnyvale as his address. According to Raymond's notes, the female guest used a personal credit card, and the two men each used a Kemet Properties credit card.

"Do you have any idea why Mister Henderson needs this?" asks Raymond.

"I think I do. Are these men still checked in?"

"No, they both checked out this morning."

"Did either of these men look like he might be Egyptian?"

"I don't know. I didn't see either of them check in or out. But I did see a Middle Eastern-looking guy in the coffee shop early this morning, and he had a suitcase with him. So, he could have been about to check out."

Raymond says, "I wonder if he paid his coffee shop bill with a credit card."

"I doubt it. All I saw him with was a cup of coffee."

Leland folds the sheet of paper and puts it in his shirt pocket as he gets up from his chair. He says, "I think I'll go over and see what Angelo remembers about that guy. Thanks a lot, Raymond. This could be important."

"Glad to help. Let me know if you need anything else. Also, if Angelo can't help you, the morning desk clerk, Ralph, is still on duty. He might remember what those two guys looked like."

Leland leaves Raymond's office and walks across the lobby to the coffee shop where he takes a seat at the butcherblock counter and says hello to Angelo. Leland orders a cup of coffee and a slice of apple pie, and Angelo brings them to him, along with a glass of water. Leland asks Angelo if he remembers seeing a Middle Eastern-looking guy this morning in the coffee shop. Angelo says that he does, and Leland asks if that customer paid with a credit card.

Angelo thinks for a moment. "I can't say for sure, but I believe that he did because he bought a bag of our special blend Columbian medium roast and put it in his suitcase."

"I hate to ask you to go to this much trouble, but could you check and see if he used a Kemet Properties credit card?"

"I don't have to check. I remember now that he did use a credit card with that name on it, because I asked him what kind of company that was."

"What did he say?"

"He said it was a company that he and his partners put together to buy some land near here. I asked him if they had bought the land yet, and he said that the deal had closed yesterday."

"Did you ask him where the land was that they bought?"

"No, I didn't ask him, but he told me that it was about seven or eight miles out toward Carleton on Highway 36."

Leland reaches over the counter and grabs Angelo by the shoulders. "Man, you don't know just how helpful you've been." Leland releases Angelo, who is chuckling at Leland's exuberance, and asks, "Did he by any chance say what they were going to do with the land they bought?"

"No. He didn't say anything about that."

Leland wolfs down his pie, hurriedly drinks the rest of his coffee, and lays a ten-dollar bill on the counter before he rushes out of the coffee shop.

As he drives back to the sawmill, Leland loudly sings one of the songs that he has been rehearsing for his album.

When Leland gets to his office, he looks though the door of Mr. Henderson's outer office to see if Mr. Henderson is in. He sees that Mr. Henderson's office door is closed, so he walks into the outer office and asks Sally if the boss is in.

"He's in, but he's on the phone with one of the customers. If you want, I'll buzz you when he's free."

"Thanks, Sally. But be sure to tell him that I've got some important news for him."

"All right, I'll do that."

Leland is in his office trying to concentrate on a blueprint for an addition to the company's milling complex when Sally lets him know that Mr. Henderson is available.

Leland bumps his knee on his desk as he jumps up from his chair to head for Mr. Henderson's office.

Before he even sits down in the boss's office, Leland takes the folded paper from his shirt pocket and starts talking. "Boss, I don't want to sound like I'm brown-nosing, but that was really smart of you to ask Raymond to check the hotel records for guests from California. Look at this." Leland hands Mr. Henderson the list that he got from Raymond.

Mr. Henderson studies the list for a moment then says, "Interesting, two men from Northern California, and one of them with a last name that could be Egyptian, 'Hassan.' And two credit cards on the account of Kemet Properties. Leland, you may already know this, but 'Kemet' is a name for ancient Egypt."

Rubbing his left knee, Leland says, "No sir, I didn't know that. But that is interesting when you put it together with what I found out from Angelo at the coffee shop."

"What was that?"

"Well, Raymond told me that he didn't personally see either of the two men from California check in or out, so he couldn't say what they looked like, but he did see a Middle Eastern-looking man in the coffee shop. So, after I finished talking to Raymond, I went over to talk to Angelo and found out that the man that Raymond had seen in the coffee shop had bought a bag of coffee using a Kemet Properties credit card."

"That was very clever of you, Leland."

"But that's not the good part. When Angelo asked what kind of company Kemet Properties was, the man told him that he and his partners had put the company together to buy some property near Libertytown."

"That *is* interesting."

"But wait till you hear this. According to what the man told Angelo, Kemet Properties had just closed on some land about seven or eight miles out of town toward Carleton on Highway 36."

Mr. Henderson says "Bingo" as he rises from his chair. He walks past his desk and starts pacing back and forth in the open area behind where Leland is sitting. He says, "I wonder who they bought that property from."

Leland says, "When I was driving back, I noticed a sign on the side of the highway advertising property in the same area where Kemet

Properties may have bought their land." He reaches in his back pocket for his wallet. He pulls out the piece of scrap paper on which he has written the name of the broker whose name was on the sign next to the highway. He hands the note to Mr. Henderson and says, "This is the name and phone number of the broker that was on the sign."

Mr. Henderson looks at the note and smiles. "Liz Baker. I know this woman, Leland. I'm going to give her a call right now."

Mr. Henderson walks back around his desk and sits in his chair. He picks up his phone and dials the number on the scrap of paper. In a moment he says, "Miss Baker, it's Mark Henderson of Henderson Properties. You and I did some business together a few years ago . . . That's right, the office complex on Bainbridge. Well, I may want to do some more business with you. I hear that you just sold a parcel to Kemet Properties over on Highway 36 about halfway between Carleton and Libertytown . . . I see . . . Well, I'm looking for a parcel about that same size in that same area . . . Is that right? Right next to the Kemet parcel. What's the price on those two parcels?" Mr. Henderson looks at Leland and winks.

"Can you hold those two parcels for me until I have a chance to come look at them? I could come by late this afternoon or early this evening if you're available. It's not going to get dark until . . . That'll work. I'll see you then."

As she hangs up his phone, Mr. Henderson says, "Leland, your excellent detective work may have not only answered our questions, but it may also make Henderson Properties some money."

"How's that, boss?"

"Miss Baker just told me that Kemet Properties bought a five-acre parcel, and there's an adjoining five-acre parcel for sale, and then another five-acre parcel next to that one. Well, I'm going to have a look at that adjoining parcel, and if it looks like I hope it does, I'm inclined to buy both lots because the price is very reasonable."

"I see what you mean, boss. If you're right thinking that a technology company is going to be located on the lot that Kemet Properties bought, then the value of all the property in that area is going to skyrocket. And

I'm guessing that you can tell from the price you just heard from Miss Baker that she and the seller don't know yet why Kemet bought their parcel."

"Leland, sometimes you shock me at how quick your mind is."

"That's from working with you, boss."

"Now you *are* brown-nosing. But let's you and I ride out there and look at that property you spotted. How about I pick you up at your house at a quarter to six?"

"That'd be fine."

At 5:42, Mr. Henderson pulls into Leland's driveway in his black 1995 Mercedes-Benz G Class SUV. Leland comes out the front door of the house in Levi's and a black Muscle Shoals Sound Studio t-shirt. He gets into the SUV and says hello to Mr. Henderson.

Mr. Henderson says, "I like that t-shirt, Leland. Did you pick that up when you went up to see Earl Gaines."

"Yes, sir. I got this shirt for me and a FAME shirt for Diane. I'm hoping to record in one or both of those studios."

Once they're on the road, Mr. Henderson says, "I've been meaning to ask you when you expect to start recording."

"Earl called me night before last and said that he's going to send me the music tracks for two of the songs this week or next so that I can start practicing for the recording. But to be honest, I'm getting a little nervous about actually beginning the process."

"I can understand that. You'll be making a record for the first time. But I'm sure you'll do very well once you get started. Do you know when you'll need to go back to Muscle Shoals?"

"Well, the good thing is that Earl told me we can do all of my vocal recordings on weekends, since we won't need to have the musicians or the background singers there when we're laying down the vocal tracks. And I figure that it won't take but a couple of hours, three at the most, of practicing to get comfortable singing the first two songs once I get the music tracks, because I already know both the songs. So, my first trip could be as soon as a week from Saturday, or the next Saturday after that."

"Let me know if you need any time off. I'll be glad to work with you on that."

"Thanks, boss, but if we can do all the vocal tracks on weekends, I'll probably go up on a Saturday morning and record on Saturday afternoon, and then spend the night and have Sunday available, too, if we need it. So, if everything goes smooth in Muscle Shoals, I probably won't miss any work time."

"That sounds good but let me know if you find out later that you will need some time off. Is Red going with you?"

"It depends on what he's working on for our carpentry company at the time. But I definitely want him to go with me for the first weekend."

"Well, regardless of how it turns out, that'll be a good experience for both you and Red."

"I think you're right, but I'm still anxious about it."

"You'll be fine."

Mr. Henderson asks Leland to find a good station on the radio, and Leland tunes to his favorite classic rock station out of Mobile. When they get a few miles out of town on Highway 36, Mr. Henderson says, "Let me know when we start getting close to where you saw that sign. Liz Baker said she'll meet us there."

"It should be between three and four miles from here."

About four minutes later, Mr. Henderson asks, "Is that the sign up there on the right?"

"Yes sir, that's it, and I see a car parked in that little dirt area in front of the sign."

"That must be Liz."

Mr. Henderson checks his rearview mirror as he slows down to turn into the dirt area and park his SUV next to the 1994 silver Cadillac Sedan de Ville that's already there. As soon as he and Leland get out of the Mercedes, Miss Baker greets them and introduces them to the man at her side. "This is my good friend, Ken Foster. He won't let me go off alone to meet men in the woods. Can you believe that?"

Mr. Henderson extends his right hand toward Mr. Foster and says, "A pleasure to meet you, Ken. I'm Mark, and this is Leland, who works with me at the sawmill. And I don't blame you for looking out for Liz's wellbeing. I'd feel the same way."

Ken shakes hands with Mark, then with Leland. He says, "Liz is misleading you a tiny bit, Mark. She wanted me to come with her for another reason as well. I'm in the travel business, and I heard that you were the main party behind the renovation of the Liberty Hotel, so I wanted to meet you and ask how the hotel's doing."

"Couldn't be better. Are you thinking about sending us some business?"

"I am. I think that the hotel is in a great location, being downtown in a quaint little city that's only about sixty miles from the Gulf. Would you mind if I came by and checked it out some time?"

"Not at all. Tell you what, Liz has my contact information, so you just let me know when you want to come by, and I'll arrange for the hotel manager to give you the grand tour. I think you'll like what you see."

Liz puts her hand on Ken's shoulder and says, "Okay, Ken. Let me give Mark and Leland a tour of these two lots that Mark asked about."

Ken says, "Sorry about that, Liz. How about if I stay here and make some business calls while y'all are looking at the property?"

"Sure, it won't take too long. The land is pretty flat once we walk up this little rise."

When they come back about a half hour later, Ken can tell that Mark and Leland are pleased with what they saw. He hears Mark tell Liz to go ahead and draw up a purchase agreement for Henderson Properties to buy both parcels. Liz smiles slyly and tells Mark that the contract is in her briefcase in the car. She says, "I had a strong feeling that you would like this property at the price I quoted you, so I had my assistant prepare a contract in case I was right about that."

Mr. Henderson winks at Leland. "Well, in that case, let me read it."

Liz walks to her car to get the contract. She comes back with the document and hands it to Mark who carefully reads it. Once he's finished, he says, "This looks fine. I'm ready to sign, and I see from the contract that you've been authorized to sign for Mister Marshall, the owner. Do we need a notary?"

Liz says, "Ken, come over here and notarize this contract for us if you don't mind."

Mr. Henderson watches Ken as he gets out of the Cadillac. As Ken pulls his notary seal from his briefcase, Mr. Henderson asks, "Ken, do you get the feeling that we're both being exploited by Liz?"

Ken smiles at Liz, then says to Mr. Henderson, "I'm used to it. We've been friends a long time."

Mr. Henderson and Miss Baker each sign three copies of the contract, and Mr. Foster notarizes them. Miss Baker hands one copy of the contract to Mr. Henderson.

Liz says, "Thank you, Mark. I think that this was a good purchase for you. I'll bring you the two signed deeds by no later than next Tuesday. You can make the payment then."

Mr. Henderson says, "Sounds good. Just give me a call before you come, and I'll have a check for you when you bring the deeds." He looks at his watch and says, "Well, I need to get Leland back to his wife in time for dinner, so we're going to head on out."

Mark waves to Ken. "Good to meet you, Ken, and thanks for notarizing the contract. Send me an invoice if there's a fee."

"No fee. It's on me. And I'll be calling you about the hotel."

As they head back toward Libertytown, Mr. Henderson says, "You know, I might have bought that land even if I didn't think that a tech company would be moving in next door. Did you see how many mature pine trees are on it?"

"Yes, sir. It looks to me like about six or seven thousand dollars' worth on each lot."

"Yeah, that sounds about right."

Leland says, "You know, I'm wondering how Miss Baker is going to feel when she finds out that the Seshat company is moving onto the land bought by Kemet Properties, and when they do, it's going to double or triple the value of the land you just bought."

"She's going to wonder if I knew beforehand that Seshat was going to locate there, and I can honestly say that I didn't, because all I have as of today is a strong suspicion about what *might* happen."

Leland chuckles. "Yeah, you might say an *extremely* strong suspicion."

"Well, I have to admit that I do feel a *tiny* bit guilty. So, I'll make it up to Liz somehow. I can send her some business that she otherwise might not get."

Leland runs his hand over the leather on his seat. "This is a really cool car. It's fancy on the inside but kind of rugged looking on the outside, and it's got four-wheel drive."

"I bought it because it reminds me of my Army days. The G Class was originally designed to be a military vehicle."

"Yeah, I can see that. It's got a military look to it."

At dinner that night, Leland tells Diane about his trip with Mr. Henderson to buy the land out on Highway 36. Diane asks what Mr. Henderson intends to do with it.

"I'm not sure, yet. The boss says that he's most likely going to build an office building on the parcel next to the Seshat property, because he thinks that the Seshat company will draw related businesses to the site. All I know is that he has pretty good instincts about that kind of thing."

Chapter Thirty-seven

LELAND GETS HOME AROUND EIGHT O'CLOCK ON THE NIGHT OF Wednesday, August 14, 1996. As soon as he walks through the door, Bret comes running up to him and wraps his arms around Leland's left thigh. Leland musses Bret's hair and says, "Hey, Bret man, were you a good boy today?"

Bret nods vigorously. "Yes, sir."

Diane comes up and hugs Leland. "Had to work late again, huh?"

"Afraid so, but we're getting a lot done. We're almost ready for Dunham. I think we'll be finished with the setup for their lumber in a few days, thank goodness."

"That's good. You're starting to look a little worn out. But right now, you need to get some supper in you."

Leland goes into the bathroom to take off his dress shirt and clean up. He comes to the kitchen table in a faded Sun Records t-shirt and sits down in front of his dinner of baked chicken, rice, and two buttered dinner rolls.

Leland finishes his dinner and asks Diane for a cup of decaf. She brings him the coffee and says, "Oh, Leland, I almost forgot. You got a package in the mail today from Earl Gaines. I'll go get it for you."

"It must be the first set of music tracks."

Diane comes back and hands Leland an envelope containing a small box. When Leland opens the envelope, he sees a CD in a plastic case. He says, "Yep, that's what it is. If I wasn't so wiped out, I'd start practicing tonight."

"Tomorrow will be soon enough."

Leland finishes his coffee and looks at the round kitchen clock hanging above the sink. It's 8:42. He picks up the CD, studies it for a moment and says, "I'm not going to be able to sleep tonight if I don't listen to this first." He stands up and waves goodnight to Bret who's walking to his bedroom in his Tweety Bird pajamas. Leland smiles at Diane and says, "I'm going to take this out to the music studio and play it."

Diane puts down the dish she is rinsing in the sink. "Not without me, you don't."

Leland extends his open left hand to Diane, and she takes it in her still damp right hand. They walk out the back door to the music studio that Leland and Red installed in the room that would have been Diane's art studio if they had not moved her studio to the space above the garage. Leland unlocks the door and walks in to turn on the lights. Diane comes in and takes a seat on a revolving stool that's sitting in front of the studio's control panel. Leland goes over to a gray metal file cabinet on a side wall and opens the top drawer. He rifles through some files, then pulls out the sheets with the words and chord charts for the two songs listed on the CD he just received. He inserts the CD into the player on a shelf above the control panel and tells Diane to hit the play button when he gives her the sign. Diane slides her stool over to a spot in front of the CD player. Leland turns on the PA system and slips on a black headset. Then he places the song lyrics on the music stand in front of the studio microphone. He taps the microphone twice then points at the CD player. Diane hits the play button, and Leland hears the beginning of the first music track.

When Leland hears his cue, he starts singing "A Tear in the Corner of My Eye" into the mic. Diane cups her ears with her hands and shakes her head. Without stopping his singing, Leland reaches over to flip a switch on the control panel that sends the music track and Leland's voice through the studio speakers as well as Leland's headphones. Diane smiles and gives Leland the okay sign.

When Leland finishes his first run-through, he takes off his headset, hits the stop button on the CD player and says, "Man, those musicians are great. This is going to be a lot of fun."

Diane says, "You sounded great, too."

"Not really, but I'll get there. Do you want to hear the other track?"

"Absolutely. What is it?"

"'I'll Be Your Lighthouse.'"

"Oh, I love that song."

Leland does a run-through of "I'll Be Your Lighthouse." When he's done, he takes off his headset, hits the stop button, and turns off the CD player. He says, "I like that music track even more than the track on the first song. They really nailed it."

"You sounded better, too. You were especially good on that one."

"Well, I wasn't that good on that one, either, but I'm getting more comfortable with the process. I'm going to ask Daddy to come over here tomorrow after work, and he can record me singing with the music tracks, and we'll play it back and see what it sounds like."

Leland turns off the sound system, lays his lyric sheets on the console counter, and waits for Diane to get out the door before he turns off the lights and walks through the door behind her. As he's locking the door, he says, "Now I'm fired up. I can't wait to get these songs down and head up to Muscle Shoals and lay some vocal tracks." He claps his hands twice then grabs Diane by the shoulders.

She smiles and says, "And I can't wait to hear those tracks on the radio."

Leland pulls Diane toward him. "You know, babe, I'm finally starting to believe that could actually happen. By the way, how close are you and your mother to having y'all's paintings ready for next month's art show?"

"We're in good shape. Melanie and Frank want to do the mother and daughter thing again, and they want us to have ten paintings ready for that. We've got twelve already, plus these two I'm working on for Dunham and the one that Mama's working on that'll be ready in a week or so, so we're going to have to choose ten out of those fifteen. That'll be hard because I like all of them about the same."

"Well, that's a good problem to have. You know, if they advertise this right, the gallery is going to be packed for that show. I mean you and Miz Beverly are famous already. Everybody's going to want to see y'all's exhibit."

"Well, I don't know about *famous*, but it does seem like a lot of people know who we are."

At 9:10 on Thursday morning, the Moore sisters come into the diner. They take seats at the counter and wave to Diane. When Diane walks behind the counter to serve them, Beth smiles and says, "We'll have just coffee, Diane, and by the way, Melanie owes you and Leland one."

While Diane is reaching over to pick up two mugs she asks, "What do you mean?"

"Well, Melanie and George had dinner with John and me last night, and Melanie happened to mention that Leland had bought you a new car for your anniversary. And believe it or not, right there on the spot, George said he would buy Melanie a new BMW just like mine for their anniversary."

Diane looks up from pouring coffee. "Wow, I can't believe that, Melanie. That's fantastic. When's your anniversary?"

"October eleventh."

Diane sets their two mugs of coffee on the counter. "Well, I'm glad that I was able to help you get a new car, if I did. Do I get a ride in it?"

Melanie says, "Absolutely. Anytime, anywhere."

"I really am glad for you. You're a good mother and a good wife. You deserve something special like that."

"How sweet of you to say that, but I need to tell you something else. Frank has been contacted by reporters from two art magazines who both heard about our fall show and wanted to know if you and Beverly were going to be part of it. Of course, Frank told them that y'all would be having another Mother and Daughter Exhibit, and both reporters said that they would come to the gallery to take photos and do interviews."

Diane wipes down the countertop next to where Beth is sitting. "Maybe Leland was right. He said that Mama and I were getting famous.

I still don't believe it, though. I'm thinking that we're more of a curiosity than anything important."

Melanie takes Diane's hand into hers. "Oh, you sweet, innocent girl. You really don't realize how big a deal you're becoming."

"I'm not a big deal, but I'll tell you who *is* going to be a big deal. Leland's going to start recording an album in Muscle Shoals in about a week and a half. He's the one who's going to be famous."

Beth leans over the counter and asks, "Did you just tell us that your husband is about to record an album in Muscle Shoals?"

"Yes, ma'am. He starts a week from Saturday."

Melanie stares at Diane for a moment. She manages a slight smile and says, "Well, that's just wonderful, Diane. I know you're proud."

"Oh, I am. Will y'all excuse me, please. I just saw the mayor come in."

As soon as Diane is out of earshot, Beth looks to Melanie and says, "Well, sis, maybe we were wrong about Leland being just a small-time musician."

"I'll believe that when I see the album in the window of Lou's Music Shop."

As Melanie and Beth pass by Diane and Mayor Steadman on their way out, Melanie says hello to the mayor and hands Diane a ten-dollar bill and tells her to keep the change.

Diane says, "Oh, thank you so much. Y'all have a nice day."

A few minutes into their walk, Beth says, "That was interesting news about the reporters coming to your fall show. It'll be good publicity for the gallery."

"It will, but I think that the articles are going to focus on Diane and Beverly and not so much the gallery."

"Well, that'll still be good for the gallery, won't it, and it'll still reflect well on you and Frank."

"Yeah, I suppose."

Two blocks later, Beth says, "I'm still having a hard time processing what Diane said about Leland. He's so easy going and seems so unambitious. He seems to just kind of float through life."

"Maybe Diane misunderstood whatever it was that Leland told her."

"I don't think so. She's pretty astute."

"Well, we'll find out eventually. I'll ask George if he's heard anything about Leland making an album in Muscle Shoals. He's the music fan in our house."

"Good idea. And I'll ask John if he's heard anything like that."

For the rest of their walk, the Moore sisters catch each other up on what their children have been up to and how they're doing in school.

That night during dinner, Melanie asks George if he has heard anything about Leland Johnson making an album in Muscle Shoals. George answers, "No, hon, but it wouldn't surprise me. Why'd you ask me that?"

"When we saw Diane today at Danny's Diner, she said that Leland will start recording an album in Muscle Shoals in about ten days."

"Well, I'll ask around and see what I can find out. But I sure hope that what Diane said is true. If it is, we could put a big sign out on the edge of town saying, 'Hometown of Recording Star Leland Johnson.'" He looks at his son and says, "Hey, Georgie, it might bring my drug stores some business, what do you think?"

Georgie nods twice and digs into his banana pudding.

Melanie pours herself a glass of white wine.

Over at the Lancaster house at about the same time, Beth and John are having dinner with their daughters.

Beth says, "John, today at the diner Diane Johnson told us that Leland Johnson is about to make an album in Muscle Shoals. Have you heard anything about that?"

"No, but I'll sure buy a copy when it comes out."

"I just have a hard time believing that it's true."

"Well, we'll know soon enough. But I heard something else about that family today. I heard that Mark Henderson's property company just bought ten acres of land on Highway 36 about halfway between here and Carleton."

"Why in the world would he do that? There's hardly anything out there."

John, who has just finished his meal, reaches for his coffee. He takes a sip and says, "Beats me. But I've known Mark for over twenty-five years now, and I've never known him to make a bad business move. So, that's probably something I should look into. And, of course, I'll also ask him about Leland's album."

Beth, who's on her way to the kitchen, says, "Okay. But if you hear anything about that album, you better tell me."

John winks at his daughters and takes another sip of coffee. He says, "Yes, dear."

At 8:30 that night, Diane hears Leland unlocking the front door. She takes Leland's dinner out from the warmer and sets it on the kitchen table.

Leland is smiling broadly as he walks into the kitchen. He hugs Diane tightly and says, "Babe, it looks like we'll be ready to handle the Dunham account by the end of this week. That means that I can start working normal hours again next week."

On his way to the bedroom to change out of his dress shirt, Leland waves his arms and says, "Glory Hallelujah."

Diane whispers, "Thank goodness" as she pours Leland's iced tea.

A sleepy Bret walks into the kitchen from his bedroom. "Is Daddy home?"

Diane says, "Yes, baby" and leads Bret to the table where she helps him into the chair across from Leland's.

Leland walks in and spots Bret. "Bret, buddy, did I wake you up? I'm sorry."

"That's okay, Daddy. Can I have some Fruit Loops?"

Chapter Thirty-eight

At seven o'clock in the morning of Saturday, August 24, 1996, Red pulls into Leland's driveway in his new red Ford F-150 crew cab pickup.

Leland gives Diane a quick kiss on the cheek as he hustles out the front door with his canvas duffle bag in hand. Diane and Bret wave to Red, and he smiles and waves back.

Leland opens the back door on the passenger side of the pickup and sets his duffle bag on the seat. As he's situating himself in the front seat and fastening his seat belt, Red says, "Well, son, you're on your way to the big time now."

"I don't know about that. I feel like I might be on my way to making a fool of myself. I'm still not sure I'm ready for this. I had a hard time sleeping last night."

"You're ready, trust me. Have you got the practice CD with you?"

Leland shows Red the CD case in his right hand. "Yes, sir."

"Well, just sit back and relax for a while. Once we're on the interstate and you're wide awake, you can practice some more, and I'll critique you as we go."

"I'd appreciate that. I had a long conversation with Earl the other night, and he told me some things that I need to work on as far as articulation and not dropping syllables at the end of a line, and how to sing on different parts of the beat, and how to make better use of phrasing, stuff like that. You know, learning how to quit doing the stuff that I can get away with in a honky-tonk but not on a record."

"Earl told you right. There's a big difference between singing for a bunch of drunks in a club and singing for a record. But I'm not worried about you because I know you can do it. And when you get in that studio, remember what I've always told you—you've got to sing it like you believe it."

"Hey, that's another thing that Earl told me to do. Have you two been talking to each other about me?"

"We might have exchanged a word or two."

"Well, I just hope that you're right about me being able to pull this off. But I promise you one thing, I'm going to give it all I've got. The boss harped on that yesterday when I told him we were going to start recording today. He said never walk away from anything feeling like you didn't do your absolute best. You'll always regret it."

"He told you right."

Once they get onto I-65 North, Leland slides the CD into the truck's CD player and dials the volume to a level where he'll be able to hear the music while he's singing.

When Leland finishes the first song on the CD, Red asks, "What do you think about the sound system in this truck, pretty good, huh?"

"Yeah, it sounds almost as good as the one in our studio. How about me, did I sound okay?"

"I'll be honest with you, Leland. I think that's the best I've ever heard you sing. You were even better than you were at our practice session the other night. But you still have a habit of sometimes tailing off a little at the end of a line. Why don't we play that track again, and you focus on holding your voice steady all the way through each line. Oh, and there's one more thing that I just found out a few days ago that you need to know."

"What's that?"

"You're going to record the first two tracks at Studio B at FAME. Earl told me that he's working on a project over there and has the studio till midnight. He said that he should be able to get to us at around five, and then we'll have till midnight to get your tracks done if we need that much time."

Leland grins. "At FAME. Well, now I really am nervous."

They arrive at FAME Recording Studios at 4:20. There's not much going on at the studio when they get there, because most of the musicians have left to play somewhere else that night. Red and Leland each take a seat in the lobby. When a young lady comes into the lobby and asks if she can help them, Red tells her that they have an appointment with Earl Gaines.

The young lady says, "Oh, you must be Red and Leland. Earl called me a few minutes ago and said that if I saw you to tell you that he was on his way."

Red says, "Thank you, ma'am. Can we look around while we're waiting for him?"

"Sure, just don't go into the studios. There might be somebody working in there."

Before Red and Leland can start to look around, Earl walks through the front door and says, "Afternoon, boys. Sorry I wasn't here to greet you. I had to take care of something. Did y'all stop to eat on the way up?"

"We did," says Red. "We ate lunch in Gardendale."

"That's good. That means that we can get right down to business. Were you able to practice much on those two songs, Leland?"

"Oh, yeah. If I mess up today, it won't be for lack of practice."

"Well, let's go on upstairs and see if we can cut a couple of hit songs."

When Earl opens the door to Studio B, Leland looks inside and says, "I still can't believe I going to be recording in here."

Earl says. "I figured it would be good if you could tell your friends that you recorded some of your album at FAME. And I'm going to let Red help me out on the production so that he can say that he helped produce two of your songs at FAME Studios."

Red says, "You don't have to do that, Earl."

"Red, I'm not just being a sweetheart. You know Leland's voice better than anyone, so you'll be a help to me."

Around 8:15, Earl, Red, and Leland walk out of the studio. As Earl leads Red and Leland back to the lobby, he says, "Guys, that was a very productive session. Once you got used to the equipment, Leland, you did a great job. I don't think it could have gone any better. I'm going to add the background vocals on Monday, and I'll overnight y'all a copy of the final version of the two songs we worked on tonight once that's done. Just keep in mind when you listen to them that they haven't been mastered yet. I'm not going to master anything until all the vocal tracks are completed. But, for now, how bout we walk over to Little Joe's Cafe and get some fried catfish."

On the walk back to FAME after eating at Little Joe's, Red says, "That was a good meal, Earl. I'm glad you took us there."

"That *was* good," says Leland.

"Thanks, guys. Are y'all heading home or staying here tonight?"

Red says, "We've got a reservation at the Red Roof Inn. We'll leave early in the morning unless you need us to do something tomorrow."

"I don't, but let's go by my car and get Leland's next practice CD. I think he's ready now to take on three songs at a time. And if we do three songs a week, that'll let us finish the album in four more weekends."

Earl breaks into a sly smile. "I can tell you now that I've had the studio musicians working on your music tracks since the day after we met at my office. And they've already been working on the arrangements for the three new songs y'all wrote. Yeah, after I met you and talked with you, Leland, I had no doubt that we were going to do this thing."

Red looks at Leland, who says, "Well, I sure wasn't that confident, but I'm awfully glad that we're doing it. And I've got no problem with doing three songs a session, especially now that you've helped me so much with my technique. Today was like going to music school."

"Well, you're a good student. By the way, the vocal setup at my studio is almost identical to the one you used today. So, you should be able to just walk right in and start recording."

Earl turns to Red and says, "You raised a good boy, Red."

"Not me. I have to give all the credit to Jeanette. She raised both of us."

When they get to the FAME parking lot, Earl walks up to a black

Corvette and opens the passenger-side door. He picks up a CD from the seat and hands it to Leland. The jewel case holding the CD is marked "LJ2."

Earl says, "This is for the next session. I'll have one of these ready for you each time you come up, so you won't have to wait for them to come in the mail. The music track CDs will be numbered two, three, four, and five, and we're going to record the songs in that order. With that in mind, when can you come back and do the vocals on the second CD?"

"I'd like to do all the sessions over the next four weekends, if that's possible, because there's a good chance that the Dunham factory that we told you about a while back could start up in October."

Earl leans into his Corvette and reaches inside the console. He takes out a small appointment book and opens it. "Okay, we're talking about doing the last four CDs in sequence with number two being done next Saturday, which is the thirty-first, and then the other three sessions will be on September the seventh, fourteenth, and twenty-first. Yeah, I think I can make that work. I'll give you a call if I have a problem with any of those dates, but now that I've seen what you're capable of, Leland, I'm anxious to get this album done and released. So, I'm going to do every-thing I can to get it done this month, particularly since that'll help both of us. And if we don't run into any unforeseen problems, I believe we'll have the album on the market in time for Christmas sales."

Red asks, "That's amazing. Do you know what label yet?"

"I've still got the same two in mind that I told you about, but I haven't approached either of them so far. My new plan is to not negotiate a con-tract for Leland until the album is mastered. I'm going to do it that way because I think that the album is going to sound so good that it'll sell itself. That'll give us some bargaining power."

Red laughs. "You can tell that after two cuts."

Earl extends his open right hand to Red. "I could tell that when I first heard your demo."

Red and Leland shake Earl's hand and head for Red's truck.

On the way to the motel, Leland says, "Daddy, once I got over the nervousness, I really enjoyed today. I think I'm going to like making an album with Earl. He really knows what he's doing. And I still can't believe that I got to record at FAME."

"Earl's the best. And don't believe for a minute that it was a coincidence that he had Studio B today. He did that just for us."

As they're walking from the parking lot to their hotel room, Leland says, "Daddy, can you do something for me?"

"What do you need?"

"When we get back to work on Monday, can you not make a big deal out of this? I mean I'm proud of what we're doing, but I don't want to make it seem like I'm anybody special. Can you do that for me?"

"I can try, but you have to remember how many of the guys at work are musicians. They're going to know that making an album in Muscle Shoals with Earl Grimes is something special."

"I guess so, but let's please try to not let it get too crazy."

Red shakes his head and says, "Son, I still don't think that you realize how big a deal this is. You stepped off a cliff today."

Leland reaches into his front pocket for their room key. As he's unlocking the door, he softly says, "I suppose so, but I don't know if I can handle getting too much attention."

Red shakes his head and says, "If getting attention is the worst thing that ever happens to you, you'll be a lucky man."

As he enters the hotel room and turns on a light, Leland laughs and says, "Yeah, I guess it beats driving head-on into a giant oak tree."

Red laughs and slaps Leland on the back. "Now, that's the right way to look at it, son."

Red and Leland take their time going home on Sunday. They eat breakfast at Shoney's in Muscle Shoals, have lunch at Golden Rule Barbeque in Birmingham, and stop for peach ice cream at Durbin Farms Market in Clanton.

Bret is sitting on the front porch when Red pulls into the driveway at 4:25. Bret waits for the truck to stop then runs to the passenger-side door and waits for Leland to open it. Before Leland is completely out the door, Bret wraps his arms around Leland's right leg and starts jumping up and down. Then while Leland is removing his duffle bag from the back seat of the truck, Bret lets go of his daddy and runs around the back of the truck to his grandfather's door. Red opens the door and steps out. He reaches down for Bret and picks him up. "Hey, you're getting heavy, Bret."

"Bret's a big boy."

"Yes, he is. He's Granddaddy's big boy."

Bret laughs. "I'm Granddaddy's big boy."

For the next four Saturdays, Leland drives to Muscle Shoals alone, practicing his vocals all the way up. Each Saturday goes smoothly. On the third weekend of the four, Leland finishes his three songs in less than three hours, so Earl and he decide to reward themselves with some barbequed chicken at Little Joe's Cafe before Leland checks into the Red Roof Inn for the night.

On the final weekend, Leland records the vocal tracks for the three songs that he and Red most recently wrote. That session not only gets started early, it only takes about two and half hours to complete.

During that final session, Leland meets two of the musicians who did the music tracks for his album. He also gets to sing live with the background singers. After the session is over, Earl invites Leland, the two musicians, and the three female background singers to come by his house and unwind.

Leland looks at his watch and says, "I don't know. It's early enough that I won't have to spend the night if I leave right away. But I guess I can come by for a little while if that's okay. It probably wouldn't hurt me to unwind some before I get back on the road."

On their way to their cars, Earl tells Leland to follow him home. Once they exit the parking lot, Earl leads Leland on a short drive to a large two-story log house overlooking the Tennessee River. Leland parks his truck behind Earl's Corvette and looks around. He gets out from his truck and walks up next to Earl, who's looking out at the river.

Leland looks at how the orange glow of the setting sun is reflecting off the slowly moving river and says, "Earl, this is beautiful. I can see why you came back to Muscle Shoals."

Earl starts walking toward the house. "Come on, I'll show you some of the inside before the others get here."

Earl leads Leland through the front door into a spacious open room with a stone fireplace and a picture window overlooking the river. "This is my living room . . . Oh, I hear some cars pulling in already, but let me show you my office while they're coming in."

Earl takes Leland into an office that Leland estimates is about four hundred square feet. Each wall is paneled in walnut and decorated with gold records, certificates, and photographs of famous musicians.

Leland says, "You know, if I didn't have to go, I'd like to stay in here for a couple of hours looking at all this stuff on your walls."

"That's okay. You can do it some other time. Come on, let's go out to the living room so that you can tell everybody goodbye."

Leland spends the next ten minutes thanking each of the singers and musicians for the work they did on the album and giving them each his business card and inviting them to call him anytime they're in South Alabama. Then he walks over to Earl and gives him a warm embrace and thanks him for everything that he's done.

Earl says that it was his pleasure. He drapes his right arm over Leland's shoulders and tells him that the fun has just begun.

As he drives from Muscle Shoals to Birmingham, Leland plays his practice CD's and sings all the songs from the album. After that, he finds a sports talk show on the radio. When that show fades away, he listens to an all-night talk show on which the two guests are bigfoot hunters from Louisiana. When he gets closer to home, he finds a familiar classic country station and listens to it for the rest of his trip.

Leland arrives home about 1:10 a.m. Sunday, physically tired but still exhilarated from completing his vocal tracks. As he pulls into his driveway, he wonders for a moment if he needs to phone Diane and tell her he's outside so that if she hears him, she won't think he's a burglar and greet him with a shotgun. Before he decides whether to make the call, Leland sees the porch lights come on. He gets out of his truck, and with his hands held high, he walks to a spot where Diane can see that it's him.

Leland hears the front door open and sees Diane running toward him in her pink flannel pajamas and pink house shoes. She puts an arm around Leland's neck and pulls him toward her. "You're home early. I can't believe it. Does that mean you finished early?"

"It does. My part of the album is done, so I can get some rest now."

"Thank goodness. I was beginning to worry about whether you were overdoing it."

"You and me both. But I feel pretty good now that I won't have to be driving the length of the state every weekend."

"Well, come on inside. I'm wide awake now. You scared me to death driving up at one o'clock in the morning."

Leland retrieves his duffel bag from his truck. "Sorry about that, babe. Want to eat some Cheerios with me?"

"Sure, why not? But be quiet about it. We don't want to wake up Bret."

Chapter Thirty-nine

Leland gets to work early on the morning of Monday, September 23, 1996. He unlocks the front door of the operations building and walks over to the alarm control panel and enters the passcode to turn off the alarm. He takes the metal staircase to the second floor. When he gets to the landing at the top of the stairs, he takes a few minutes to look out at the expanded operations area.

"Good lord, this place is getting big," Leland says to himself. "It's probably twice as big as when I started here. I need to recalculate the total square footage of the company buildings and work area and send that and some new photos to Mister Baker so that he can increase our insurance coverage."

When he gets to his office, the first thing Leland does is write himself a note to contact Mr. Baker. Then he picks up a folder of documents related to the Dunham account.

At 7:55, Leland is sitting at his desk computing the potential profit margin for the Dunham account when he hears the unmistakable sound of Mr. Henderson walking down the hall. A few seconds later, Mr. Henderson walks into Leland's office and says, "Morning, Leland. How'd your Muscle Shoals session go on Saturday?"

"It went great. And that was the last one, thank goodness. My part's done. All that's left is adding some background vocals on one of the tracks, some horns on one other track, and then the mastering."

"I know you're glad that all that driving is over."

"I am. But except for those longs drives, it was one of the best experiences I've ever had. You wouldn't believe how much I learned from Earl about the music business this month."

"I know what you mean. Sometimes when you finish something you've never done before, you almost want to go back and start over so that you can make use of what you learned doing it the first time."

"That's exactly how I felt driving home on Saturday. I'd start my next album right now if they'd let me. Of course, that's not going to happen. We'll have to wait and see how this one does before I'll know if I'll ever do another one."

"Well, I've got a good feeling about this album."

Leland holds up his crossed fingers. "I hope you're right."

Mr. Henderson says, "In any case, let me know as soon as you get a copy of the final version. I want to hear it as soon as possible. But there's something else I need to talk to you about today, so let's have lunch together at the country club. Today is gumbo day. Can you leave around 11:30?"

Leland takes a quick look at his desk calendar. "Yes sir, I can do that. Do you want me to come by your office a little before then?"

"No, I'll come by here and get you."

Before he gets back to what he was doing when Mr. Henderson came in, Leland runs down a mental list of what the boss might want to talk to him about. He gives up when he realizes how many possible topics there are. He starts his computer back up and picks up where he left off on the Dunham calculations.

When they get to the Libertytown Country Club, Mr. Henderson leads Leland to a table in a far corner of the dining room.

"Have you been in here before, Leland?"

"A couple of times with the band, playing for parties, but never to eat."

"Well, the food's good. Some of the members are a little too snooty for my taste, but I still like to eat here once or twice a week. And one day I'll probably start back to playing golf. I've only played here a few times, but I like the course. It's very scenic. And the course is easy enough that

I can get a decent score without a lot of practice."

Leland says, "I didn't know you were a golfer."

"Been playing since I was a kid, just not much in the last few years. I started taking lessons when I was twelve at the Youghiogheny Country Club in McKeesport. I played on my high school golf team, and then I played on the Pitt team my freshman year."

"Why just one year?"

"I joined the National Guard and didn't have time for golf anymore."

"How long were in the Guard?"

"All the way through undergraduate and graduate school. Then, when I graduated from Pitt, I went on active duty in the regular Army. And after I finished my active duty, I served two more years in the Guard. But enough about that. I want to give you some good news about the land I bought over on Highway 36."

"What's the news?"

"I just got an offer from Kemet Properties to buy my ten acres, and I'm going to take their offer. It's too good to turn down. They've offered a hundred and fifty thousand for the two lots, and Kemet will let me keep the timber rights for three months after the closing. That means I can still harvest those pine trees we saw. Of course, that works to their benefit, too, because they've got to clear the land, anyway."

"Well, I don't blame you for taking that offer. That's over twice what you paid for the property, even without the timber rights."

"And once the deal closes, I'm going to pay you a five-thousand-dollar finder's fee, because it was your seeing that for-sale sign on the highway and your having the insight to talk to Angelo about the mysterious coffee house customer that led me to the purchase."

"Nah, you probably would have bought the property, anyway."

"Maybe, maybe not. But you're getting the finder's fee. You can use it to pay down the mortgage on your new house."

Leland smiles. "Well, thank you. I really appreciate it. Diane's going to light up when I tell her that tonight."

"Now that we settled our business, let's eat. I'm hungry. I'm getting the gumbo. Would you like a bowl? Lunch is on me."

"I can always eat gumbo."

Mr. Henderson signals to the waiter, who comes over and takes their order. As the waiter walks off, Mr. Henderson looks at his watch. "David Dunham is going to join us in a few minutes. He wants to talk to you about what's going on at their factory."

"I hope he doesn't want to change anything. We're all ready to go full speed now."

"I'm pretty sure he doesn't want to change anything . . . There he is now. We can ask him."

Leland and Mr. Henderson stand up to greet David Dunham. David shakes their hands, then the three of them take their seats.

Leland says, "I understand that you want to talk with me about something, David. I hope that it's not about anything we've done wrong."

"Oh, no. You guys have been great. You're way ahead of schedule on your part. But as of tomorrow, we'll have a skeleton crew cranking up the factory equipment and building a few of each of our products to see if everything is working properly. I want you to come over one day next week so I can walk you through our manufacturing process."

"I'll be glad to do that. I'm fascinated with furniture-making."

"Yeah, I've seen some of the cabinets that you and your father built, and if Mark wouldn't shoot me, I'd probably offer you both positions with our company."

Mr. Henderson says, "Don't even think about it, David. But before I shoot you, would you like a bowl of gumbo?"

"Absolutely."

On the other side of the dining room, the Moore sisters are having lunch with two of their former classmates from prep school. Beth nods her head toward Mr. Henderson's table and asks Melanie, "What do you think that's about? This is the first time I've ever seen Leland in here."

Melanie says, "Beats me. But I'm guessing it has something to do with wood. What do you think, Belinda?"

Belinda Murphy looks over at the men and says, "I don't know either, but Leland looks awfully cute in that dress shirt and tie."

Beth says, "And Mark Henderson looks more presentable than usual."

Melanie says, "Yeah, maybe Beverly's dressing him now."

On his way out, Leland sees the Moore sisters. He smiles and waves to them.

As Beth is waving to Leland, she says to Belinda, "You're right, he does look handsome today."

At 8:50 on Tuesday morning, the Moore sisters come into Danny's Diner. They're both a little damp from the sprinkle that started a few minutes ago.

"Goodness," says Melanie as she gives a slight wave to Diane. "I've got a chill."

Beth points toward a table and says, "Me, too. Let's sit at that table over there. It's right under the heater vent."

The sisters take seats at a two-person table near the front window. Earline walks over and asks what they would like this morning.

Beth says, "Just coffee, Earline. By the way, how have you been?"

"I'm just fine, thank you ma'am. I'll be right back with your coffee."

Diane comes over to say hello to the sisters.

Melanie says to Diane, "We finished putting up the Mother and Daughter Exhibit yesterday, and it looks even better than the first one. You and Beverly did a great job on those paintings. I wouldn't have believed it, but your painting just keeps getting better."

"Why, thank you. It's so nice of you to say that. Mama and I are both looking forward to the show."

Beth says, "We saw your husband over at the country club yesterday at lunch, and our friend Belinda Murphy said he looked cute in his dress shirt and tie."

Diane nods. "Yeah, he does look good when he's all cleaned up. I wish I could get him to dress better when he's not working, but that's a lost cause. Anyway, he was at the country club to have lunch with Daddy Mark and David Dunham. And he brought me some good news about the land that Daddy Mark bought on Highway 36."

"What was that?" asks Beth.

"Daddy Mark got an offer to sell the ten acres that he bought, and he's going to make a pile of money on the deal."

Beth says, "Really? Who made the offer?"

"Leland says it was a real estate investment company from California."

Beth looks at Melanie, then back at Diane. "From California. What are they going to do with the land? Does Leland know?"

"I think that he knows something, but he won't tell me much. Says it's too soon, whatever that means. But we'll also make some money on the deal, because Leland is going to get a finder's fee for locating the property."

Beth says, "That's good that y'all are also going to make something on the deal. But I just can't think of anything that you could do with land way out there, except maybe build a factory of some kind."

"I'll bet that's it," says Melanie, nodding. "Somebody's going to be building a factory out there." Then she laughs and says, "Why don't we set up a pool at the club on what kind of factory it's going to be."

Beth says, "I'm in. I say it's going to be a textile mill."

"That sounds like a pretty good guess," says Melanie. "What do you think, Diane?"

"I don't know, but I have a feeling that it's not going to be a factory. I think it'll be something like an office building." She laughs. "But what do I know. Y'all are probably right about some kind of factory."

"Let me ask you about something else," says Beth. "Now, I don't want to be nosy, and you don't have to answer if you don't want to, but with your art career going so well, and with all the other things that are going so well for you and Leland lately, why are you still working here?"

Diane smiles. "Oh, I don't mind you asking me that, but the truth is I want us to pay off our mortgage as soon as possible, so I told Leland, and I also told Theo, that I'm going to keep working here until we pay the house off. Besides that, I enjoy working here. I like seeing nice people like y'all every day."

Diane looks toward the front door. "Excuse me, please. Another customer just walked in."

After Diane leaves their table, Melanie whispers to Beth, "Can you believe what we just heard about that land sale. Every time we turn around, somebody in that family is making money off something. I heard from George last night that Beverly had just sold her house for a huge profit to a couple who moved here to work at the Dunham factory. The husband's going to be making furniture, and the wife's going to work in the office."

"That *is* a cute little house. Red and Leland did a good job of fixing it up," says Beth.

Earline brings their coffee. As she sets the mugs on the table, she asks, "Is something wrong? Y'all look kind of worried."

Beth says, "We're fine, Earline. We were just sitting here thinking about having to walk home in the rain."

"Oh, you'll be all right. Judge Bailey says it's just a passing shower. He's usually right about those things. Y'all let me know if I can get you anything else, okay."

Chapter Forty

On Thursday morning, Leland calls David and asks if next Wednesday afternoon would be a good time for him to visit the furniture factory. David tells him that any time after two would work, and they agree that Leland will come by the factory at two thirty on Wednesday.

At 2:25 Wednesday afternoon, Leland stops his truck at the entrance to the Dunham factory. He tells the security guard who signaled for him to stop that he has an appointment with David Dunham.

The security guard looks at the top sheet of paper in the clipboard that he's holding. He says, "Mister Johnson, you can park in one of the visitor spots in front of the main entrance."

"Thank you, sir. Have a good day."

Leland parks in a spot right in front of the entrance door and gets out. He walks to the door and presses a button under a sign that reads, "Please Press Button and Wait for Door to Open." When the door opens, Leland walks into the main lobby where he's greeted by David Dunham. Leland laughs and says, "My Lord, David, this was like coming onto a top-secret military base. Is there something I don't know about what y'all do here?"

"We'll see. But strict security is a company policy set by my father a long time ago. He likes everything buttoned down. That way, nothing comes in that we don't know about, and nothing goes out that we don't know about."

"That makes sense, I guess. Maybe we need to make the sawmill more secure."

"I don't know about that. It's kind of hard to imagine someone sneaking out with a twelve-foot-long one by six."

Leland smiles. "You'd be surprised."

"Anyway, let me show you our factory. Let's take a walk outside first, and I'll show you how we warehouse the lumber that we get from your company."

The two men walk out a side door onto a concrete sidewalk. David leads Leland to a large warehouse behind the main building. He opens the front door and motions Leland in. When Leland enters the building, he can tell that it's climate controlled. He looks around and sees that the lumber in there is separated and stored by dimensions, shape, and species of wood. The floor is brown-stained concrete, and Leland can see that the walls have been fireproofed. There is a sprinkler system in the ceiling above the lumber.

"Very impressive," says Leland, "Y'all take very good care of your lumber."

"It's the most important item in this complex. That's why we chose your company to be our supplier. We want only the best wood to work with, and we want it cut right. Now, let's walk over to the parts warehouse next door, so that I can show you what our guys do with the lumber."

Leland follows David into another large warehouse where he sees dozens of labeled compartments inside of each are different parts from which to build furniture. Once again, the building is climate controlled, the floor is stained concrete, the walls are fire resistant, and there is a sprinkler system.

David takes Leland back into the main building and leads him to where the wooden parts are assembled into the different items of furniture. They stand there for a few minutes watching two craftsmen assemble a Georgian-style dresser.

Then David takes Leland to the sanding room, the glazing and staining area, and the spray rooms. David explains to Leland that the factory's sawdust is captured and sold to paper companies, and the lacquer over-spray is captured and shipped to Dunham's Pennsylvania factory where they have the lacquer recycled.

David leads Leland to the upholstery department and then to the shipping warehouse where completed items are stored in compartments until they're loaded onto trucks. At the door of the shipping warehouse, Leland asks, "Will you keep a big inventory in here once you get up to full speed?"

"No, we'll keep on hand maybe a dozen or so of each item, because almost all of our furniture is made to order and shipped out right after it's built."

David watches Leland walk from compartment to compartment, inspecting the various pieces of furniture that the skeleton crew has produced.

"David, this stuff is near perfect. The only other furniture I've ever seen that was this well-made is what y'all put in the Liberty Hotel."

"I'm glad you like it because I've got an offer for you."

"What's that?"

"Mark told me that you and Diane still need a few items for your house, and I want to help you with that. Tell me what you need."

"Well, for certain, we need to replace the funky double bed in one of the guest bedrooms, and we need some kind of small sofa or loveseat for our foyer. Are you going to make me a good deal on those? I hope that's what you're getting around to."

"No, that's not where I'm going. Where I'm going is that in consideration of your getting your production line and your milling shop ready for us well ahead of time, we're going to give you a bed and a loveseat. We don't have any sofas yet, but we've got two loveseats here that are just like the two that are in the lobby of the hotel. They're the model that our company has been making for about sixty years that everyone seems to like. One is upholstered in heavy-duty green damask and the other in dark burgundy leather."

David points to a spot to Leland's left. "The bed that I'd like to give you is that walnut Queen Anne queen-size bed over there. The two loveseats are up there near the loading dock. You pick the one you want, and it's yours."

"Are you sure about this, David. That's some very expensive furniture."

"Not compared to the money we're making in that extra time you gave us."

Leland walks to where the loveseats are positioned next to each other, and he carefully looks them over. He chooses the one that is upholstered in dark burgundy leather.

David tells him that the loveseat and bed can be delivered to his house tomorrow.

"That'd be great, but it'll have to be after four thirty. That's when Diane usually gets home."

"Not a problem. I'll schedule the delivery for five o'clock tomorrow, and I'll see you and Diane at the art gallery on Friday, and she can tell me then how wonderful I am."

Leland chuckles. "I'm sure she will. She'll probably run up and hug your neck. I don't know what to say, David. If there's ever anything I can do for you, just let me know."

"I'm going to hold you to that, Leland, because there's bound to be some carpentry work that'll come up after we move into the house that we're buying downtown."

"I don't know. Emma's got that house in great shape. But, if y'all do find anything that you want to change, give me a call, and I'll be right on it."

Chapter Forty-one

On the following Friday afternoon, Leland stops his pickup in front of the Main Street Gallery. Diane gets out of the truck, blows Leland a kiss, and enters the gallery. Leland drives away to find a parking spot.

When Diane gets inside the gallery, she sees that a crowd is standing around the refreshment table in the lobby with drinks and snacks in hand. Frank Dupre sees Diane and walks her way.

Frank gives Diane a warm hug and says, "Darling, I'm so glad you're here. Everyone's been asking about you and your mother."

"Am I late, Frank? I thought you were going to start the reception at five thirty."

"That was the plan, but people started coming in around four thirty, and before I knew it, I was overwhelmed by a hungry, thirsty mob. So, I told our intern Anna to start serving early."

Frank motions to a man and a woman who are conversing with Melanie. The three of them walk over to where Frank and Diane are standing.

Melanie says hello to Diane.

Frank says, "Diane, I want you to meet two good friends of mine. Doctor Joe Sabatini is a former colleague of mine. He's now the dean of the art department at Langston College over in Georgia, and he's spending this weekend at my place. And this lovely young lady is Linda Atmore who is an assistant professor of art at South Alabama."

Joe is short and stocky with longish gray hair and a dark beard. He's wearing blue jeans, a black t-shirt, and a tan corduroy sport jacket with elbow patches. Linda is about Diane's height and thin with long, straight black hair and very little makeup. She's wearing a simple light blue summer dress and a matching blue headband.

Diane shakes hands with Joe and Linda and says, "I'm so glad to meet y'all. Have y'all looked at any of the paintings yet? Some of them are just great."

Joe smiles at Diane's question.

Frank says, "Diane, sugar, these are our two jurors for the show. They came in yesterday afternoon and studied *all* the paintings very assiduously."

"I don't understand," says Diane, looking puzzled.

Frank looks at Melanie. "Melanie, did you not tell Diane this would be a juried show?"

Melanie blushes. "No, I don't believe I did."

"Sorry, Diane," says Frank, "We should have told you that this show would be a competition. We had Joe and Linda come in yesterday and pick a best in show, and a second and third place, and honorable mentions for both the paintings and the photography."

Frank looks at his watch. "We're going to announce the winners in about forty minutes or so, Diane, so why don't you just mingle in the meantime." Diane looks around. "Okay. I've got to find Leland and Mama, anyway. Looking at Joe and Linda, she says, "It was so good to meet y'all. I hope y'all enjoy this evening."

Diane sees Leland standing just inside the front door. She turns to Frank and the others and says, "There's my husband now. Y'all please excuse me."

Linda and Joe are both smiling as Diane walks away. Linda says, "What a sweet girl."

Joe says, "She is. It's so refreshing to see someone with that kind of talent be so demure. Frank, I'm sure you remember how many students we've had who had very little talent but were completely full of themselves."

"Oh, do I. Bless their deluded little hearts."

Just as Diane gets to Leland, Beverly sees them and walks over and hugs them both. She says, "Can you believe this crowd. And it's not even five thirty yet."

Leland says, "Like I've been telling you two, you're famous now. They're here to see y'all."

"Surely not," says Beverly, looking around the room.

"Where are your parents, Leland?" asks Diane.

"They ought to be here shortly. Look, there's a woman over there who's talking to Frank and pointing our way."

Beverly and Diane peer over to where Leland is looking. Beverly says, "Oh, that's Bonita Franklin. She's a reporter with the *Courier*. She's been to our other shows. She just has a different hair color now. Her hair used to be blonde."

Leland says, "Oh yeah, I recognize her now. I've seen her on the news. She's the one who interviewed Daddy and me over the phone about our Grammy nomination. She did a nice article on us. I need to thank her for that."

Leland excuses himself and walks over to speak to Bonita Franklin. Frank shakes hands with Leland and introduces him to Miss Franklin.

Leland says, "Good to see you, Miss Franklin. I want to thank you for the nice article that you wrote about my Daddy and me."

"Oh, that was my pleasure. How's your songwriting career going?"

"Pretty well right now. I just recorded an album of songs by Daddy and me."

"He recorded the album in Muscle Shoals," says Frank.

"That so. Well, I came here tonight to cover your wife and your mother-in-law, but maybe I should talk to your dad and you while I'm here."

Leland looks around for Red. "Yes ma'am. Daddy should be here soon, and you can talk to us whenever you want after he gets here."

At 5:45, Frank reaches over and picks up a brass dinner bell from the reception desk. He rings the bell until the crowd quiets to a low murmur. He calls out, "If I can please have your attention, everyone, we'd like to begin the award presentations."

Frank, Melanie, Joe, and Linda all walk to a wooden dais that has a microphone attached to the top and a speaker built into the front. Frank stands at the microphone and welcomes everyone, then he introduces Melanie, Joe, and Linda. The audience applauds after each introduction. Frank motions to Joe, then moves back from the dais and lets Joe take his place.

Joe says, "I am so honored to have been chosen, along with Professor Atmore, to judge this show. As you can see, there is a great deal of talent on display here this evening. So much talent, in fact, that we had a difficult time deciding just which of those talented painters and photographers should get an award. If it were up to me, I'd give all of them awards. But since that's not what we were charged to do, I'll announce the recipients of the painting awards, and Professor Atmore will announce the recipients of the photography awards. And remember, this contest has a rule that no single painter or photographer can receive more than one award. That means we'll have eighteen different award winners today.

Joe looks toward Frank, who has taken a position about six feet to the right of the dais. He says, "When I call your name, please come up to where Mister Dupre is standing. He'll hand you your award, and your picture will be taken during the presentation of the award. I'll begin with the six honorable mention award winners in the painting competition. They will each receive a ribbon and a check for fifty dollars."

Joe calls out the names of the six honorable mention recipients, and they each walk to where Frank is standing and receive their ribbons and checks and have their photos taken.

Next, Linda comes to the microphone and announces the honorable mention award recipients for the photography competition, and those six people come up and receive their awards.

Then Joe walks back to the dais and tells the audience that the third-place winners will receive a ribbon and a one-hundred-dollar check, and the second-place winners will receive a ribbon and two hundred dollars.

After the third-place winner in the painting category receives his award, Joe announces that the second-place winner is Beverly Henderson for her painting of the Clark County fishing pond. When her name is announced, Beverly looks at Diane, who is smiling and applauding. Leland pats Beverly on the back as she's walking up to accept her award.

Linda announces the third-place winner and second-place winner for photography, and Frank hands the winners their awards. Then Linda tells the audience that the two remaining awards are for best in show in the painting competition and best in show in photography.

Joe comes back to the mic and says, "First, I'll announce the winner for best in show in the painting competition. This winner will receive a trophy and a check for three hundred dollars." Joe looks around the room very slowly. Then he takes a deep breath and says, "Diane Johnson for her painting entitled 'Main Street.'"

Diane turns and looks at her mother. Beverly eyes glisten as she pulls Diane to her side and whispers, "I'm so proud of you, baby."

Once the award presentations are over, several people come by to congratulate Diane and Beverly, including some of Diane's former high school classmates. Emma Crawford briskly walks over to give Diane and Beverly congratulatory hugs, as does Jeanette Johnson, who got to the event just in time to see them receive their awards.

Leland, Red, and Mark are all standing against a side wall, talking about tomorrow's football games and taking everything in. Mark says, "I'm glad I got here in time to see Beverly get her award. I didn't know there was going to be an award presentation."

Leland says, "Neither did Diane or Miz Beverly. They thought this was just going to be a show."

Red says, "Well, I'm proud of both of them. They deserve the recognition, award or no award."

"Look," says Leland. "They're about to be interviewed now by the newspaper lady and a couple of more reporters."

"First of all," says Bonita Franklin to Diane and Beverly, "I have to introduce you two to Angela LaRosa from *Alabama Arts and Crafts Magazine* and Doug Chambers from *Wiregrass Arts Magazine*. They're going to listen in on my interview and take notes for their columns, and those two photographers over there are going to be taking photos of y'all and your paintings for their magazines. Is that okay?"

Beverly looks over to see where the photographers are standing. She puts her right arm around Diane's shoulders. "Sure. Anything to help Diane's career."

Diane looks around at the magazine reporters and photographers. She takes a deep breath and nervously says, "I don't know, Mama. This is kind of intimidating. But I guess it'll be all right. Just stay close by."

Miss Franklin says, "Well, let me start with Beverly. Beverly, just how proud are you of Diane winning best of show."

Beverly says, "Before I answer that, Diane and I want to thank Frank Dupre and Melanie Pebworth for all they've done to help us. Without them, none of this would have happened.

"Now, as to Diane's winning best of show, I've got mixed feelings about that. On the one hand, I've always disliked art contests because I've never thought that art should be treated as a competitive sport. But, on the other hand, I love seeing Diane's talent being publicly acknowledged by two respected art experts. So, I guess I have to say that overall, I'm pretty proud of my girl."

Diane puts her arm around her mother's waist and says, "And what about those two experts acknowledging *your* talent?"

"Well, I've won awards before, and I've never felt comfortable about it. But this is probably the least uncomfortable I've ever felt about receiving an award, because we did it together."

Frank walks up with a broad smile on his face. "Excuse me, y'all. Sorry, Bonita, I hate to interrupt, but I just had to come tell these two ladies that their paintings have sold out, except for the two that weren't for sale."

Miss Franklin says, "No problem, Frank. I'll put that in my article."

Beverly and Diane look at each other. A flash goes off as the photographer from *Wiregrass Arts Magazine* snaps their photo. The photographer turns to Doug Chambers and says, "The expressions on their faces were precious."

Bonita Franklin is still interviewing Diane and Beverly when Leland sees David and Emily Dunham walking toward him. When they get to where Leland, Red, and Mark are standing, David says, "How's it going, guys?" He looks around and says, "Man, there's a big crowd here tonight."

Red says, "You just missed seeing Diane and Beverly win awards."

Mark adds, "Yeah, and Diane's was for best in show."

Emily looks at Diane and Beverly, who are still answering questions from Miss Franklin. She says, "I'm sorry we missed that, but I couldn't get David off the phone with some timber guy."

"Hey, those timber guys keep us in business," says Mark, smiling. "Don't give David a hard time about that."

"All right. But I still wish we'd been here to see them get their awards."

David asks, "Leland, how'd Diane like the loveseat and bed that we sent over yesterday?"

"Oh, she couldn't believe it. She was crying, she was so happy. And those pieces look great in those two rooms. So, don't be surprised if she comes over here and hugs your neck."

Sure enough, when Diane ends her conversation with Miss Franklin and sees David and Emily, she runs over and gives David a warm hug. She says, "Oh, David, that furniture you gave us is *so* beautiful. Thank you, thank you." Then she gives Emily a hug and says, "You two are so nice to us."

Emily says, "Well, you and Leland are easy to be nice to. But I've got something to tell you that may be just as exciting for you as winning your award today."

"Really? What's that?"

"That garden painting that you did for us is now hanging in the lobby of one of the best hotels in Monte Carlo."

Diane looks at Beverly, who reaches for Diane's hand and says, "See, Leland was right, baby. You're going to be famous."

Diane turns back to Emily. "Thank you so much, Emily. I don't know what to say. Can you get me a picture of it hanging in there?"

"Sure. I'll give the manager a call tomorrow."

"Oh, and one more thing, Emily. How far is Monte Carlo from Paris? Daddy Mark has promised to take Mama and me to Paris when things are not so hectic for him. He's going to take us to all the big art museums."

"It's a pretty good distance, probably about nine and half hours by car. But you can get there a lot quicker by train."

Diane looks at Leland, who's shaking his head and smiling broadly. Diane says, "Oh, Leland, honey, I almost forgot. Bonita Franklin wants to interview you and your daddy."

Red says, "Y'all excuse us, please" and takes Leland's arm. "Let's go, son. We've got to start selling some albums."

When they get to Miss Franklin, Red tells her about how Leland went up to Muscle Shoals for five straight weekends to work on the album with Earl Gaines, one of the best producers there is, and how Earl projects that the album will be out before Christmas.

Leland tells Miss Franklin that Earl called him last night and confirmed that the album title will be "Songs from Creek County." Leland adds, "Earl also told me that the label approved the design that he and Diane came up with for the album cover. The cover is going to have a picture of Diane's depot painting on it."

Miss Franklin says, "Why, that's wonderful, Leland. I'll add that to my notes about Diane. Could y'all get me an advance copy of the album so that we can put a review in our paper before it comes out."

Red winks and says, "Only if you promise us a good review."

Miss Franklin laughs. "You know I can't do that, Red, but I really can't see how it would be anything else."

Red, Jeanette, Leland, and Diane all stop by the Henderson house after the show to eat chili and grilled cheese sandwiches. Mark is in the kitchen heating the chili that he made last night. He says to Beverly, who's grilling the sandwiches, "David told me that Emily and he are going to come by for a while. They need to go by the hotel first to take care of some business, but they should be here in about thirty minutes. So, let's set places for them, too."

Beverly asks Diane if she wants to take some chili home with her, and Diane says that she does, and she also wants a grilled cheese sandwich to take to Earline, who's watching Bret.

"Earline is such a good friend to you," says Beverly. "I'm sure she could be doing something else on a Friday night."

"She's the best. But she loves to stay with Bret, and, besides that, she's got a late-night date with her boyfriend. So, I won't be keeping her from anything. And she always brings a book so that she can study once Bret gets occupied with something. She's in her second year over at Carleton Community College, so I've told her that she can study at our house when she's tending Bret, and that she can use my computer."

"That's thoughtful of you. What's she majoring in?"

"Business. And she wants to go to South Alabama after she gets her associate degree and study business there."

Beverly says, "I've always been crazy about Earline. I like her spunk, and her attitude."

Diane says, "Oh, she's got some spunk all right. She's fun to work with."

"Well, since she's going to be seeing her boyfriend later, take two grilled cheese sandwiches, one for him. And I'll put a bag of chips and a dill pickle in the bag with them. And just between you and me, let's plan on helping Earline with her expenses once she gets to South Alabama."

Diane kisses her mother on the cheek and says, "You bet."

David and Emily arrive at seven thirty. As soon as he walks through the door, David says to Mark, "Thank goodness you've got food. I haven't eaten anything since breakfast."

"Excuse my husband's manners," says Emily to Beverly.

Beverly says, "That's all right" and takes Emily by the arm and leads her to the dining room. "We're almost finished eating, but y'all take your time."

When David sits down at the dining room table, Red asks him how things were at the hotel.

David spoons some chili into his bowl and answers, "I don't want to say anything to break the spell, but things couldn't be any better. Phil did us right when he hired Raymond to run the place. But we didn't go by there tonight to do any serious business. We only went by so that Emily could take a couple of new knick-knacks up to the large penthouse suite."

Emily stares at David. "David, those weren't knick-knacks, they were antique Chinese vases."

David looks at Mark. "Like I said, knick-knacks."

Mark laughs. "Don't look at me, David. I'm not getting into this discussion. But, while you're here, I want to tell you in front of everybody how grateful I am for those two young couples you brought by to look at Dunham Place lots. Both couples signed sales contracts, and they can start building as soon the street and utilities are completed and inspected. I gave them both the contact info for our two approved builders, and I recommended John's bank for their financing."

David says, "Both those couples are good people, and how can I resist promoting a development called Dunham Place? And you probably already know from talking to them that the two husbands will be on our production line, and one of the wives will be in our accounting office. The other wife just got her degree in education, so she'll be looking for a teaching position."

"Yeah, they did tell me all that. You let me know if I can do anything to help the one who's looking for a teaching job."

"Thanks. That's very kind of you. I also want you to know that I have at least two, and possibly three, more prospects for you. They'll all be down here within the next two weeks. I'll take them over to Dunham Place and show them around."

Mark nods as he swallows the last bite of his grilled cheese sandwich. "So, that'll potentially be four or five lots sold, and I've sold three others to people from this area. That'll make seven or eight of the fifteen lots. And once they start building, it'll be no time before the rest of the lots are sold."

Red says, "Boss, I've got to give you credit. That development was a good idea. It'll be an improvement to the city on top of making you some money."

"And it'll give us some neighbors," says Diane.

Jeanette has finished her meal and is standing at the buffet looking at Diane's best in show trophy. "This is just beautiful, Diane. Are you going to put it in your studio?"

"Yes, ma'am. And Mama's going to hang her ribbon in there, too. And Miss Franklin is going to send us a picture of the exhibit. So, when we get that picture, we can display those three things together. We just need to find a good place for them."

Mark lifts his glass of root beer and holds it up high. "Here's to my two favorites artists. I'm proud of both of you."

At 8:15, Diane and Leland tell Beverly that they need to get home so that Earline can leave. They say goodbye to the group and tell Mark how good the chili was. Beverly goes into the kitchen and comes back with a brown paper bag containing the two sandwiches, the chips, and the dill pickle.

On the way home, Leland says, "What a night. You win best of show, your mother wins second place, and we both get interviewed by Miss Franklin."

"Did you and your daddy also talk to the magazine reporters?"

"*He* did. The two photographers were taking my picture while he was talking, so I don't know what he told them. But I'm glad he talked to them. He's better at that kind of stuff than I am."

"He is, but you're going to have to get better at it fast, because you're probably going to be interviewed on the radio and maybe on television."

"Let's not get ahead of ourselves. The album might be a complete dud."

"No, it won't. It's going to be a top ten album."

Leland reaches over and pats Diane's hand. "Okay, babe, if you say so."

Diane laughs and says, "So." Then her expression gets serious. "I wonder why Melanie didn't say much to me tonight."

"She's jealous."

"Jealous of me? Why? She's so smart and pretty, and so talented. She's got no reason to be jealous of me."

"Well, she is smart. But you're prettier and more talented." Leland runs his right hand though his dark wavy hair. "And you've got a better-looking husband."

Diane kisses Leland's right cheek. "Well, I agree with that last part."

Chapter Forty-two

It's a few minutes after ten o'clock in the morning on Tuesday, October 22, 1996, and the members of the Liberty Hotel Company, LLC are meeting in Mr. Henderson's office. Three of the other four members are present, and Sean Henderson is on the speaker phone.

Mark Henderson hands a document to each of the other three members who are present and tells them that Sean has been faxed his copy. "Gentlemen, this is our quarterly report for the third quarter of nineteen ninety-six, which is the first quarter of operation for the hotel. As you can see, the gross revenues were about twenty percent over what we projected; and from our reservations list, there's no doubt that next quarter will be significantly better. What this means is that the hotel will make a small profit this year, which none of us expected, and we'll have to decide today or at next quarter's meeting whether we want to make a distribution of that profit or just leave the money in the bank for the time being."

Judge Bailey says, "There's no reason to wait three months to decide on that. I move that we don't make any distributions until the accrued profits are over a hundred thousand, because I think we need to keep a cushion of at least a hundred thousand in the operating account."

David seconds the motion, and Mark asks for a vote. The members vote unanimously to wait until the hundred-thousand-dollar cushion accrues before there is any further talk of a distribution of profits.

Mark says, "Boy, that was easy. Does anyone have any other hotel company business to discuss?"

Phil says, "I think we ought to invite Raymond to our next meeting and somehow show him our appreciation for the good job he's doing. How about we hold the January meeting at lunchtime in one of the private meeting rooms at the country club and invite Raymond and his wife to have lunch with us? And I say that we should reward Raymond by having the hotel company buy him a country club membership and pay his annual dues."

"I like that idea," says David.

"So do I," says Phil. "Not just to reward Raymond, but because it would be beneficial to the hotel for the manager to do a little hobnobbing with the town's power brokers."

Mark says, "I agree." He gets up and walks over to his desk where he looks at his calendar. "I propose that we hold a meeting at the club at lunchtime on January 15, 1997. I'll make the reservation. Any objection?" Mark waits a moment. "There's no objection, so I'll make the reservation for us and invite Raymond to meet with us on that date."

David says, "Before we break up, I'd like to make another announcement. As of tomorrow, our factory will be fully operational. We still need to hire some more production employees, but we'll have all our departments in operation as of tomorrow morning, and we'll be turning out furniture at a pretty good rate."

Phil Bernstein slaps David on the back, and Mark says, "That is no insignificant announcement you just made, David. Your factory is going to have a big impact on our city and this whole area."

"That's right," says Judge Bailey. "Thanks to Dunham, Libertytown is going to be known all over the world. Mark showed me a photo of that brass plate that y'all are going to attach to the bottom of your furniture that says, 'Custom made by the Libertytown, Alabama Division of Dunham Fine Furnishings Corporation.'"

Ron Anderson looks at Judge Bailey and nods his head twice. "You're right about that, Hollis. Now, we've got to put some pressure on the mayor to get all the potholes on Main Street repaired."

"Hear, hear," says Sean over the speaker phone.

Phil says, "Speaking of Mayor Steadman, he told me something yesterday that could also have a positive effect on Libertytown. He said that the Defense Department had contacted him to discuss a training center that's going to be jointly built by the Defense Department and a company out of California on some property not too far out on Highway 36. The official who called him wanted to know the potential of the city annexing that area so that the training center would fall within coverage by the fire department, the sanitation department, and the police department."

Mark writes a note on his memo pad and says, "I think I know exactly where that center's going up. What did Bob tell him?"

Phil laughs and says, "Bob said he'd start working on it right away. And we all need to use our influence to get that annexation done as soon as possible."

Sean's voice comes back on the speaker phone. "Wouldn't that mean that the city will have to increase the size of those three departments?"

Mark says, "It would, but with the additional tax revenues that'll be coming in soon, that won't be a problem." Mark turns to Phil and asks, "Does Bob know what kind of training is going to be done there?"

"He said the Defense guy kind of danced around that, but he did say enough for Bob to conclude that it'll have something to do with computer technology training for the military."

Mark smiles. He thinks to himself: *That's why Seshat bought that ten acres from me instead of just five. This training center will need space for dormitories and a dining hall on top of the training facility and parking lot. And they're also going to need standoff distance around the whole thing for security purposes.*

Out loud, Mark says, "Hollis, can we humbly request that you take the lead on this annexation that the mayor wants?"

"Absolutely. I've got some acreage out that way myself."

Chapter Forty-three

On Thanksgiving Day 1996 at the Henderson house, Mark and Beverly are joined for dinner by Red, Jeanette, Diane, Leland, Bret, Emma, and Mel. Once everyone is seated at the dining table, Beverly says the blessing. After she finishes, she says, "Now Mark wants to say a few words while Diane and I get everyone served."

Mark looks around the table. "On this day of thanks, I don't know how I can express how truly blessed I feel, but I'll try. Obviously, the thing that I'm the most thankful for this year is being married to Beverly and being a part of this extended family. And, as Red and Leland know, this year is going to be the best year our company has ever had, due in no small part to the work they've been doing to get us ready for the Dunham account. On top of that, the Dunham Place development couldn't be going any better, the Liberty Hotel is way ahead of where we thought it would be, Leland and Diane built their new house, Beverly and Jeanette are both enjoying their retirement, Beverly's and Diane's art careers are going unbelievably well, and Leland has finished recording his album which will no doubt be a big success. Folks, I just don't see how things could have gone any better for us this year, and I'm glad that we're all here together today to humbly give thanks to God for all that he's blessed us with."

"Amen," says a smiling Red.

Emma takes Mel's hand in hers and says, "And thank you so much Mark and Beverly for inviting Mel and me to be with y'all today. We're going to miss y'all when we move. But I did get some good news from Brad last night. The Air Force approved his request to be transferred to Eglin. So, we'll be just a little over an hour away."

Diane sets down the gravy boat that she's carrying and goes over to hug Emma and then Mel. "I can't believe y'all are going to be so close. We'll have to visit each other every chance we get."

Red sets his empty iced tea glass on the table and leans back in his chair. He looks at Leland and says, "Well, folks. I feel like we may have already gotten overloaded with good feelings today, but I'm going to have to lay some more good news on you. Earl Gaines got Leland signed to Dubyar Records, and his album is going to be out in time for Christmas sales." Everyone at the table starts clapping and congratulating Leland. Diane gets up and kisses Leland on the cheek and then Red.

Red says, "Thank you, darling. But here's the topper. I've got an advance copy with me, and y'all will see that it just happens to have the cover on it that was designed by Diane and Earl, with Diane's depot painting on the front."

He hands the CD to Diane to look at and pass around. Red continues, "And I'm going to be dropping that CD off at Jumpin' Jeff Foster's house tonight so that he can play it on his afternoon radio show tomorrow. I'm also going to take one to Bonita Franklin on Monday so that she can publicize it in the *Courier*."

Diane studies the CD cover for a moment, then she reads the notes on the back. She hands the CD to Beverly. Then she lightly slaps Leland on the back of his head and asks, "Why didn't you tell me about this, Leland?"

Red laughs. "Don't blame Leland. I didn't tell him until about half an hour ago. I wanted to save it until we could tell everybody else at the same time. By the way, Earl sent me enough copies that I can give one to each of y'all. They're out in my truck."

Mark says, "That was awfully nice of Earl. Do you know much about the Dubyar label? Is it a good label for Leland?"

"Oh, yeah. It's owned by a big-time media guy named W. R. Gandy from north Mississippi. He's got connections all over the world. He added the Dubyar label to his media company a few years ago, and they put out a first-rate product. Leland's in good hands."

"Can y'all get Dubyar t-shirts for Bret and me?" asks Diane.

Red laughs. "I don't see why not."

After Thanksgiving dinner, Diane is helping Beverly clean up her kitchen when Beverly says quietly to Diane, "Remember back when we talked about going out to Salem, Oregon and visiting Burton's gravesite?"

Diane stops putting dishes in the dishwasher. She turns excitedly to Beverly and asks, "Do you mean you found out where it is?"

"I did. Mark's friend Victor out in Northern California helped me find it. And I also found a museum not too far from Salem where some of Burton's paintings are on display, including one of his Monterey paintings. I can't wait for you to see them. You'll see how similar your style is to his."

Diane hugs Beverly and rocks her side to side. She says, "You are the best mother ever. When can we go out there?"

"Well, now that Bret is old enough that he can get along without his mother for a few days, we can go anytime. But we'd best wait until after the holidays are over and the weather's better. It'll be easier to travel then. So, let's plan on going sometime in early April. You can tell Theo tomorrow that you'll need a few days off in April, and we'll work out a schedule."

"Well, you know I don't want to wait, but that probably would be the best time to go. Does Daddy Mark know that I want you to take me out to Oregon?"

"He does, and he thinks that it would be good for you."

"He's so sweet. You're so lucky."

"But there is something else that I need to tell you. The museum director that I talked to about Burton's paintings sent me a print of one of his Malibu series and I had it framed. I was going to give it to you for Christmas, but I think that this might be a better time."

"Are you kidding me, Mama? Where is it?"

"Come with me."

Beverly leads Diane to the library where she opens a closet door and picks up an eleven by fourteen walnut frame. Beverly hands the frame to Diane, whose hands are shaking, and Diane looks at the print that the frame contains. The print is of a seascape in which the roaring ocean waves are crashing hard against a tall rock wall that overlooks a somber beach. The twilight sky lights up the clouds over the ocean in shades of pink, purple, and orange. The colors are reflected on the surface of the ocean. The only figures on the beach are an old man and his black dog. They're standing at the water's edge looking at the sunset.

"My goodness, Mama, I just love this picture. And this is my father's painting."

"It is, and you should see the original. It'll take your breath away."

Still staring at the print, Diane says, "Now, I really can't wait to go out there."

"I promise you we'll go in April."

Clutching the print in her right hand, Diane reaches her left arm around Beverly and pulls her close. Diane says, "Thank you, thank you. This is the best present ever."

Beverly gives Diane a quick peck on her cheek and says, "That's because you're the best daughter ever."

Diane releases her mother and starts walking toward the family room. She says, "I've just got to show this to Leland. I'll be right back."

Beverly smiles and goes back to the kitchen to finish her cleaning. As she's wiping down the kitchen counter she softly says, "Thank you, Jesus, for looking after us."

Diane leaves work an hour early on the Friday after Thanksgiving so that she can be home to hear Jumpin' Jeff Foster's show on the radio. At four o'clock, Diane and Bret are sitting together on the sofa in their family room staring at the front of the stereo system's radio, waiting for Jumpin' Jeff's show to start. Leland, who is off that day along with all the other sawmill employees, is in his workshop with his radio also tuned to Jumpin' Jeff's station.

The commercial for Lou's Music Shop fades out, and Jeff Foster comes on the air. "Welcome everybody once again to the Jumpin' Jeff Foster Show broadcast every weekday afternoon from historic downtown Libertytown, Alabama and covering all of Creek County. I hope that you all had a good Thanksgiving yesterday.

"Some of you may have heard that Libertytown's own Leland Johnson will soon be coming out with his debut album on the Dubyar record label. The album is called 'Songs from Creek County,' and all the songs on it were written right here in Libertytown by Leland and his father Robert C. 'Red' Johnson, a well-known musician in his own right.

"Well, folks, let me tell you that I am fortunate enough to have right here in my grubby little hands an advance copy of that album. I've already listened to it twice, and I can tell you that every song on it is great. With that in mind, every other song that I'll be playing for the next two hours is going to be one off that album. If you like what you hear, please be sure to tell Leland and Red the next time you see them, and also be sure to put in an order for the album at Lou's Music Shop. Let's see, the first track that I'm going to play for you today is called 'I'll Be Your Lighthouse,' and here it is."

Diane bounces up and down on the sofa as the first few notes of the song come through the stereo's speakers. Bret laughs at his mother and follows suit. Leland's voice comes over the radio, and Bret stops bouncing. He listens attentively and then points at the radio and yells, "Daddy's singing on the radio."

Diane looks at Bret and yells, "Daddy's singing on the radio."

Out in his workshop, Leland is singing along with the radio and trimming a one by six with his table saw.

Diane's phone rings just as Leland's song is ending. Diane answers the phone. It's an excited Emma saying that she just heard Leland on the radio. She says how much she and Mel loved that song when they heard it on the CD that Red gave them, and she wants to know when the album will be out so that she can buy some for Christmas gifts. Diane describes to Emma how excited Bret was when he heard his daddy's voice on the radio and tells her that she'll call Earl tomorrow and ask if there's a date yet for the album's release.

As soon as Diane gets off the phone with Emma, the phone rings again. This time it's Stephanie, a former high school classmate of Diane's, who says that her exercise class was listening to the Jumpin' Jeff Foster Show when Leland's first song came on, and they all went crazy over it. Stephanie goes on to say that the whole class has decided to stay at the Y listening to Jumpin' Jeff's show until all the songs off the album have been played.

When Leland comes into the house from his workshop at around seven to eat dinner, Diane tells him that she has gotten at least six calls from people raving about the album. As Leland is walking to the sink to wash his hands, he grins and says, "It is pretty good."

Chapter Forty-four

The Moore family are having their Thanksgiving dinner on the Saturday after Thanksgiving Day, as is their tradition. Having dinner on Saturday instead of Thursday allows Dr. Horace Moore and Dr. Andrew Moore to keep their clinic open, with a skeleton crew, on Thanksgiving Day. It also allows the Moores' kitchen help to spend the holiday with their families.

Sitting at the long dining table with Dr. Horace Moore and his wife Sarah are Dr. Andrew Moore and his wife Abigail, as well as John and Beth Lancaster and their two daughters, and George and Melanie Pebworth and their son.

Horace asks everyone to bow their heads, and he renders a simple blessing by which he thanks the Lord for the food they are about to eat, for the love that the family have for one another, and for the good health that the family have been blessed with.

The amens are said, and Sarah rings her silver dinner bell. Shantell and Denise, her kitchen help, carry loaded silver food trays from the kitchen, and Sarah thanks them as they walk around the table distributing winter salads to everyone. Shantell and Denise finish serving the salads and quietly retreat to the kitchen to prepare to bring out the entree.

Andrew watches the two young Black girls walk away in their dark green skirts and starched white aprons. He says, "I like those girls.

They're very orderly in what they do, as well as being excellent cooks. You're lucky, Sarah. It's hard to find good help these days."

Sarah says, "You're so right. We're very lucky. Mildred in my bridge club was complaining the other night about having trouble finding a decent cook."

Horace laughs. "Lord help those poor friends of yours if they ever had to cook their own meals."

"Don't be a smarty pants," says Sarah.

The family quietly eat their salads and then the main course. While awaiting dessert, Beth asks, "Did any of y'all happen to hear Leland Johnson on the radio yesterday afternoon?"

When no one answers yes, Beth says, "Jumpin' Jeff Foster was playing songs from Leland's new album all afternoon. I figured that some of y'all might have heard the show."

"Why didn't you call me?" asks Melanie.

"I called you twice, but the line was busy both times."

"Oh, that's right. I was on the phone for over an hour with the county cultural arts director. Well, anyhow, what did you think of the album?"

"Well, you know that I'm no fan of country music. It's a bit low class for my taste. But I thought that the album was well done. I can see how some people might like it."

George looks at John. "Well, John, now that Leland's album is being played on the radio, I guess we need to go ahead and order that sign I was telling you about."

John smiles and nods.

Horace asks, "What sign is that?"

George says, "The big sign that we're going to put out on the edge of town saying, 'Hometown of Recording Star Leland Johnson.'"

Horace and Andrew laugh. Melanie shakes her head. Sarah glowers at George.

Horace says, "I hope you're not joking, George, because I think a sign like that might be a good idea if the album turns out to be a hit."

"No, sir, I'm dead serious."

Melanie says, "Well, I think a sign like that would be tacky. And besides that, I'm getting a little tired of hearing about Diane and Leland Johnson, aren't y'all? I mean, we're talking about television, newspapers, magazines, and now radio. And this is a couple who about a year ago were living in a little trailer on the side of the highway."

Beth leans in and adds, "Oh, they're nice people all right, but they're just not as big a deal as everyone is making them out to be."

Horace stares at his daughters and shakes his head. Then he slides his plate to one side and makes room on the table for Denise to set down the saucer holding his slice of pumpkin pie. He thanks Denise and looks over at Abigail Moore. He asks, "Mother, what do you think about this sign business?"

Abigail takes a sip of the coffee that Shantell just brought her. In her slow, cultured Southern drawl, she answers, "Well, as long as the sign is tastefully done, I would have no objection. I remember that Leland Johnson boy from when he and his father worked on our pool house. They were both very well-mannered, and they were always on time. And they did an excellent job." She turns to her husband. "Please pass the sugar, Andrew dear."

Horace looks around the table before he taps the edge of his pie saucer twice with his fork. With a twinkle in his eye, he says, "Well, that settles it. If Mother says the sign's okay, then it's going up. Now, on to more immediate things. Fellas, are we still going deer hunting in the morning?"

John firmly answers, "Oh, yes sir."

George looks at Melanie and smiles as he adds, "And Leland and Red are going to join us."

THE END

. . . I could jump aboard that old midnight train;
ride the rails to anywhere it goes
till it pulls into the station of some town I don't know.
I could ride aboard that old midnight train.

One day you'll look around and I'll be gone,
Cause there's something in my soul that must be free.
Now, that don't mean I didn't like your company.
I just know when it's time to move on . . .

From track 14 of *Songs from Creek County*